ROWDY Boy

CLARISSA WILD

Copyright © 2020 Clarissa Wild
All rights reserved.
ISBN: 9798684164958

This is a work of fiction. Names, characters, places and incidents are either the product of the author's imagination or are used fictitiously. Any resemblance to actual events, places, organizations, or person, whether living or dead, is entirely coincidental.

All rights reserved. No part of this book may be reproduced, transmitted in any form or by any means, electronic or mechanical, including photocopying, recording, or by any information storage retrieval system. Doing so would break licensing and copyright laws.

PLAYLIST

"Icy" by Kim Petras
"No Shame" by 5 Seconds Of Summer
"Youngblood" by 5 Seconds Of Summer
"Teeth" by 5 Seconds Of Summer
"Cruel Intentions" by Valerie Broussard
"I feel Like I'm Drowning" by Two Feet
"Pass That Dutch" by Missy Elliot
"Her Lies" by Asaf Avidan
"Somebody" by Hurts
"Muddy Waters" by LP
"Hourglass" by SURVIVE
"Dance In The Dark" by AU/RA
"Pneumothorax" by Blueneck
"In The Woods Somewhere" by Hozier
"So You Wanna Start A War" by Klergy with Valerie Broussard
"Beat Me" by Davina Michelle
"Bloc Party" by The Pioneers (M83 Remix)
"Bad Kingdom" by May and Robot Koch
"Angry Too" by Lola Blanc
"High Enough" by K.Flay

DESCRIPTION

Rude boys play best.

I've always known how to make girls fall to their knees.

When I open my mouth and play my music, they line up to scream my name.

Cole Travis, rock star and high school legend.

Fans beg me for a dirty smile and a filthy kiss.

And I give them everything they could ever want.

All these years, I thought it was enough.

Until her.

Monica Romero, the new girl whose wistful eyes hide a closed-off heart.

A heart I know belongs to me but one I can never have.

She doesn't know me.

My band.

My reputation.

Not even my name.

But she will remember me…

Because if I can't have her…

No one will.

PROLOGUE

Monica

I wasn't looking for trouble, but no matter what I did, it found me.

When I moved schools, I thought my life would be different, that I'd finally get to turn a new page … be a better me.

But no one can escape their past. Or their own heart.

And my heart pounded with fury for the only boy I knew I should never, ever crave.

Cole Travis.

The moment he laid his eyes on me, I was his.

He looked like the devil incarnate with his ash-black hair and dark, soul-crushing stare that could make any girl scream his name. And I knew right then that boy would end up breaking my heart.

Still, I made the plunge.

I didn't know then how far I'd fall …

But he did.

He was counting on it.

***

Cole

I always knew how to make the girls fall.

It was easy to get them on their knees.

All I had to do was open my mouth and play my music.

I came alive when they lined up to scream my name, begging for a dirty smile and a filthy kiss. Girl after girl, I gave them what they wanted, and they fawned all over me.

But it was never enough. I always wanted more … and I did anything to get it, no matter how many hearts I had to break.

I was bad, and I knew it every step of the way.

But I simply didn't care.

Nothing mattered.

Not my education.

Not my popularity.

Not my career.

Not even my fucking heart.

Until *her*.

ONE

Monica

When I pull into the parking lot of my new school in my Range Rover, panic sets in. Black Mountain Academy is one of the most prestigious private schools around here, even more so than my previous school, Falcon Elite Prep. All the rich, spoiled kids attend here, and now that includes *me*.

But I'm grateful for the opportunity to start over.

Now all I need to do is muster the courage to get out of my car.

A hand on my shoulder makes me jolt up and down in my seat. "You've got this."

I turn my head to look over my shoulder at Sam, who's smiling in the back seat. She came all this way with me just to be a good friend and wish me good luck.

"I know," I say, nodding a few times to force myself to believe my own words.

"And if anyone harasses you or bullies you, you know I'm gonna be right there to whoop some ass," she adds, making a fist to pound into her other hand.

I snort. "You sound like me now."

"You've turned me into a proper bitch," she says, and we both laugh.

"Good. It's about time I found my own bitch back."

"That's what I wanna hear." She squeezes my shoulder. "Go on then. Your cousin is waiting for you."

I take a peek outside where Ariane, with her long, curly blond hair and her cute short school skirt, waves at me from the pavement.

"My God ... that *thing's* related to you?" Sam mutters. "She looks like she just stepped out of that Stepford wives movie."

"Tell me about it," I groan. "But I guess you don't choose your family, or I would've traded mine long ago."

She snorts. "Is your entire family as feisty as you? Because now I'm starting to wonder if they would've traded your ass too."

I throw her a look. "HA. Ha. Wait until you meet her," I say, and I grab my bag from the back and open the door.

"Oh, boy," Sam responds as she gets out too. "Whatever is she hiding underneath those pearly curls?"

With a snort, I slam the door shut. Somehow, with our banter, she always manages to calm the storm raging in my heart. No more anxiety; I've got this.

"You ready?" Sam asks from beside me.

"As ready as I'll ever be," I say with a sigh.

"You give 'em hell," Sam says, patting my back. "And if anyone bothers you, you call me, alright?"

"Right." I nod, blowing out my breath before I throw my bag over my shoulder and walk off.

"I'm gonna call my mom to come and pick me up," she says. "When you're done with class, text me about your day. Tell me how it all went down."

"Course," I reply. "Thanks."

I don't like saying goodbye, especially not to my best friend, and especially not when she's looking at me like that. She's worried we'll see each other less and less … until we no longer have time for the other.

But I won't ever let it get to that point. She'll always be my best friend, and nothing can ever come between us, not even a different school.

"Love ya, bitch!" I tell her, sticking out my tongue, and she says, "Love you right back, bitch!"

Then I turn around and walk toward Ariane with my head held high.

"Hey, girl, I'm so glad you're finally here!" she says, immediately hugging me, but in a weird non-touchy way, almost like some kind of ritual I wasn't aware of. "How are you feeling today? Excited?"

"Yeah, of course," I lie, but I don't want to come across as ungrateful, so I don't tell her the truth. I'm already glad she was willing to help me out.

"So this is our school, your new school ... Black Mountain. Our colors are red and black, and our mascot is a cougar. Remember that. It's important, especially if you want to try out for cheerleading. We'd love to have you." She winks.

God no. That shit makes me wanna vomit.

We walk toward the building. "This is the main entrance, there's the gym, and that's where the cafeteria is." She points at all the doors. "I already went ahead and got your roster for you so you won't be held up at registration." She whips out a piece of paper from her pink bag and hands it to me. "I've circled all your classes today, so you won't get lost. The numbers are really easy, it's just front to back, top to bottom, so A1 is the first room downstairs."

"Got it," I reply as we go inside, but I'm not really listening because the place is huge, and I'm taking in as much as I can.

"We have lunch in the cafeteria at twelve; you can sit with my friends and me," Ariane says as we stop in front of the cafeteria door. "Our table is the one in the middle, there." She points at one table, but I have no clue which one it is, so I'll guess I'll find out once it's time to find her.

"Oh, and Mr. D gave me permission to give you a teacher's bathroom pass," she says. "So you'll have some privacy." She smiles. "I know how hard it is for you."

I give her an awkward smile, as I don't like talking about these things. I guess my mom told her about what happened, probably because Ariane was curious about why I was switching schools.

"But they're unisex bathrooms," she suddenly says, and I look up in surprise.

"Wait, what? Unisex?"

"Yeah. But it's fine. You'll be like the only one there," she says, waving it off. "I think."

Why do I feel like she doesn't really know?

Oh, boy.

She hands me the pass. "Thanks," I say, as I don't want to appear ungrateful for her effort to give me a sort of haven.

"You're welcome!" she says with a super cheerful voice.

We walk by most of the classrooms, and Ariane points out some things about each class, such as where the drama club is and how to sign up (like I ever would), and where the math club meets, where the theater is, and at what time the music club starts. She's meticulous in her explanations, almost as if she's afraid that if she skips a single item on her list, I won't know how to find stuff for myself. She's always been like this, and it makes me wonder if she thinks I'm dumb, or if she just hangs with a lot of dumb people. Probably the latter.

"Okay, and that's the tour!" she says cheerfully. "If you have any questions or problems, anything whatsoever, you know you can always come ask me, right?"

"Of course," I say, shrugging it off, but I didn't listen to half of what she was saying anyway. I just looked around and marveled at the beauty of the building, and the uninterested looks of all the other students as though they didn't even care I was there. And it was amazing. No one here knows who I am or what I've been through, and that feels so good. Not one second did I want to disappear.

Until ... *him*.

A few seconds peeking into the band practice room is all that's needed to make my jaw drop.

Right there on the stage is the most gorgeous black-haired boy I've ever laid my eyes on. His jaw razor-sharp, his lips thick and kissable. Three distinct moles—one on each cheek and one on his chin. Brows slanted, cheeky, as though he's perpetually daring someone to look at him—someone like me.

He casually plays the guitar and sings his lungs out with a beautifully raspy voice. Suddenly, he adjusts the mic, and his green, devilish eyes land on me.

This moment, this one second feels stuck in time.

As though the world comes to a standstill, and all that's left is him and me ... and my heart that's about to be thrashed to hell by the likes of him.

A filthy, dirty smirk forms on his face.

My fucking God.

My heart just skipped a beat.

"Monica? Monica!" Ariane's suddenly right in front of me, snapping her fingers as though she's trying to call for a butler. "Hello? What's going on? What are you ...?" The moment she turns her head, she's silent, and then she mutters, "Oh …"

"What's his name?" I ask.

She grabs me by the shoulders and pushes me aside, breaking the connection I had with that one boy who made my heart throb without ever touching it.

"No," she says in a way that reminds me of a stern mother speaking to a toddler. "Not *him*."

"What? No, I wasn't—"

"I saw you look," she says. "You *don't* wanna go there."

I don't think my cheeks have ever been redder, but there you go. "I'm not—"

"He's bad. Like, *really* bad. I promise you, he's the worst kind of asshole. Trust me on that," she says, still clenching my arms as though she's trying to stop me from going inside. "Don't talk to him. Don't get anywhere near him."

"Why not?" I ask, confused as to why she'd go to that length just to warn me.

"Everywhere he goes, he leaves damage. He's nothing but trouble."

I wonder if she means he damages property … or girls' hearts.

She pulls me along into a new hallway. "I promise you, there are plenty of hot guys here, and they'll treat you much better than he ever will. I can introduce you to one if you like. I know some guys from the football team that are still single." She winks.

"I'm good," I say, holding up my hands. "No boys for me."

"Oh, right …" She stops in her tracks. "I'm sorry, that was inconsiderate of me."

I wave it off as if it's no biggie, even though it is. But I don't want to make it a bigger deal than it already is. "It's fine."

"I won't push you to do anything, so tell me if I go too far, okay?" she says.

"Thanks, I really appreciate you giving me a tour and helping me get settled here," I reply.

She leans in. "If anyone bothers you, you let me know." She looks me in the eyes as if she wants to find my soul. "You know …"

Yeah, I know what she means.

"I won't let it get that far, promise. No boys for me. I've learned my lesson." I roll my eyes.

"Boys only break your heart anyway," she adds lightheartedly, but she has no clue—none at all—and it shows. "Oh, I think it's about time for your first class to start," she suddenly says. "C'mon."

Before I know it, she's pulled me all the way upstairs, right in front of a classroom. "English!" she says. "The bell will ring soon, and I have something I need to take care of before my first class, so I gotta go if you don't mind."

"Oh, it's fine. Thanks so much for all your help," I reply. I wonder what's so important that she needs to take care of right off the bat when school hasn't even started yet.

"You're welcome, but if you need anything else, just send a text. I'm always available." She sends me some fake kisses. "Gotta run, love. Bye!"

"Bye!" I wave her off, but I'm not really looking because all I can think of is that boy I just saw … and the way he looked at me that almost promised trouble.

I don't think I'll be able to stay away, even if I tried.

***

Cole

Sweet fucking mercy.

Those eyes.

The way she watches me adjust the mic, as if I'm touching myself instead of the mic, makes all the blood rush to my dick. Fuck.

I haven't even had a proper look at her ass or her frame yet, but a small glimpse has me turned on.

I'm already hooked, and I don't even know her name.

Do I need to? Maybe. For now, all I need to know is that she's interested in me … and I'm definitely interested in her too.

I don't care who she is or where she came from. She's new, and fresh meat always gets me excited. It's not often new girls step onto the Black Mountain property. Once the new school year starts, there's an influx of new girls, but they're all so young and inexperienced.

Unlike this girl.

I could tell from one glance that she's been through a world of trouble ... and still, she looked like she was ready for more.

Ready for *me*.

Someone pulls her attention away from me, and the spell is broken.

But I'm far from done with her ... and I like a challenge.

Especially when I haven't had one in a long time.

"Oh, Cole ... won't you just sing one song? Please?" a girl in the back asks, interrupting my train of thought.

I hadn't even noticed her sitting there in one of the seats. I wasn't paying attention, and I still don't really care.

"No," I say, clearing my throat as I lower my guitar. The girl who watched me from the doorway is gone, and so is my smirk.

"Aww ..." The girl in the seat makes a pouty face. "But I came all the way here to watch you practice."

I raise a brow. "Tough luck."

She makes a face as though she didn't expect me to be such a bag of dicks. Most fans only like me when they hear me sing and play, but when the mic drops and my personality comes out, they finally realize the truth. I'm not someone they should admire. I'm an asshole.

I don't like being one, but right now, I don't have time to play for a single girl when I need to practice. And I can't do that with a fan watching my every move. I'll make mistakes and stumble over my words, and that's fucking bad. I can't let any fan see it.

"Don't you have class, uhh …?" I don't even know who she is.

"Judy." She giggles, tucking her hair behind her ear. "And yeah, but it can wait."

Suddenly, the bell rings, and the girl instantly gets up. "Shit."

Bet she didn't think that through.

"I gotta go, but I have tickets for your next concert, so I'll see you there!" she says, blowing a kiss at me before leaving through that same door where that one girl was peeking through. Maybe I'll fuck her backstage later … with the other girl on my mind.

I can't help it; I'm a grade A bastard. I enjoy mindless sex with girls who're only with me because I'm popular, because I'm in a band, and because I can sing and play the guitar. They all fall so easily for the image I've crafted, and none of them ever get beneath the surface.

Just as it should be.

I tuck my guitar back into the case and snap it shut. Time for my next class, where I'll most likely have fifteen other girls fawning over every breath I take. I try to ignore them, but it's so damn hard when they're hanging on every word uttered from my lips. It does something to a guy's ego, and I'd be lying if I said I didn't like it.

BANG!

I look up. Ariane smacked her bag on the front table.

"Don't," she says.

"What? Get to class?" I raise my brows and smirk at her.

"You know what I'm talking about."

"No, I don't. What do you want now?" I snarl.

"Nothing. I want absolutely *nothing* from you." She folds her arms. "But *she* doesn't either."

"*She?*" I cock my head, and a mischievous grin automatically forms on my face.

"Don't pretend you don't know who I'm talking about," she says. "I saw you looking at her."

Oh … *that girl.*

Ariane eyes me down with that violent look that she always has when she's contemplating calling the headmaster or murdering someone. Who knows when she'll get to that last option, but no way am I going to wait around and see.

"Stay away from her."

I shrug and throw my bag over my shoulder, clutching my guitar case firmly in my other hand. "Whatever."

"I mean it, Cole!" she says, stomping her foot.

I pause and cock my head. "Why do you care so much?"

"I … I don't," she says, trying to hide a blush behind those luscious blond curls of hers, but I know better. "But she doesn't need your shit."

"Right," I say. In one ear and out the other, as my mom always says.

"Cole!" When she grabs my leather jacket, I stop and jerk myself loose from her grip.

"Don't," I growl, and I throw her a harsh look.

She immediately backs off, as she should.

No one fucking touches me, especially not her.

"You *can't*," she says through gritted teeth. "You hear me?"

"You think I'm gonna listen to you?" I scoff. "You've got some nerve."

"Cole, please …" Her lips grow thin, and the concerned look on her face throws me off. She knows how to pack enough punch in her words to go straight for the jugular, and I fucking hate it. I hate that after all this time she still manages to get to me.

"I don't even care," I say. "And neither should you."

When I walk off, she calls after me. "She deserves better than you."

That hurt. And for a second, she almost makes me wish I didn't exist. But then I realize who she is, and I snort.

"Or maybe she deserves *all* of me …" I say, glancing at Ariane over my shoulder. "And you just wish you did."

Her lips twitch as she struggles to hide a sneer, and I can't help but smile at the thought.

Fuck her. And fuck everyone trying to contain me.

She doesn't want me fucking with the new girl? Too bad because I've already decided…

I'm going to fuck with both of them.

TWO

Monica

When the other students start pouring in, I stay behind and wait until the teacher arrives. "Ah … Monica, right? Welcome to your new school."

"Thanks," I reply as he walks inside.

"C'mon." He beckons me to step right in front of the class. "Everyone, quiet please. We've got a new student, and she wants to introduce herself."

Oh, God.

Everyone sits down and stares at me, and it feels awkward as hell. Am I the only one who never prepares for these things?

"I, uh …" My eyes suddenly land on a pair of eyes I recognize, and they twist my stomach into knots. That boy with the guitar and his icy cold stare.

"Gonna say something or what?" another student hollers from the back, and some begin to laugh.

"Dexter, stop it," the teacher grumbles. "Give her a chance."

My cheeks turn pink, but I quickly compose myself.

"I was just thinking about how I'm going to introduce myself, that's all," I say. "I'm Monica Romero. Nice to meet y'all." When there's silence all around, I shrug and add, "That's about it, really."

I don't want to tell them anything about me.

I don't want to tell them what I liked to do … because it's not who I am anymore.

And I certainly don't want anyone to know the real me.

I'm trying my best not to look at the boy with the guitar right now, but he's straight out staring at me like he's trying to peer into my soul, and I can't fucking take it.

A girl with big bushy hair in the front waves, and says, "Hi, Monica."

"What … that's it?" another boy replies, leaning back in his chair.

"If that's all she wants to say, then that's fine too," the teacher interjects. "C'mon, give her a warm welcome. You'll be spending all semester together, so there's plenty of time to get to know her." He gives me a gentle nudge toward the class. "Go on and find an empty seat."

One swift glance across the empty spots and I realize I have two options … sit down beside the girl in the front nodding at the chair to her left ... which is unfortunately situated right behind the boy with the ash-black hair who is giving me a deadly stare ... or sit down right next to him.

I gulp.

Neither is good, but if I have to choose, I'd rather sit behind him than next to him.

Because let's face it ... even though he looked sexy as hell, I'm nowhere near ready to get that close to someone like him. Someone who clearly knows how to seduce girls with a single smile. Not me. I won't fall for the trap.

That's what I tell myself as I quietly sit down behind him and grab my books without drawing too much attention to myself. I used to like it but not anymore. I just want to be the silent girl, the one no one notices, the one no one really knows. Because it sure as hell beats being the girl *everybody* is talking about.

"Hey," the girl beside me whispers, "I'm Melanie, but call me Mel."

"Hi, mell." I smile at her, hoping to make a good impression even though I'm terrible at them. "Nice to meet you."

"Your intro was so short," she says. "But don't mind the boys, they're just messing with you."

"I won't," I reply. "Got those at my old school too. I've learned that lesson long ago."

She smiles. "Why'd you leave? If you don't mind me asking?"

My heart skips a beat and images of Bobby and me in

his room flash through my mind, but I quickly push them away. "My dad had a new job somewhere else."

"Figured it was something like that," she says. "What does he do?"

Shit. Now I gotta make up even more lies.

"He's a CEO." Well, it's the truth. He just never switched jobs, but she doesn't need to know exactly where he works. "Got a better offer elsewhere, so here we are." I smile it off like it's the most unimportant shit ever.

"Well, I'm glad you made the switch. I think you'll fit right in here," she says, whatever that means. "If you want, I can help you get on track with the assignments. We're currently reading Shakespeare."

"Sure," I reply. Even though I've read almost all of his work, I don't mind her thinking she can help because she might just be my next friend at this school. And I definitely need more friends at this school than just my cousin.

"You sure you wanna do that, new girl?"

I smelled his scent before he even turned around in his seat, but my God … that voice is just as low and husky as I imagined it being.

"Shut up," Melanie barks at him.

"That's the kind of girl she is," he says, raising his brow.

"No one asked you a damn thing," Melanie says, and she boldly slams her books onto her table.

"No … she doesn't have to," he says, and he's looking straight at me now with those same seductive green eyes that almost make my heart stop.

"Hi," he says.

"Um ... hi," I mutter back.

I don't know what's gotten into me. I'm normally never like this, and I always know what to say. But the minute he turned around, I forgot every single word I wanted to say.

"I didn't quite catch your name. What was it again?" he muses.

"Monica," I reply.

"Monica," he repeats in such a salacious way that it makes the hairs on my skin stand up. "Nice."

Did he just approve ... of my name? *Wow*.

"Cole Travis," he says, licking his lip. "But I bet you already knew that."

"Ughh," Mel grunts, rolling her eyes so far they almost end up in the back of her head. "You're so full of yourself."

"Says the girl who immediately jumps on the new girl like a shark on fresh bait," he quips.

"I am *not*," she retorts. "I'm just trying to be friendly, that's all."

"I don't mind," I interject, laughing a little to ease the tension.

His eyes narrow. "So ... you don't know anyone here?"

I shake my head. "Not yet, anyway." Is this his way of inviting me to get to know him? Because I may or may not take him up on that offer. I shouldn't, but a guy like him would be hard to deny.

"My cousin goes to this school, that's about it," I explain.

His eyes narrow for a second. "Interesting."

Then he turns around again. Just like that, without saying another word. Weird.

"Ignore him, he's always looking for trouble," Mel says.

"Ignore her, she's trying to stir up shit," he retorts without even looking back at us.

It feels super awkward to be in the middle of this fight. "Did you two …?"

Her eyes widen, and she looks as if she's seen a ghost. "Oh no, God no, I would never," she says. Leaning forward, she beckons me to do the same. When I do, she whispers, "He's a player. He uses girls and treats them like trash. I'd stay the hell away from him if I were you."

"You're talking shit about me again, aren't you, Melanie?" Cole turns around again.

"Guys," the teacher interrupts us, and we all quickly focus on our books. "Stop talking, please. Open your books to page eleven and read the first paragraph."

While staring at her book, Mel darts glances my way, and she starts penning something down on a piece of paper. Then she chucks it onto my table.

I pick it up and make sure the teacher isn't watching before opening it. It's her phone number with some text underneath that reads: *Add me*.

After mouthing, "Thanks," I quickly grab my phone, but right as I'm about to punch in the numbers, the note is snatched out from underneath my nose.

It's him. "You don't need this."

"Hey!"

He spins around in his seat again, right as the teacher looks up at me, and says, "Eyes on the book, please!"

With a frown, I lower my eyes, but I won't let Cole get away with this so easily. "Give it back."

When he doesn't respond, I tap on his back.

"What do you want?" He's playing me now.

I sigh. Whatever he thinks he's doing, I'm not playing this game. "Give. It. Back."

"I don't know what you're talking about." He glances at me over his shoulder with that same aloof gaze, but instead of being seductive, it's now infuriating as hell. Or maybe both. Definitely both, goddammit.

"Yeah, you do. Stop playing around," I reply.

"I'm not playing, but I can. You wanna hear it?" he says with a devilish smirk on his face. "We have band practice at four."

I frown and try not to look excited because a tiny part of my heart just did a little jump, but I have to ignore it. He's the kind of guy you'd steer the hell clear from after going through what I went through.

"I could give this back after you've watched us practice …" He flaunts the tiny paper between two fingers, casually flicking it back and forth like a pen. "Or I could keep it."

I try to snatch it out of his hand, but he immediately retracts and gives me a coy smile. "Nuh-uh, that wasn't part of the deal."

"I don't make deals, especially not with boys."

He raises a brow. "What do you have against boys?"

"Nothing," I say, looking away when the teacher is onto us again.

I'm not gonna tell him shit.

There's silence for a while, but when the teacher's back to mumbling some things about the text we just read (which I didn't read because of Cole), I tap his back again.

"I need that number," I say.

"No, you don't," he says.

Goddammit! Why is he so annoying? What is he trying to achieve?

"I get it. I'm the new girl, and you like making me the butt of jokes," I say, "but it's not funny anymore."

"Joke? Who says I'm joking?" he muses without even looking at me. "You want this back?" He holds up the tiny paper again. "Come and get it."

Is that a challenge?

If this was any other day in my old school, I would've stood up, punched him, snatched that paper from his hand, and taken the time-out in detention like a big girl. But I'm the new girl now, and I can't afford to misbehave.

So I stay down and ignore him. Maybe I can convince Mel to give me her phone number again later when Cole isn't bothering me.

"Fine, I'll keep it then," he mumbles. "I have enough groupies at the band practice anyway. You won't be missed."

"Fuck you," I reply. "Asshole."

Suddenly, he turns around in his seat, his green, smoldering eyes piercing straight through me. "What'd you say?" he says through gritted teeth.

"Mr. Travis, is there anything you'd like to share with the rest of the class?" the teacher interrupts. I thought he'd never notice.

"No, sir. I'm just saying hi to the new girl."

This is his way of saying hi?

"You can do that after class," the teacher says, clearing his throat. "We'll continue with page thirteen now. Fifteen minutes. I don't want anybody talking."

Cole's silent again, but I'm not. "My cousin was right about you. You are an asshole."

I don't even care anymore what he says. He's already ruined our first meeting. He's clearly only out to play games with me, and I'm not up for it. Assholes will always be assholes, no matter how pretty they are.

THREE

Cole

Asshole.

That word ... I've heard it so many times before, but I never had the urge to defend myself and show them I'm not. But I do now, more than anything. And I don't know why.

Why the fuck would it irritate me so much that she called me an asshole?

Why the fuck do I even care that she's here at all?

I smack my pen onto the table and look away, blowing off steam, but nothing I do can stop the voices in my head from repeating what she told me.

Asshole.

I'm a fucking asshole, and I know it.

I do it on purpose because I wanna see how far I can go.

Because they'll always come back to me because I'm popular, because I'm in a band, and because they can't help themselves. Nothing I do ever has any effect.

But this girl ... she doesn't play by those rules.

And the fact that she doesn't fangirl over me like all the others makes my stomach churn.

When the bell rings, I pick up my shit and chuck it into my bag, right as she passes by. Her hips sway as she walks, and she has this arrogant attitude to her, but not in an I'm-a-hot-cheerleader-and-I-know-it kind of way. No ... this is a girl who knows she doesn't need anyone to make it. A girl who doesn't want the attention of boys but gets it anyway.

And it's infuriating to the point that it makes me want to snap.

Why?

I don't even fucking know her.

But I want to ... I want to know what made her this way.

I follow her out the door and grab her shoulder, spinning her around.

"Don't call me that," I say. "Ever again."

The look in her eyes changes as they widen, and her pupils dilate, her body growing rigid under my touch, the hairs on the back of her arm standing up. She backs away from me as though I threatened her with a knife.

"Don't touch me," she says quickly but softly, almost as if she can't get the words off her lips. Those pretty lips quiver with fear right at this very moment.

Is she scared of me?

I frown, confused. No girl has ever had that reaction. Most of them fawn over me, beg me for attention, a touch, a kiss, anything. But she … it's almost as if she hates me already.

But she doesn't even know me.

And for some unknown fucking reason, I want her to, more than anything right now. I don't know why I'm having such a visceral reaction to her calling me an asshole. It normally doesn't faze me … but this time, it's different. And I'm not fucking used to shit being different.

"Whatever your cousin told you about me, it's not true," I say.

She puts on a defensive stance. "I think I'd believe her over you."

Of course she would. They're family after all. But who in this school would ever tell the new girl I'm the asshole? There's only one person I can think of …

"You're being lied to," I reply, licking my lips in anger.

"Yeah, well, I could say the same about you," she says, clutching her bag closely as though she's using it as a shield to create distance, and it makes me want to rip it away. "What do you want, Cole?"

I swallow. I don't fucking know either, and I hate that she asks because I don't want to think about the answer.

"If you bully me, I'll call you out," she adds. "And you're an asshole for stealing my shit."

"It's just a fucking note," I reply.

"It was a big deal. In case you hadn't noticed, I'm the new girl," she hisses. "That was the first friendly conversation I had with that girl, and you stomped all over it. Why? You jealous or something?"

She's so fucking direct, and I both love it and hate it at the same time. I don't know why I did what I did. I wasn't jealous. Maybe I like being the asshole because everybody loves me, and no one ever calls me out on it ... until her.

"You want a phone number?" I say. What I'm doing is wrong, but I do it anyway. "Here." I fumble in my pocket and take out a bunch of scribbled on torn pieces of papers that I've gotten today from several different girls. Fans. Groupies. It doesn't even matter because they're all the same to me. "Have at it." And I chuck them at her.

They all fall to the floor like a cascade of confetti. None of them manages to make her move. "Go on. Plenty of girls to be your friend."

She shakes her head with such disappointment that it stings like a motherfucking knife cutting me to pieces. And I don't even fucking know the girl. What is wrong with me?

"You know what, never mind," I say, and I turn around before I make an even bigger mess. "Call me whatever you want. I don't care."

"Clearly, you do," she calls after me.

I glance over my shoulder, and she's standing there, arms folded like she's the queen of the motherfucking hallways. And it makes me want to turn around and make her regret every single word.

But I don't.

Instead, I slam someone else's locker closed and march off. I have a bone to pick with another girl, and it's not going to be pretty.

I immediately make my way to the classes she attends, walking past every door to gaze inside and see if she's there. Drama class. Of course she'd be there. Perfect opportunity to polish her skills.

"Ariane," I growl, stepping inside.

She's talking with one of her friends, but the moment she hears me, everyone grows quiet. They all stare at me for a few seconds, and I take in their judgmental looks with rage. She nods at them, and then they leave, all passing me with snooty looks on their faces as though they know exactly what kind of guy I really am.

They don't know shit, and neither does she.

"You think you can turn her against me?" I growl.

She folds her arms and clears her throat. "Nice way to say hi."

"I'm done playing nice with you," I reply, stalking toward her. "What did you tell her about me?"

She inches away from me just a bit. Not enough to become untouchable, but enough to make a point. "I don't know what you're talking about."

I smash my fist on the table next to me, and she jolts up and down in shock. "Don't fucking play around with me! You talked with her, that new girl."

"So? You're forbidding me from talking to people now

too?" She raises a brow, and it makes me want to yell.

"I never told you to do jack shit. But you just can't stop it, can you?" I growl. "You have to insert yourself into everything."

She puts her hands against her side. "I warned her about you, big deal."

"You had no right." I point at her, wishing I could rip out her heart. But she doesn't have one.

She splutters. "Pfft ..." And she rolls her eyes. "As if you can't get any other girl in this school."

"That's not the fucking point, and you know it," I reply.

"Oh, yes, it is. You want to own every girl you meet. And now you're surprised one of them fights back?" She scoffs.

"You always make shit up," I say, biting my tongue because I'm about to flip out. "You always do this, always get in my way."

"Poor you. It's just one fucking girl."

"You've already turned her against me for no goddamn reason," I say.

"Oh, I have *every* reason," she replies, and she looks over her shoulder at her girlfriends who seem eager to eavesdrop.

I don't fucking care. Let them hear just how fucked up Ariane is.

"She's your fucking cousin, isn't she?" I scratch my chin, but it doesn't take away the sting. "You should've fucking told me. Any other secrets you're keeping from me?"

She makes a face and shakes her head. "None that you

ever need to hear about."

"Right …" I knock on the table a couple of times out of frustration. "You know, I always thought you were one of the nicer ones. Guess I was wrong about you too."

I turn around and march away before I do something I regret. The table behind me scoots, and suddenly, she's right in front of me, blocking my way.

"Cole, stop. Please." She sighs. "Look, I'm sorry. I just … I'm trying to protect my cousin, okay?"

"By telling her *I'm* an asshole?" I say through gritted teeth. "Thanks."

"Cole …" She places her hand on my chest and starts playing with my shirt in a way that only fuels my anger. "Please understand, I'm only doing what's right."

"What's right for *you*, you mean," I retort, and I grab her hand. "Don't even try."

"What? This?" With her other hand, she curls a strand of my black hair around her finger and starts playing with it. "You know I know you like it. You like the attention. That's why you're so upset."

"Stop it," I growl.

"Why?" She leans in and whispers into my ear, "So you can run back to your countless other fans to get you off?"

That's it. I shove her off me. "Shut up. Always trying to slither your way in. You should look in the mirror sometime. Maybe you'd finally see the snake you really are."

The look in her eyes turns icy cold. "You don't deserve any girl, let alone her or me. I won't let you go anywhere near her."

I cock my head. "Is that a threat?"

She's all up in my face now. "Don't you even dare," she hisses through her teeth.

A part of me wants to ignore her every word, but a part of me wants to take her up on this dare, just to prove I'm not at all who she says I am, and just to get her to be even more upset at me.

Biting my lip, I say, "Any one of those girls would stand in line to suck my dick and say thank you when I'm done. I can get any girl I want, even *her* ..."

She pauses and glares at me in shock.

SLAP!

Fuck.

My cheek stings and feels hot in a second, and I grab my face.

"You're a disgrace, Cole Travis," she spits, and she storms off out the door.

Where little Miss New Girl just watched every second of the show.

FOUR

Monica

I didn't stay.

I couldn't.

The moment Ariane slapped him across the face, I was stunned. I was only going to find her because I needed to talk to her about Cole and that she was right to warn me … and then I find him there, yelling at her.

No wonder she slapped him.

I only overheard a small part of their conversation, but it was enough to believe her when she told me he was a grade A asshole.

When she left, she ran straight past me without even blinking. But I could see the tears in her eyes.

His … his were thunderous. As though he just got

caught in the act of being a monster … and I was there to witness it all, and the look he gave me was nothing short of vicious. Like he wanted to attack me for even daring to look.

I did the same thing Ariane did, fleeing the scene before I'd say or do anything that would make it worse. I didn't see her for the rest of the day … I didn't see Cole, either, despite the fact that we shared at least two other classes.

I don't want to know what he was doing, nor do I care. I just worry about Ariane, but she hasn't replied to any of my texts. I hope she's okay.

Sighing, I roll across my bed and grab my phone again to check in. A new message grabs my attention, and I swiftly click the button. It's Sam.

Sam: Bitch, why aren't you telling me how your day was?!?!?

I snort. Always so chill. Not.

Mo: Bitch, chill. I was busy.

I put my phone down again, not expecting her to answer soon since my reply came so late, but then there's a new PING, and I check it right away.

Sam: With what? Studying? Don't tell me you've turned into one of those bookworms, pls
Mo: Course not. But class exists, remember

Sam: Right. Forgot. LMAO
Sam: Calling you. Pick up

A few seconds later, the phone rings, so I pick up.

"Finally," Sam mumbles.

"Oh, stop it, bitch," I grumble back.

We both laugh. "Well, it feels like ages since I last saw you," she says.

"It's been one day. Stop freaking out," I reply.

"I can't! I miss my best friend," she says, doing some fake sniffles to make me feel guilty.

"I'm not dead," I reply. "I'm just going to a different school."

"Exactly, which means we can't gossip during class or tell each other all the dirty shit we saw."

"You can still tell me in text," I say.

"That's different," she replies. "And I still miss you."

I roll around on the bed again. "I miss you too."

"How was it?" she asks.

"Ugh …" I groan, and she immediately laughs.

"Already regretting it, huh?"

"No, yes, but no. I mean, it's better for me, in a way. No one's staring at me, you know? And no one knows me there, so that's good. Well, except Ariane of course. But she won't tell anybody … I think."

"She'd better not, or I'll come sucker punch her myself."

I snort. "Should we swap names? Because you're acting like me now."

"I gotta protect my girl," she says. "I want them to treat you better."

"I know, I know." I sigh. "But it's fine. I mean, the first day went … okay."

"Okay? Oh, God." I can almost hear her roll her eyes at me. "Spit it out."

"What?"

"Everything," she snarls. "I know when you're lying, so don't even try."

"Fine. There's this boy."

"A boy?" she gasps. "NO! Monica, no fucking way, we talked about this."

"Relax." I go to sit up. "Nothing happened. He was just a jerk. That's all. I'm not even ready for any boy stuff whatsoever."

"Okay, good," she says. "I don't want you getting hurt."

"I know," I reply.

She was there the night it happened. Even though she wasn't there in time to prevent it, she did come to my rescue when I begged her to, and she's been there for me through it all, even helping me get back to school and all. She's the kind of best friend most people could only wish for. We've always got each other's back.

"We should meet up soon. Maybe grab some ice cream too," Sam says, and I can practically hear her drool. "What I wouldn't give for a tub of chocolate ice cream right now."

"Sure," I reply. "And how're things with Nate?"

"Oh, well, he's doing great, I suppose. Finally got his

dad to agree to let him enter some rap contests."

"Really? That's amazing," I reply.

"Yeah, Nate really wants to try to see if he can score an agent. The whole college thing was never really for him, you know."

"Right." Nate's got such a difficult history. With him being involved in a girl's death last summer, I really didn't expect his father to ease up on him, especially since he wanted Nate to get a football scholarship. But you can't stop someone from living their dream.

"Anyway, we're doing okay … despite the fact that you're not here."

"I still live in the same house, Sam. You can still come and visit me," I reply.

"I know! It's just not the same."

I smile. It's good to hear that I'm missed. Beats already having a bully on day one of school. "God, sometimes I wish I could just snap my fingers and get a whole tub of ice cream delivered to my door."

"Girl, same," Sam replies.

"No, but, I mean …" I sigh. "It's really hard, going through school without your best friend by your side." Shit's getting real now, I can feel it in my bones. "I hate being the new girl. And I miss knowing where everything is, who everyone is." I swallow to stop myself from tearing up. "It's just hard, and sometimes I wonder … what if I hadn't made this stupid decision?"

"It's not stupid," she says. "Don't tell yourself that.

There's nothing to regret. You made the right decision for *you*. You needed this. So stick with it. It'll get better, I promise. It'll feel like you own the place in no time."

I laugh. Even when I'm feeling down, she always manages to cheer me up. "Thanks."

"You're welcome, bitch," she replies, making me laugh again. "Now stop crying and go get some ice cream for two. Promise me you'll eat it all."

"What?"

"I can't come, I have homework to do," she says.

"Ah, boo!" I yell.

"I know, but it is what it is. So we'll talk soon, okay? And we gotta meet up ASAP."

"I'll text you some dates and times," I reply.

"Great. Have fun eating all that ice cream without me!" she yells, and then hangs up.

Bitch. Always trying to make me miss her even more.

I get off the bed and pick up my wallet as well as my keys. Better make good on that promise.

Suddenly, my phone buzzes again, and when I check it out, I'm surprised it's an unknown number.

Hey, it's Melanie, from class, remember? I got your phone nr from Ariane. She said you were her cousin. Sorry about what Cole did. I didn't wanna run off and leave you there by yourself, but I had to call my mom for something important.

A smile forms on my lips. I thought I had to go get her phone number again myself, but she beat me to it. Damn.

Mo: Hey, thanks! Glad you got my nr. I was trying to get the note back from Cole, but he wouldn't budge. Ariane was right when she said he's an asshole

Mel: No worries. He tries to mess with literally every girl he meets. Just ignore him

Mo: Will do, definitely

Mel: Some of us from school are meeting up at this club later. There's an indie concert with lots of different bands playing. Thought you might like it

Mo: Are you kidding? I'd love to!

Mel: Great, meet me there at 8. I'll text you the address

Not long after, I get another text with an actual address in it, and it definitely makes this day a whole lot better.

Someone knocks on my door, and I lower my phone.

"Monica?" Mom enters my room. "How was your first day? Did it go well?"

"Yeah, sure. Fine," I lie.

I don't want to worry her. She's already worried enough about me.

"You sure? I mean, you came home, and you didn't even grab a Coke like you normally do," she says, stepping farther inside.

I clear my throat. "I was just busy texting, I guess." I

shrug. It didn't cross my mind.

She frowns. "With who?" A sudden smile overwhelms her face. "Did you make new friends already?"

"Mom." I roll my eyes. "It's just school."

"I'm just happy you're doing okay," she says. "Is it a girl … or a boy?"

Of course she'd worry about that. "Relax, no penises involved."

She makes a face. "I didn't say that."

"No, I know, but I know what you mean when you ask," I say. "You can stop worrying about me. I'm fine."

"I just don't want anyone to … well, you know …"

Use me. I get it. She won't say it out loud. It's like this forbidden word that never gets uttered, but we all know it's hanging in the air.

"I know, I know. There are no boys, so don't worry. Just assholes." I laugh it off, but it's not really that funny.

"Okay," she mumbles. "I trust you."

That means a lot to me. I just hope it's true.

"Soooo … about that friend I made. She kind of invited me to a party tonight," I say, tucking my hands into my back pocket. "It's not a big deal. It's just an indie concert in a club."

"Oh." My mom makes a weird face that I don't know how to describe because it shows all kinds of emotions, from surprised, to worried, to angry, to fearful.

"Are you … sure you're ready for that?" she asks. "I mean, what if it goes wrong again?"

I swallow back the nerves. She means well, but sometimes it's almost as if she blames me for what happened. "I don't want what happened to me to hold me back. I want to be happy again, Mom. I just want things to be normal."

She nods. "I understand. You're a teen."

I don't know whether to take that as a compliment or an insult.

She grabs my shoulders, and says, "If you think you're ready, then it's fine by me."

I smile. "Thanks. That means a lot to me."

She pulls me in for a big hug. "I'm proud of you, always. Remember that. Nothing will ever stop me from loving you."

"I know," I reply. "I love you too, Mom."

"What time does it start?" she asks.

"Um … in like three hours, so there's plenty of time."

"Will you be eating dinner with us?" she asks hesitantly.

"I'd love to," I say with a genuine smile.

Dinner at home. Before, I never used to consider it my favorite place to be, but right now, normalcy is the only thing I crave.

***

A month earlier
Falcon Elite Prep

Breathe.

Just breathe.

You can get through this.

It's just school. It's nothing special. You've walked down these halls a million times before, and you can do it again.

The little voice inside my head sounds like my mom. It doesn't make it any easier.

It feels as though her hand is on my shoulder as I approach the school doors. She told me she'd be here, in spirit, walking right alongside me. Even though I brushed it off when she said it, now more than ever do I need her strong voice supporting me.

This school and all the pain it harbors for me … is my biggest hurdle yet.

It's the first time in months that I'm back here, back where I left behind everything I ever knew and cared about, just so I could repair what another had broken.

Just so I could mend my heart and heal the scars a boy left on my soul.

A boy whose name even now I refuse to say out loud.

He broke me.

He broke the trust I had in people, and now it'll take months, maybe even years, to rebuild.

At least, that's what my therapist told me, but I don't know if that's true in my case.

I take a deep breath and stare down the door I once walked through clutching that same boy's hand. This time it'll be different. I won't ever let a boy trick me like that again.

Clutching my books close to my heart, I push past the door and enter the big hallway to our school. Kids are bustling all around, people are chatting near the lockers and going up and down the stairs, and watching them go about their daily lives is overwhelming.

Because all this time, I stood still.

Going to intense therapy for so long really did a number on me.

But I know I can do this. This is still the same school as it always was. At least, that's what I tell myself while I walk down the hallway, trying to keep my bearings.

I feel as though everyone's looking at me, and it's making me uneasy.

The more steps I take, the more the buzzing hallway grows silent.

And when I look up, several students gape at me as though I'm a living ghost. But it's just *me*.

I'm now *that girl*.

That girl who was used by a boy named Bobby. Whose drunken, drug-induced haze was put on camera for all the world to see. That video of him doing all those disgusting things to my body was shared around the school as though it meant nothing. As though my life meant nothing to them, and it was all a cheap trick to get some laughs and attention.

And it hurts ... because all these students are still looking at me.

That one video is etched into their brains like a permanent tattoo, and nothing I do or say will erase it from their minds.

It doesn't matter that Bobby went to juvie. It doesn't matter that Lila, who helped spread the videos and brought him his victims, is also doing community service.

None of it will undo what happened to me.

And all these people know who I am ... and what happened to *this girl*.

And I stop moving in the middle of the hallway. I'm frozen to the floor, my body shaking. This isn't me. I was the bubbly girl, the girl who took every challenge head-on, who wasn't afraid of anything, and certainly not any boy. But that was the old Monica. And the old Monica no longer exists. All that's left is a broken shell of the girl she once was.

And I feel it in my bones—everyone's looking at me, judging me. They're whispering things I can't hear, but I know they're talking about me.

Tears stain my eyes, and I blink them away. I told myself I could do this, that I was ready, but am I really? Am I really willing to fake my way through my education and pretend nothing ever happened?

No.

I turn around.

I can't. I just can't.

My feet march faster than tears can flow, and I quickly make my way outside again so I can breathe.

"Mo?"

Sam's voice makes my heart shudder, and I turn my head.

She's standing near the door, clutching her bag over her shoulder. That same worry is in her eyes that's always there when she knows I'm in deep shit.

I don't think I've ever been in deeper shit, and we both know it.

"Are you okay?" she asks.

She wouldn't be my best friend if she didn't know exactly what to ask to make me fall apart.

And I shake my head, tears flowing freely. "No. I can't do this. I can't go back."

***

When Mom opens my door, I sit up straight in bed. The book I was reading drops to the floor. I try not to look guilty, but I know I do. After running from school, I've been home all day, avoiding the inevitable, and she knows.

"Mom, I—"

She holds up a hand. "No more excuses."

I lower my eyes. I got caught in the act. I'm not trying to hide it. I just … wish I could've kept my promise to her.

"I'm sorry," I say.

She sighs and sits down on the bed, grabbing my arm. "Stop apologizing."

"I promised you I'd try. But …" I rub my lips together. "When I saw all those people, I just froze."

"Oh, honey," she murmurs, pulling me in for a big hug. "I know things have been hard on you. I'm so sorry it has to be like this." Her body grows rigid. "If I could get my hands on that boy, I would've strangled him myself."

"Mom!" I gasp, leaning away to look at her.

She grabs my face with both hands. "You know I'd do anything to protect you. And I'm sorry I failed you."

Tears stain my eyes. "You didn't fail me. But I can't … I can't go back there."

She gives me a heart-wrenching smile. "I know, honey."

She's been trying to tell me for months that it'd be beyond hard to return, and that it would never be like it was before, but I wouldn't listen to her. I didn't want to believe her because it was easier than facing the truth.

But I saw it with my own eyes now. I don't belong there anymore.

"That school may not be the right fit for you anymore. But there are options. Your cousin's school is close by. You could go there," she says.

I frown. "But then … I'd leave everything behind."

"Exactly. It'd be good for you. A fresh start. Somewhere new, where no one knows you."

My heart feels like it's bleeding. "But what about Sam?"

"Sam will understand," she says, grabbing my shoulders. "You need to do what's best for *you* now." When she sees my hesitation, she continues. "You can stay friends. You just won't be able to see each other every single day. But you can see each other every other day," she adds, smiling.

"Yeah …" I say, but a tear still manages to escape my eye.

"I think it'll be good for you," she says, brushing away the tear. "I'll go ahead and call your cousin. I'm sure she'll be willing to help out. What do you think?"

I nod, and she immediately hugs me again. "It's gonna be okay. I promise."

But it's not. Even though a new school means no prejudice and no one who knows I'm *that girl*, it still means separating myself from everything I ever knew. My friends … my life.

I'll be starting all over if that's even possible after everything I've been through.

But I gotta give it a try because I deserve to move on. I deserve to be happy.

FIVE

Monica

Now

After dinner, I go to the address Mel texted me and wait outside.

"Hey!" She's right behind me, and I'm a bit startled when she calls out. "I'm glad you made it. Please tell me I didn't make you wait too long."

"Oh no, I've only been here for like five minutes," I say with a fake but cheerful smile.

"Cool." She returns my smile.

She opens the door and lets me inside first. It's loud and noisy, but there's no guard inside and no one to take tickets, which surprises me.

"It's a free concert to get donations for charity," she says when I look confused.

"That explains it. I was expecting a ticket counter," I reply.

"They have these free indie concerts every month. The club pays for them to play," she explains.

"Cool. Who's up tonight?" I ask. "Any bands I know of?"

She rubs her lips together. "Hmm … maybe …" She giggles to herself.

Now I'm really curious. "What?"

"Oh, fuck." She points at the stage. "If I knew TRIGGER was gonna play right now, I would've come later," she scoffs.

When I look at the guy on stage, it's as though the whole room has gone icy cold.

It's *him*.

Cole Travis, with his dark hair all gelled up and combed back, playing the electric guitar and singing into the microphone, right there on stage. The only thing he's wearing is a pair of black leather pants and a blazer … no shirt … which puts his thick, taut abs on full display, and it's making me swallow … hard.

Suddenly, he stares back at me with that same smoldering gaze, lighting my whole body on fire.

Fuck.

Something tells me this isn't going to be a fun and easy night out.

***

Cole

I love the way the girls hang on my lips as I sing the notes to our dirtiest song yet. How they scream my name between every sentence as if they're begging me to give them a simple glance. Performing is one of the only things that can truly get me going.

Until I spot *her*.

The girl with the long, dark hair cascading over her shoulders and that wistful stare that could crush a guy's soul if he dared to get close.

What the hell is she doing here?

She's in the back of the room near the bar next to Melanie.

So she managed to find out what her phone number was after all …

I smirk to myself.

And here I was, thinking Monica would give up easily. Guess this one's got more bite in her than I thought.

She glares at me with contempt in her eyes, and I know damn well why that is. I was a complete asshole to her, and now she's here watching my fucking show. She must be pissed as hell that we're performing here tonight, judging from the grumpy look on her face.

It's the first time I've ever seen any girl look at us like that, and I can't say I like it, but I don't hate it either.

There's something about her that's so defiantly pretty that I can't stop looking even though I should be paying as much attention to my actual fans standing in the crowd. She captures my attention without even trying, and it's annoying as hell.

I run my fingers through my hair and scream out the last few notes to the chorus. Sweat drips from my eyebrows as I give it my all. Any night we play, we play our best because you never know who might be watching and who might be offering us a deal.

But this girl … this girl's eyes have me in their grip, and I can't fucking look away no matter how much I try. Not even as I grip my junk while singing, making all the girls in front of me squeal their lungs out.

Nothing seems to faze her.

Why?

And why do I care so much?

I shouldn't even be thinking about Monica. If I even try to get close to her, I'm sure Ariane would stir up plenty of rumors about me just to punish me.

I'm already a bad guy as it is, and I'm not about to make it worse. Especially with one of Ariane's friends being in the crowd too.

As the song ends, I put the microphone back on the stand, and my tongue darts out while staring at her, just like she's staring at me. My eyes fall to her lips as I imagine ravaging them until they're swollen and pink, and all the other filthy things I could do to those pretty lips.

But I don't like that she's looking back at me as though she wishes she was somewhere else. And it makes me want to lash out.

So I grab the nearest girl standing at the edge of the stage and whisk her up into my arms, smacking my lips onto hers as if I already own her when I don't even know her damn name, and I don't fucking want to.

But my eyes … they still can't stay focused on anything other than Monica and the scornful look on her face, even while I'm kissing another girl.

But I don't fucking care.

I hope she fucking looks as much and as hard as she can.

Because that's the closest I'll ever get to her jealous little heart.

***

Monica

I can't stop looking. Can't stop homing in on his eyes when his tongue licks his bottom lip. Can't stop picturing all the things he could do to me with that same tongue.

But this boy is so much sin wrapped in a single package that I cannot, under any circumstances, ever unwrap.

So I falter and force a frown on my face to send a signal that I'm not interested, and I'm not to be messed with. Even when I secretly am.

But then he picks another girl from the crowd and smashes his lips to hers, and my jaw practically drops. A pang of unwanted jealousy hits me in the stomach.

I don't know this boy, and I certainly don't nor should ever want to.

Yet I can't help but wonder if he did that on purpose to mess with me. Or has he always tried to grope one girl while looking at another?

Because his eyes never stop boring into my soul.

Fuck.

"Earth to Monica. Hello?" It's only when Mel snaps her fingers right in front of my face that I finally manage to break the connection between Cole and me. "Are you okay?" she asks, laughing a little.

"Yeah," I reply, clearing my throat. "Is it hot in here, or is that just me?"

"Um … no, not really," she says, looking confused. "I was just about to order drinks. Want something?"

"Ahh … just a Coke, please," I reply, and I fish in my pocket to grab some cash for her to pay for the drinks with. "Here."

"Keep it," she says, waving it off. "It's on me."

I smile as she walks off, but my eyes instantly resume gawking at Cole. I wish I could stop. I *should* stop. But something about him forces me to look, forces me to find him wherever he goes. But it isn't a pretty sight. He's practically ravaging a girl right behind the curtains off stage but close enough that I can still see. He gropes her butt and kisses her voraciously in a way that makes my stomach churn … and my mouth water at the fantasy that it could be me in her shoes.

I don't know what's wrong with me.

"Here you go," Mel says as she hands me my drink.

I almost gulp it down in one go.

Mel's eyes widen as she stares at the glass. "Boy, you're really thirsty, aren't you?"

"Yeah, thanks," I say, leaving a few sips in so it's not awkward. "It's just really hot in here."

"Are you sure you're okay?" she asks, raising a brow. I don't know how to reply, but she immediately adds, "I can see you staring at him, you know."

I choke on the Coke and swallow it down so fast my eyes water and turn red. "Staring? Me? No, I was just—"

She snorts. "Save it, girl, I know a crush when I see one."

Now I wished I hadn't gulped down that Coke because the bile is rising in my throat already at the thought of someone catching me staring at Cole fucking Travis … and thinking it's a crush.

"I don't have a crush," I explain.

She holds up her hands in surrender. "Relax, I won't judge you. You aren't the first." She rolls her eyes. "And you definitely won't be the last."

Jesus. Are there so many girls pining over a guy like him?

Mel takes a sip of her Coke before continuing. "But I need to warn you. You really don't want to go there, trust me. Last year, he had a huge falling out with his ex because she accused him of cheating." She searches the crowds for someone. "She's not here, but she has one of her friends spy on him and tell her everything he does." She points into the crowd at a blonde, swaying back and forth to the filler music. "Right … there."

"Kind of obsessive," I reply.

"Word," Mel says, taking another big sip. "Boys like that are nothing but trouble."

"Right," I mutter as I move my hand until the Coke begins to swirl in the glass. Still, my eyes can't stop trying to catch a glimpse of this same bad boy. Like a cigarette—a dirty, filthy addiction that I can't say no to. Occasionally, anyway.

SIX

Monica

When I drop onto my bed, I breathe a sigh of joy. It was such a long night with Mel, and I enjoyed every second of it. Dancing, drinking, partying ... staring at a forbidden boy.

I roll around on the bed and bury my head in my pillow, forcing myself to forget, but no matter how hard I try, his face keeps drifting to the forefront of my mind, along with vivid imagery of every single kiss he gave to that girl ... and how I wished I was her instead.

Fuck.

I'm really done for, aren't I?

Nothing sadder than a girl with a hopeless crush.

Especially when that girl should not be anywhere near boys right now, let alone falling for them.

Shaking my head, I open my drawer and take out my vibrator. Better take care of this craving right now before I do something I'll regret tomorrow at school when I'll most likely see that handsome face again.

But even as I bring myself satisfaction, I can't stop thinking about those sinful green eyes and that sexy glance he shot my way as he kissed someone else. Something about that turns me on like nothing else, and I moan out loud and whisper his name while I come.

I lie down on the bed with my hands to my side and stare at the ceiling, wondering if I'll ever stop crushing on the wrong guys.

Probably not.

I get up and clean the toy before burying it deep in my drawer again. I brush my teeth and throw on some pajamas before hopping back into bed. But even as I drift off into sleep, I dream about Cole and all the dirty, filthy things he'll whisper in my ear if I ever let him get near.

***

Back at school, I try to blend in as well as I can while still trying to find the way to all my classes. It takes some time to get used to the layout as well as the amount of time I have to find the next class. But I have Mel to help me out when needed now. We don't share all our classes, but I can text her anytime and ask for directions. She even offered to help me catch up on homework and topics, which is really nice of her.

The bell rings, so I hastily search for my math books in my messy locker. Right then, two girls position themselves right beside me, one of them opening up her own locker.

"Were you at that party last night where TRIGGER was playing?"

"Fuck yes, of course I was there," the other girl replies, rummaging in her locker. "Cole was soooo good. I can't believe he goes to our school. We're so lucky."

I try to pretend I don't exist while still listening to the conversation.

"Did you hear? That girl he was kissing there was invited to the back," the girl says. "Apparently, she gave him …"

I peek from the side of my locker door and watch the girl make a back and forth motion with her hand in an O-shape and her tongue pushing against her cheek. And it makes my eyes widen.

"Noooo, really?" the other girl slams her locker shut, and I quickly hide behind mine again. "Shut up."

"Yes, really," the girl says, "I saw them go backstage myself."

"You have to tell me more," the other one says, and the two lock arms and march off.

I nudge my locker door aside and let it shut slowly as I stare at the girls walking through the hallway. I'm completely dumbfounded by what I just overheard. I mean, I saw him kiss that girl, but I didn't think he was gonna invite her to the back … Let alone that she'd suck his dick.

Even though these boys are sexual devils, and they often do these things at concerts, especially when there's a popular band playing, rage still bubbles to the surface, and I close my locker with a little too much fury.

"You look cheerful."

I shriek but then cover my mouth with my hand to stop the rest from escaping. It's only my cousin. "Jesus, you scared me."

"Sorry." Ariane snorts. "I wasn't like, trying to."

"I know," I reply. "I just ..." I sigh and throw my bag over my shoulder.

"Something wrong?" she asks. "You seem off today."

My lips part, but I don't know how to respond, so I stutter a little, "No, yeah, I'm fine. It's nothing."

She narrows her eyes. "Are you sure? You sure gave that locker door a piece of your mind."

"I hate math. That's all," I lie.

"Oh! I completely forgot!" She places her hands against her cheeks. "Math!"

"What?" I mutter.

"We share this class together!" she squeals and grabs my shoulders, hyping it up like it's a big deal when it's just math. "Ooh, I'm so excited to have my cousin in the same class as me!"

She hugs me so hard she almost squishes me, and I struggle to breathe. That's when I notice him; Cole Travis. He marches through school in his tattered down black-and-red striped school outfit that's ripped in several places, and when he runs his fingers through his slick dark hair, almost all the girls in his path swoon against the lockers.

A cloud hangs above his head, and the look on his face predicts thunder. But the worst part is that he's walking straight toward us.

With those ice-cold green eyes, he's glancing back and forth between us, and now I can't tell who he's coming for. But one thing's for sure—shit's going to hell.

The closer he gets, the taller he appears, and it almost feels as though he's going to barge straight into us before he comes to a full stop, towering over us.

"What the fuck did you do?" Cole barks, pointing at Ariane. "Or was it you?" When he directs his full and utterly fierce attention at me, I'm at a loss for words. "Which one of you was it, huh?"

"Cole, what the hell are you talking about?" Ariane asks.

"Shut your damn mouth," he snarls.

Ariane leans away in disgust. "Jesus, tone it down a little. The whole school can hear you rant."

"I don't fucking care!" He's so enraged he's on the verge of violence. "One of you spread those rumors."

"What rumors?" She folds her arms. "I don't know what you're talking about."

"Was it you then?" He looks at me again, and I feel like a goddamn homing beacon.

My lips part, but I don't know what to say. No boy has ever made me stutter before. But this boy ... damn near every time he looks at me, I get choked up as though he has his hands wrapped firmly around my throat.

"I … I …"

He cocks his head. "Well?"

"She doesn't know what you're talking about," Ariane says, grabbing his arm to push him away.

"Bullshit." He shoves her away and lunges at me, cornering me against the lockers behind me. "I saw you there. At the club. With that girl … What's her name?"

"Melanie," I mutter, clutching my own damn clothes as if they're my only saving grace… because they're quite literally the only thing hovering between him and his hands right now.

He's all up in my face, practically sniffing me to catch me in a lie. And it works because I'm already sweating heaps.

"You two did it, didn't you?" he says through gritted teeth. "You don't even know me, and you already start telling people what went on behind the curtains?"

"I don't know what you mean," I say, my lips quivering.

"Cole! Leave her alone!" Ariane says, tugging at his shoulder, but it's no use. He's far stronger than she could ever be.

He completely ignores her and slams a hand on the locker beside my head. I try not to jolt up and down when he leans in closer, our faces mere inches away from each other. "I saw you looking at me on stage when I grabbed that girl and kissed her. It was *you*, wasn't it?"

"No one spread any rumors!" Ariane growls at him.

"Stop fucking *lying*!" he yells in her face, and he whisks his phone from his pocket and holds it up for us both to see.

It's a text from one of his buddies from the band with a picture of the girls' bathroom attached. Someone wrote on the stalls with big fat letters the name of the girl who sucked Cole's dick and that she liked it … and that she's a whore.

My phone suddenly bleeps.

"Go on then … look at your phone," Cole challenges me.

There's a pause as he cocks his head and waits. I reach for my phone and check it out. It's Mel.

Mel: OMG, did you see this? See, I told you not to get close. This girl just got named! I'm so glad this wasn't you.

The text has that same picture attached. A picture like this easily turns into rumor, spreading through the school like wildfire.

"Do you get it now?" Cole growls at me. Then he pushes himself off the lockers. "That's what happens when you play with fire." He makes a face and shakes his head at both Ariane and me before storming off.

But his behavior and the forced proximity to the worst bad boy at school certainly left its mark on me.

"What just happened?" I mutter, completely dumbfounded by what just went down.

He managed to get some girl on her knees for him, and now the whole school knows. Not only that, but he parades around like it's his goddamn school, and no one does anything to stop it. Is this normal here? Or is this just because he's in a band and popular?

He sure seemed pissed that everybody knew.

Ariane grasps my arm, and says, "Ignore him. He doesn't know what he's talking about. You weren't even there. He's always trying to start some shit."

For a second there, I almost tell her, but then I remind myself she wouldn't take it well if I went somewhere without asking her to come too. So I keep my mouth shut and let her accompany me to class.

"I know you're still thinking about him," she says.

My lips part, but I don't get the time to form an answer. "Don't. He's not worth your time. When I see him again, I'll give him a big ole slap to teach him a lesson not to threaten women."

She makes an obvious fist even though I know for sure that if she did manage to muster up the courage to do it, he probably wouldn't even flinch.

"He knows he's bad, and he doesn't care," she says. "Now you know why I said what I said."

"What's that then?" I ask as she throws her arm over my shoulder.

She smirks. "That Cole Travis is a giant fucking bastard."

SEVEN

Cole

I readjust my mic and fiddle with my guitar, but it won't tune the right way, and it's pissing me off to the point that I tear it off my shoulder and throw it on the stage.

"Cole ... really?" Tristan sighs.

"Yeah, fucking really," I growl back. "Nothing works."

"Maybe if you focused, it would work," he says, running his fingers through his ruffled blond hair that always looks like he just rolled out of bed. "Look, just because it's just the two of us today since Michael's still in class and Benjamin had to go to the hospital with his mom doesn't mean you can slack off."

"I'm not slacking off!" I snap. When the look on his face changes, I sigh, and say, "Sorry. I don't mean to snap at you."

"I don't think you're here, to be honest. Is it because of those texts?" he asks, sitting down on the stage.

I nod and sit down beside him. "Yup. You know how it goes. One minute, I'm flirting with some girl, and the next thing you know, it's all over social media and the entire school knows."

He pats me on the back. Not gentle, more like a slap. "When are you gonna learn to ignore all that noise?"

"Never," I say, glancing at him over my shoulder. "It's impossible."

His brows rise. "Because you play into it."

"Do they ever write about you like that?" I ask, throwing him the same look back.

He knows damn well it's a rhetorical question, yet he still answers. "No, but that doesn't mean I don't know what it's like to be in the spotlight. I'm in this band too, remember?"

"I know." Rolling my eyes at his obvious dig. "Forget it." I avert my eyes.

I can't say it to his face, so I won't say it at all … but we're not alike. People look at him, and they see a cute drummer. People look at me, and they see a rock god. Someone they want to get to know just to feel good about themselves. Not to really *know* me … but to be popular, and I fucking hate it.

Maybe that's hypocritical of me.

I'm a douchebag, and I enjoy it most of the time.

But sometimes … I just wish girls would want the real me. The guy underneath all that fame.

I sigh to myself and get up from the stage. Right then, I notice that same girl from the concert, the one I made out with, standing in the room. She's been watching us … or me … but for how long?

"Wait a minute," I mutter. Her eyes widen as I march toward her, and she tries to flee, but I'm quicker than she is, and I block the door with my body. "Eavesdropping?"

"No, I swear, I wasn't." She tucks her hair behind her ear. "I was just … looking for you, that's all."

My eyes narrow. "Why? What do you want?"

"Nothing, I just … I wanted to tell you how much I liked being with you after that concert." Her eyes trail off. "You know, the kiss." A blush grows on her cheeks.

"Okay," I reply. It does nothing for me. That kiss meant nothing to me except a momentary distraction from what was really on my mind … the new girl. And I honestly do not care about this chick. "That's it?"

"Yeah," she says. "If you want, I can come see you again." Oh God. I don't like where this is going. "Maybe we can—"

I hold up a hand. "Look, I'm gonna say it up front. I don't date."

Her eyes widen, and she looks around as though she's seen a ghost. "I was … I thought—" she mutters, stumbling through her words.

"You thought what? After one kiss?" I frown.

"Well, we had such an amazing time backstage, I figured—" She starts to blush, which is my cue to put a stop to this nonsense right this minute.

"No, sorry," I say, averting my eyes. I knew I shouldn't have done it, but I couldn't stop myself. I was drunk on the music ... and on the need to kiss someone instead of that girl staring at me from the crowd.

Monica.

Just thinking about her makes me want to storm out of here and find her.

And I don't know why.

Why the hell am I so obsessed with a girl I don't even know?

I shake it off when the girl in front of me sighs. "And here I was, thinking I could tell everyone."

I frown. "What do you mean?"

"Well, you know, *you* ... the greatest rock star in school and little ole me." She giggles with a slight uptick in her tone halfway through. "It would surely be a good story."

My eye twitches, and my lip curls up. I can't believe what I'm hearing.

"I just ... like you a lot, you know. Everyone does."

"So that's it, huh?" My fist balls, and I lower my head to hide my rage.

"No, not all, I mean, you're good looking, you're sexy, you're popular."

"Popular," I repeat. "That's why you wanted me to kiss you?" I look at her. She's smiling gently, unaware of the coils inside my heart, twisting it into a knot further and further until no one can break the bonds. "Because I'm popular?"

She tries to grab my hand, but I pull back.

That's when it hits me.

The rumors.

They weren't started by Ariane or her friends.

They were started by *her*.

"It was you," I growl.

"What?" she mutters.

"You spread those rumors," I growl.

"Rumors?" She gasps. "But I—"

"Don't," I hiss. "I don't wanna fucking hear it."

"Cole," Tristan mutters from the back, trying to intervene, but I don't even care anymore.

Yes, I'm a fucking hypocrite. I fuck and kiss girls for fun, but for them to go around my back and spread rumors about shit that didn't even happen takes the cake.

"You wanted everyone to know, didn't you? To be popular," I spit. "Get out."

That kiss didn't mean shit to me. It was just a fun thing to do. But these girls … they're only in it for the fame.

"But I can give you what you want. I know you like them easy, and I'm always available. I don't mind sharing, and—"

"GET OUT!" I yell, pointing at the door.

She sucks in a breath and immediately runs off.

"Cole!" Tristan barks, sighing out loud.

I turn my head toward him. "What?"

"Really? Maybe tone it down a little?" he asks. "Every fan we lose is one we won't get back. You know that."

"I'd rather not have any fans at all than one like her," I say through gritted teeth.

"Fine. Whatever. Don't direct your anger at me. I'm not your fucking problem, okay?" he says, sighing. "Now, can we finally get back to practice?"

My mind still reels from the adrenaline coursing through my veins. I tell myself I don't care, but I do. Popularity. I used to dream about it, but now I wish it away. Every fan I've gained is one more person I can't ever trust. Because all they care about is getting an inch of that fame.

I'm merely a tool for them. A way to get to the top.

A kiss with me is nothing but an exchange.

This is why I don't get close. Why I don't *let* anyone get close.

I sigh out loud and hop back onto the stage, brushing it off again, even though it happens time and time again. I pick up my guitar, checking for any damage, but luckily, it's unscathed. No thanks to me. I should really stop taking out my frustrations on this beauty. She's the only thing keeping me from quitting ... and the only thing that has never failed me.

"Ready?" Tristan asks as he sits down behind his drums, casually throwing his sticks.

I adjust the mic and play some strings before nodding.

We play our best song together because it's the easiest

one to do with just two of us here. Michael and Benjamin don't mind if we practice without them. We'll need the extra playtime for the big show coming up next week. We'll be playing on a stage for a few thousand people, which is a huge deal for us. It could be our big break, and everything we've worked so hard for. The one way trip to true stardom.

But as we play our tune to the beat, I suddenly spot the girl from my class. Monica.

And she's looking straight at me with those same eyes as before, those eyes that beg me to unravel the secrets layered behind.

Eyes that drive me mad.

For me, she stopped walking. For me, she paused her daily life.

Just to take a peek.

And it makes me want to show off.

So I smash the strings of my guitar and sing even louder, our eyes connected like the music tethers us together. It's bold, but I want her attention. I don't know why, but I'll do anything for it. Anything to keep her from looking away.

And she knows. She bites her lip, clutches her bag ever closer, tiptoes around on her feet like she doesn't know whether to stay or to run.

She's indecisive ... And she hates it.

Her eyes are on fire as she glares at the target of her rage. Me. An indescribable, unmistakable connection forged between us by that simple look that could destroy anything in its path.

And she fucking hates that it's there.

I know the feeling too damn well.

All my disappointment in myself staring straight back at me.

It's like looking into a mirror and not liking the person you see.

And for some reason, I can't stop wanting to show her just how good I can be, because the more I do, the more she'll hate me. And I need her to fucking hate me. Because it's the only thing keeping me from destroying her.

Every note that slithers from my lips is one creeping into her ear like a whisper in the night. Her body leans toward me as though she can feel my tongue drawing a line through each of her crevices. And when her eyes close, I can almost hear her gasp.

The song rises to its peak, and so does my energy as I'm swept away in the magic that is her and me. And even though there are no fans watching this performance, I play like my life depends on it. I sing my fucking guts out until I'm left without breath. I torture myself … and her … just to feel alive.

Her body sways, and her lips part. It's an invitation, one the devil inside me would gladly accept. It's tempting … and easy. Too easy.

Her foot scoots a little closer to the door. Just an inch. But I saw.

And it's enough to make me stop dead in my tracks, mid-song.

My penetrative stare makes her stop. Her body stiffens. Her mouth shuts again, and her lips are thin slits, just like her eyes.

Then she walks off.

Just like that.

And I'm left with the inexplicable need to scream.

Was it that easy to break the spell? Or did I force her to?

One simple, forceful gaze. That's all it took to make her run for the hills.

One foot. One simple forward-inching foot. That's all it took to make me want to storm off stage and drag her back inside.

Into the dragon's den.

I lick my bottom lip.

She wouldn't survive a day.

EIGHT

Monica

My feet are walking, but it feels as though something is carrying me through the hallways.

My mind isn't present even though I'm storming out like I've made up my mind.

Something about the way he looked at me made me do a U-turn.

He was playing that way, so seductively, with his eyes boring into mine, to get a reaction out of me. Not just to practice with his band, but to show off. To show me what I'm missing out on.

And for some reason, it captured my attention, made me stop when normally I never would.

Something about that guy forces me to see him.

Eye contact with him was all that was needed to stop me in my tracks. The mere sound of his voice blaring through the microphone called me like a siren luring me in. His eyes were blazing, lips talking dirt like he was whispering them straight into my ears.

And even though we were both fully clothed and not even in touching range, it felt like filthy, raunchy sex.

My body instinctively inched closer.

And then he shut me off.

Just like that, he broke the connection we had with a fiery rage unlike anything I'd ever seen before, and it made me finally come to my senses. I swear if I hadn't left right then and there, he would've stormed off stage to force me out.

But my heartbeat is still going crazy fast as I run out of the building and into the open air. The wind hits me hard, and I take a few seconds to catch my breath. The hot sun burns on my skin as I stare up at the sky, wondering what the hell I'm doing.

I shouldn't get distracted by a boy like him.

He's all trouble and nothing good.

Still, I can't stop seeing his face in front of me, his eyes penetrating my soul.

Shake it off, Monica. He's only doing it to taunt you. Don't let him get to you.

"Hey, Monica!"

My eyes burst open. It's Mel. She beckons me to come over to where she's sitting on a blanket in the grass with a couple of friends I haven't met yet. "Sit down with us."

Smiling, I approach the group as Mel introduces me to them.

"This is Monica. We have a few classes together."

"Hi," I say to everyone.

"Sit, sit," Mel pats the blanket. "Don't be shy. Tell them about yourself."

"Yeah, Monica," one of the girls says. "It's nice to meet you." She holds out her hand and we shake. "I'm Becky."

"Hi, Becky. I'm the new girl," I say, laughing awkwardly.

"We know," a guy to my right says. "It was hard to miss."

"How?" I raise my brows. I thought I was blending in quite well.

"Relax, I'm just messing with ya," he replies, and he winks. "You're already fitting in."

I smile back at him as he opens his mouth again, "Name's Troy."

"So what brings you to Black Mountain Academy?" asks another guy in the back, who's casually leaning on his elbows.

"Don't answer that. Jason's just trolling you like he always does," Mel says.

"I'm just curious," he interjects.

"It's fine," I answer. "I needed a ... new start." I shrug. I'm not about to tell some random people I've never met before my entire life's history, but a tiny inch of truth can't hurt, right?

79

"A new start? From what?" he asks.

From what?

From …

Images from my previous school flash through my mind. All the people. Parties. Bobby.

I swallow, suddenly choked up.

"I …"

Everyone's hanging on my words, but I don't know what to tell them. I don't know if I could ever say it out loud. Or if I even want to.

"Don't answer if you don't want to," Mel says, placing a hand on my back.

"Yeah," I reply, letting out a sigh of relief.

I don't want to think about it.

"You know, you look like you could use this." Some guy in the back suddenly pulls out a blunt he was smoking and tries to hand it to me.

All I can do is stare. Stare at the implications of taking a whiff. Of the effects it will have on me. Of all the things I wanted to forget.

My stomach churns, and I suddenly feel ill.

I stumble to get up from the blanket.

"Hey, what's wrong?" Mel asks.

"Nothing, I … have to go," I reply, trying to look at all of them, but I'm dizzy all of a sudden and can't get my bearings. Mel grabs my arm and helps me stay standing. "Whoa, don't fall."

"It's okay, I'm fine," I reply.

"Sorry, I only wanted to offer you a smoke," the guy says, sticking the blunt back into his mouth.

My skin feels prickly, icy and heated at the same time, as though I've just taken a cold shower and jumped straight into a hot tub. My brain is melting with the possible scenarios playing out in my mind, all of which are nightmares I never wished to imagine.

But to me, they are as real as can be.

Mel grabs my shoulders, the mere touch of her fingers on my skin, making me jolt up and down. She frowns as she looks at the goose bumps on my skin, and asks, "Hey, are you okay?"

I shake my head. I came here to escape it all, and now I'm confronted by it again. It never stops.

"Was it the question? I swear, they're not normally like that. They're just excited there's a newbie."

"I know," I say, looking away because it's not about that. Not at all. The question set me off, yes, but it's the drugs that do me in.

I can't. I just can't.

I shake my head again, and say, "I'm sorry for wasting your time."

And then I turn around and walk off.

I can't look back even though I can feel her eyes practically boring into my back, begging me to come back.

I won't. I cannot associate myself with people who use, not in any way, or any amount, no matter how small or lighthearted the occasion. It reminds me too much of what happened to me. Of Bobby. Of my own past self, someone I no longer want to be.

So I run back into the school. Tears stain my eyes, but I push them away. I couldn't stay there, and I hope Mel isn't mad about it because I'd hate to lose her as a friend.

I don't even want to think about this, yet I am. Why can't I let this go? Why can't I leave this behind me and be a new me? Forget all of it ever happened and continue with my life?

I'm so consumed by my own thoughts that I don't look where I'm going, and the moment I make a turn into a hallway, I bump into a big, muscular guy whose rock-hard body easily knocks me down.

With an oompf, I land on the floor on my backpack.

Laughter ensues.

Then I look up.

It's him.

Cole Travis.

And the look he gives me comes straight out of the devil's playbook.

He's surrounded by his buddies, one I recognize as a band member who was there when they were practicing. Behind them, a few girls tag along, giggling, waiting eagerly for them to do something. Anything. Good or bad.

"What the fuck was that?" one of his buddies with brown crew-cut hair balks.

I scramble up from the floor. "Sorry, I wasn't looking."

"You should be sorry!" one of the girls shouts over the

crowd while I pat down my dress. "Do you even know who you bumped into?"

When I'm finally up on my feet again, I come face-to-face with Cole. I didn't realize I was this close to him. The lines on his forehead crease as he frowns at me, clearly annoyed that I'm here and dared to bump into him.

"What are you doing here?" another band member with blond, wavy half-long hair growls.

It's the one who was practicing with him a while ago, but I don't know his name.

"None of your business," I retort.

The girls start to laugh.

"What a joke," one of the other guys with brown crew-cut hair says.

I make a face. "I already apologized."

Cole cocks his head and checks his watch while tapping his foot. "Guys—"

"You're such a fucking wuss," the guy spits at me. "Apologizing? Don't make me laugh."

"Hey," I say. "No need to—"

"To what? Laugh?" he says, and the girls laugh in conjunction like puppets on a string.

It's disgusting. They're only here because these guys are popular, following them around just to leech a tiny amount of fame. As if being around a celebrity suddenly makes you famous too. It's so ridiculous, and they don't even realize what they're doing. I won't ever be one of those girls. And I certainly won't ever swoon in public over the likes of Cole

Travis.

"Dude, just stop," Cole growls at his buddy. "And Lindy? Shut up." Cole glances over his shoulder at one of the girls laughing at me.

"No, she needs to learn a little respect," the guy says, stepping forward. "New girls don't parade around this school, acting as if it belongs to them."

I cross my arms. "I didn't know it belonged to *anybody* at all."

"Yeah. Us. You'd better show a little respect," he retorts.

"Respect?" I say with a tsk. "Good to know you've claimed this school. I wonder how the teachers and principal feel about that."

"Don't mess with us," the guy hisses, pointing his finger at me as though it will add a threat to his statement.

"Michael," Cole growls, and he grabs Michael's arm, but Michael jerks himself free before Cole has a shot. "No. She needs to apologize properly and mean it."

I narrow my eyes at him, trying not to feel intimidated, but it's hard. All his groupies and friends are watching, and the twisted look on Cole's face makes it hard not to get lost in rage.

I want to scream. Fight. Punch. Kick. Make a scene.

But that wouldn't help me.

All it would do is make me more hated.

Especially by the countless fans who walk these very hallways.

It would be like career suicide but in high school.

Still, it hurts to be the target of their games. To have these people watch eagerly in anticipation of my demise as if I'm part of the show.

"Who are you even? Just some random girl thinking she can talk to us? No chance," Michael says, and all the girls giggle again like it's funny, but it's not.

Now I know what Sam felt like when she was being bullied.

"You're a *nobody*," he adds. "Why did you even want to go to this school? You've got no friends. You're running away from something, and I wanna know what it is."

My eyes widen.

Panic seeps through my veins.

Run.

Run.

Run.

The word plays over and over in my mind, and I can't escape the message it brings.

I should've run when I had the chance.

Should've fought when I had the time.

But I can't change what happened. I can't fix what someone else broke in me.

All I can do is try to ignore it and move on.

But the tears still well up in my eyes.

Suddenly, the look in Cole's eyes shifts. His body grows rigid.

"Michael!" Cole intervenes, and he grabs Michael's arm

and jerks him aside. "Enough."

It's as if he's reining in the dog meant to maul me.

Well, it worked.

I glare at Cole, who doesn't say a word to me. One simple look, that's all he gives me.

One soul-crushing, searing look.

"Fuck you all," I say through gritted teeth.

The girls laugh. The boys laugh. Everyone laughs. Except Cole.

But they got what they wanted. They got to me.

They made me remember why I came here. Why I ran.

They made me break down.

And I hate that I let them, so I turn around and march off even though I can still feel Cole's coal-hot eyes burning into my back.

I won't glance.

I won't turn around.

I won't even grace him with my middle finger.

Because even though he's not worth a tear, they still made me shed one.

***

Cole

The hallway is filled with rumors and chatter, people whispering about how bad this whole scene was, but none of them take a stance. None of them dares to speak up.

Just like me.

I was dead silent while my boys and the fans following us tried to fall in line as though they had to protect me from imminent death. Ridiculous. They made it a big deal, made her feel uncomfortable ... and then made her cry as a final nail in the coffin.

"Yeah, run, little girl!" Michael calls after Monica.

I immediately grab his arm and turn him my way. "Stop."

"What?" he growls, jerking himself free.

The look on his face makes me want to punch him, but I refrain because he's my bandmate, and I need to be on good terms with all of them. Otherwise, we'll never succeed in chasing our big dream.

But at what cost?

"You're beating a dead horse," I say as he looks around at all the girls eyeballing him. There are not as many as who usually follow me, but enough to make him want to show off. That much is obvious.

"So what?" he scoffs. "I was just having some fun. Besides, she ran into you, remember?"

I shake my head. "I don't fucking care." And I turn

around and yell at the crowd, "Party's over."

The girls pause and stare at me for a moment; almost all of them hanging on my every word.

My pupils dilate, and I make a shooing motion with my hand. "Scram."

Finally, they leave us alone. But it still doesn't chill the fire blazing in my heart.

"Really, Cole? Chasing away fans?" Michael says.

"They're not fans; they're groupies," I growl back, turning my attention toward him. "Don't ever try to protect me again, got it?"

He makes a face. "What's your problem?"

I don't want to fight. But the way he behaved makes me want to punch his jaw.

I've never felt this way toward my bandmates, and it terrifies the living shit out of me.

So much so that I turn around and walk away.

I don't know what to do with this turmoil snaking its way through my head. This isn't me. I never used to care about anything, let alone one silly girl.

Yet I can't stop thinking about Monica and the look in her eyes the moment Michael mentioned her running away from her old school. They flickered with a kind of fear I've never seen before.

Something … vicious … and feral.

As though it would kill her to remember.

One moment she was feisty and ready to defend herself, but that one question knocked her off her axis. Why?

And why do I care so much that I want to know the answer?

Ruminating, I go up to the teacher's area where there's a private unisex bathroom that I'm allowed to use to escape the fans. The teachers don't want me going into the regular bathrooms to prevent a traffic jam from everyone hoping to snap a dirty pick of my visits. It surprised me too that people would really sink that low …

Not as low as me, though, when I hear sniffles coming from the teacher's bathroom.

I pause. Who is in there crying?

My hand instinctively hovers over the door handle because I'm curious to know who it is.

Right then, the noise stops, and the door opens right in my face.

A girl comes full stop right in front of me.

And not just any girl …

Monica.

She has access to the teacher's bathroom too?

Interesting.

Standing in the door opening, she stops mere inches away from me, her body frozen to the floor as though she's seen a ghost.

I can't take my eyes off her, can't focus on anything else but the sparkle in her reddened eyes, the fleeting happiness that has now been whisked away. I can't look away. Can't do anything but stare at her as she stares right back at me for a few seconds, before her fingers reach for her eyes, and she briskly wipes away any trace of her tears.

"What are you doing?" she asks. "Did you follow me?"

My lips part, but I don't know what to say, so I say the first thing that pops up into my head. "I needed to take a leak."

She raises a brow. "In the teacher's bathroom?"

"Yeah … I have a pass." I hold it up between two fingers. "To keep the fans at bay."

She snorts, and her eyes narrow. "Right. I thought this was a women's only bathroom."

I lean in closer and point at the sign above the door. "Unisex."

The moment the word sex leaves my lips, she gulps. Hard.

It almost makes me want to put my hands against the wall, trap her inside, and kiss her, right then and there. But then I remember what my bandmates did. And what I *didn't* do.

I sigh out loud and rub my lips together. "Look, I just wanted to apologize for Michael. He was out of line."

She glares at me, looking unamused. "Really?"

"Really," I repeat. "He's an asshole."

"You two perfectly match each other then," she replies.

Fuck. I hate this. Even though I've behaved like an asshole, I'm not like him. And I hate that she'd compare us.

"I'm trying to apologize, okay? Don't make this harder," I say out of spite.

"That's a shitty apology then," she scoffs.

"I know I have shitty friends," I retort. "But you walked into me, not the other way around. Maybe you should watch where you're walking."

"Wow …" she mutters, shaking her head. "You really tried, didn't you?"

She tries to push past me, and I know I fucked up again.

I'm not used to this kind of interaction.

To apologizing.

Girls usually throw themselves at my feet. Nothing I do is ever wrong to them, not even when I show them the door.

But this girl … she genuinely despises me, and I hate that.

So I grab her arm and make her stop. "Wait. Sorry. I didn't mean to—"

She looks at my hand wrapped around her wrist. We both do. And when I realize what I'm doing, I release her. The look in her eyes is murderous. And I get that. I deserve it.

What I don't get is that she doesn't run. "You didn't mean to what?" she asks.

I can't let this get to me. Even if I'm the asshole and my friends are too, I have to distance myself, no matter how hard it is. I can't get fucking close, not to anyone.

I step closer, and say, "I didn't mean to offend you."

She makes a face like she doesn't believe it's true.

Maybe it is, maybe it isn't, but when everything was said and done, I still hated seeing the hurt on her face, and that speaks volumes.

"I didn't know you were so …"

"Fragile? Weak?" she fills in the blanks with a twinge of hatred as though it comes easy.

But the words she chooses surprise me. I wouldn't paint her as weak or fragile at all. "Complicated," I say.

She smiles, and the sight could fill a thousand hearts and light them on fire. And even though I thought my icy heart had been frozen for a long time, it still manages to crack under the weight of her smile.

Suddenly someone grabs my shoulder, turning me around. "Dude, what are you doing? We don't have time for girls," Tristan says.

I frown and chew my lip. He's right, even though I wish he wasn't right now. I don't want to jeopardize my band with another girl, not again, not with my reputation.

I avert my eyes, and without looking at her, without even saying another word or taking that leak I needed, I walk off.

NINE

Cole

Days later

I haven't seen Monica since she ran into us. I don't know if we're both purposely avoiding each other, or if she just happened to disappear. Maybe the reaction of my bandmates really did scare her off.

Some days, I feel guilty for not intervening sooner, but if I had, they'd accused me of being on her side instead of theirs. And that would get in the way of the band.

Anything for the band.

With my spoon, I twirl it in my dessert, but I'm not remotely hungry, so I stop, pick up my tray, and waltz to the bin next to the cafeteria door to throw it all out. Fuck this shit. I don't even know why I'm eating here when we could be practicing … away from all these eyes that are on me every second of the day.

Just one glance over my shoulder, and they're all swooning with smiles, waving at me like they're waiting for me to wave back. I like fans when I sing, but I don't like the pressure it brings in daily life.

Gotta get used to it, I suppose. One day, we're gonna be even more famous than we are now, and then photographers and tabloids will be talking shit about us too. Right now, it's just people on social media that are hyped about us, but apparently it's enough to get people to recognize you on the streets and beg for an autograph or a kiss.

"Hey."

The sound of Ariane's shrill voice is like the strings on a guitar snapping in two.

"What are you doing here?" I bark over my shoulder.

"Wow. I'm allowed to be in the cafeteria, asshole," she says, folding her arms. "Is that the way you greet people nowadays?"

"Not people," I say, putting my tray away, "but definitely you."

She narrows her eyes at me. "Ha-ha, always the funny one."

"I don't joke around," I reply stoically, and I turn around, but she keeps tagging along behind me.

"Look, I just wanted to tell you that I think you did

great."

"What, my show?" I mutter. "I don't care about your opinion, Ariane. Not anymore."

"I meant with the situation in the hallways. You know, with Monica."

I come to a full stop, and she bumps into my back. She wasn't there, I'm positive, as I looked everywhere to see if she was watching. "Who told you about that?"

"Dude, everyone saw …"

I turn around and corner her. "I don't appreciate your girlfriends keeping tabs on me, Ariane."

She raises a brow. "And I don't like not knowing what's going on when it's the talk of the day."

My eyes twitch. "You never stopped being a gossip girl …"

"And you never stopped being a manipulative bastard," she retorts. But then she puts her arm around my neck, and says, "But I'm proud of you."

I throw her arm off my neck. "Don't."

"What? You managed to stay away from her and actually chased her off. Well done."

Chased her off? Fuck no.

I shove her against the wall and point at her. "I don't need your fucking approval, and I sure as hell didn't do it for you," I growl. "Now back the fuck off."

She holds up her hands. "It's cool. I don't care that you don't do it for me. I just need you to stay away from her. That's all."

"Why do you care so much?" I narrow my eyes at her. "What's so special about her?"

Her pupils dilate, and her body stance grows rigid. "Nothing. Absolute nothing, that's exactly my point." She steps forward and throws her hands around my neck again, twirling my hair. "Not as interesting as I am anyway …"

I frown. Now my interest is piqued. But I don't want Ariane's arms anywhere near me, so I shake her off, and growl, "I don't need you or your bullshit. Just leave."

She shrugs and licks her lips. "Suit yourself. I gave you a choice."

"Bullshit," I spit. "And you know it."

"Don't say I didn't warn you, though," she adds.

"What did you say?" I growl, cocking my head.

She looks away. "You heard me."

"Or what? Are you threatening me?" I put a hand up against the wall to block her exit. "You're gonna spread more rumors?"

"If you don't want *me* …" She lifts her eyes to meet mine in an infuriatingly seductive manner. "Then you can go fuck yourself."

She pushes me off her and walks off with bouncy hips, flaunting her middle finger as though it's her single most powerful weapon.

Well, fuck her.

I don't like being threatened, especially not by the likes of her and especially not with more reputation-destroying gossip.

She's already gotten to me one too many times.

Maybe it's about time I stopped listening to anything she says and started listening to the devil in my heart. I thought I was doing the right thing by protecting Monica from the boys and me by steering clear to focus on the band.

But fuck that noise.

Because if Ariane wants me to stay away from her …

I'm going to do my very fucking best to get closer than close.

So close, the whole school will be talking about us.

Just out of spite.

***

Monica

Music class would normally be something fun and enjoyable, but not when you've got dozens of girls stacked up against the door to peek through the window at the two band members of TRIGGER sharing this class.

"This isn't even the biggest group I've seen," Mel whispers in my ear. "One time, there were about triple this number waiting at the door. It's normal insanity."

I snigger. "Do they follow them everywhere?"

"Yup, whenever fans have a free hour, they start stalking TRIGGER." She rolls her eyes. "And every year, it gets worse and worse."

"And the teachers and school are all okay with it?" I ask.

"No, of course not, but there's not a lot they can do against teenage hormones," she says, and we both laugh. "They're probably hoping the boys finish school quickly and don't come back."

"Same," I add, and we laugh again.

"Did you know, the lead singer even has his own pass to the teacher's bathroom?"

I almost choke on my own words. "Wha …? I … no, that's weird."

"Yeah, apparently Cole can't even pee without hordes of girls waiting to catch a glimpse."

"Yikes," I respond.

So he was telling the truth when I almost bumped into him a second time right in the teacher's bathroom doorway.

"Attention, please," the teacher says, clapping his hands so we shut up. "Open your books to page fifteen."

I don't think I've ever read about music, but there's a first for everything. When I took this class, I'd imagined we'd be singing our lungs out, but maybe that part comes after we finish reading the book.

"This assignment will be in pairs," the teacher says. Right then, everyone begins to bargain with one another, whispering who's going to partner with who. But then the teacher speaks up again, "I'll decide who partners with who." Then he gazes at me.

Anyone but Cole.

Please.

Anyone but him.

"Monica, you'll work together with Cole."

My eyes widen.

Fuck.

Fuck.

Fuck!

Just my fucking luck.

I don't even hear what the teacher is saying anymore or who Mel is paired with because all I can think about is Cole, sitting in the corner of the room near the window. I've never seen him wear his uniform according to the school's dress code. Something about him always has to stand out. Today, it's a leather jacket.

His head is slightly turned toward me, a half-smirk on the schmuck's face as though he owns the place. His lips part, and his tongue dives out to wet his lips, and it suddenly becomes hard to breathe.

Get your act together, Monica. It's just an assignment, nothing else.

"Go on then, go find your partners, and we'll start the assignment," the teacher says.

But all I hear is the word "partner" over and over again.

That isn't a word I'd ascribe to Cole Travis, ever.

Nor did I expect to have him look me straight in the eyes again after our last conversation. I thought he was finally apologizing for his friends, and then he vanished as though it meant nothing. Not a single look or word was uttered. Nothing. It was like I didn't exist anymore, and it confused me.

So then why is he looking at me with those hungry eyes again like some wolf ready to devour me? And why is it so hot in here all of a sudden?

I muster the courage and hold my breath while I march toward him and sit down on the empty seat beside him.

"You sure you wanna sit down there?" he asks with that same husky voice that manages to push all my buttons.

"Why, what did you do?" I ask, wondering if he placed some kind of booby trap or something.

"You're asking the wrong question," he says, leaning back in his chair with that same casual swagger he always has. "The question is … what am I *going* to do?"

I gulp, my body freezing up as he moves closer and places a hand on the back of my seat.

"You sure got the wrong partner, didn't you?" he mutters.

"Can we just start?" I ask, pointing at the book in front of him, which remains untouched.

"No," he says, eyes still completely homed in on me. "I'd rather look at you."

Jesus Fuck.

That made my whole body tingle.

Did he really just say that?

No, he's just messing with me, I'm sure of it. He saw me gravitate toward him the moment he started playing music. He noticed the attraction. And now he's using it against me to play me. To humiliate me.

"We're in class, and we're supposed to learn," I reiterate, trying to get some sense into him.

"I already know everything about music. Go ahead, ask."

I raise a brow at him, and he does too in such a playful way that it's hard not to smile.

He points at me. "See? I knew you could smile."

"Cole, really?"

"What? I'm not here to learn anything," he replies. "And I don't think you are either."

"I took this class because I like music, that's it," I reply, opening my own book.

He narrows his eyes. "You tell yourself that."

"What, you think I picked this school or class because of you?" I snort. "I didn't even know you went here. As a matter of fact, I didn't even know your band existed at all."

His smile disappears, and there's a twitch right below his eyes. "Didn't look like it when you were staring at me at practice."

"Like I said … I enjoy good music, that's all," I say.

"So, you think I'm good?"

I sigh, trying not to let his obvious taunts get to me. I open the page to the chapter we're supposed to be working on. "Can we get to work now?"

"Not interested," he replies.

"Well, then why are you even here?"

He shrugs. "Easy credits."

I snort and roll my eyes. "What a surprise."

"What?" he scoffs. I focus my attention on the book instead of him, but within seconds he grabs it off my table and holds it hostage. "You think I'm a bad guy, don't you?"

"Don't start this now, please," I say, and I look around class to see if I can find the teacher, but he's busy with another group. Everyone's working hard except for us, and no one seems to notice. "Give it back."

"Tell me the truth." His voice is darkened, and he looks serious. Not his usual mischievous self. The same way he looked at me in the hallways when he apologized for his friends' behavior.

"Fine, yes, you are a bad guy," I reply, sighing. "Happy now?"

He looks at me, dead serious. "No."

"Then what do you want?"

He leans back in his chair again, casually waving the book back and forth. "Want this? I'll give it back if you do what I ask."

Nothing's ever easy with Cole Travis. "How about you give me back my book?"

"I will …" That familiar smirk comes back. "If you come to my show Saturday."

I make a face, confused as hell why he'd want me to be there.

"No ifs, no buts," he adds. "Just be there. That's it."

Is this some sort of trap? It has to be. No way would Cole Travis himself invite some random new girl to one of his gigs unless he's trying to bait me. But for what?

"This is a joke, right?" I ask.

"No joke," he says. "In fact, after the show, talk to the bouncer. He'll let you backstage."

He licks and then bites his bottom lip while his eyes briefly dart to mine, and for some fucked-up reason, I can't stop thinking about how sexy that was… and how much it makes me think of what those lips would feel like pressed against mine.

I swallow hard. Maybe it isn't a joke … maybe he actually likes me?

Is that why he's been such an asshole?

Not that I want to be backstage with a guy like him. The last time I saw him go backstage with someone, it ended in school-wide rumors, and I don't want to be the next girl in his long line of willing victims.

I sigh. "Why do you want me there? So you and your buddies can jump me when I get there?"

He snorts. "Is that what you think of us?"

"Well, I've met a few assholes in my life, but …"

A grin spreads on his face. "None as big as me." He winks, and for some reason, it makes my heart beat faster as he leans in and places the book back on my desk. Suddenly, the look on his face turns darker. "Believe them when they tell you …"

"What?" I mutter, wondering what he means.

"That's it, class! Back to your own seats now," the teacher says, and before I know it one of Cole's bandmates is tapping his foot right behind me, annoyed that I've not moved yet.

"You're in my seat," he says, running his fingers through his shoulder-length wavy blond hair.

I haven't even had the time to move or get an answer from Cole, but whatever. I still get up and sit back at my own table again, but my eyes can't help trawl off to Cole's. He's staring right back at me over his bandmate's shoulder. But not in a sweet, casual way, no, this stare ... this is one that makes all the girls beg. One that says ... *Do you dare?*

But I don't think I have a choice anymore.

My heart's already made the choice for me.

TEN

Monica

Saturday

I'm standing at the end of the room, far away from the stage, clutching my phone in my hand. A part of me already regrets that I'm here.

I check my phone and reread the messages Mel sent me. She didn't have time to come, I asked, but she was busy with her friends. She even invited me to come over too for a sleepover, but I said no because Cole personally invited me.

Because he genuinely wanted me there, and for the first time ever, it felt like he meant it. And I didn't want to disappoint.

But now I'm starting to regret that decision. I'm all by

myself in a club I've never been to, with people around me that I've never met. No one pays me any attention, luckily, but I still don't feel like I belong. It makes me clutch my phone even harder, in case I need to call someone to come and pick me up.

Don't be such a wuss, Monica. You came here for a reason. You can do this. Get over yourself.

I swallow hard and approach the crowd. Cole and his bandmates are already on stage, as I came late because I was still going back and forth with myself about whether I was going to go or not, seeing how it went last time. I'm glad I made it in time for their last act, though.

Cole's looking at the crowd with so much joy in his eyes. It's clear he loves doing this. Being a rock star is his thing. The way he shakes his body to the rhythm between singing his notes gets the crowd going, and when he throws off his shirt and chucks it at a girl, she goes nuts, along with all the other squealing girls in the crowd.

I hide my laughter behind my hand as I don't want to ridicule them, even though it's funny to watch. This used to be my vice too, back when …

I choke up and force myself to stop thinking about it.

That was the old Monica.

And the old Monica no longer exists.

I'm just me, and I wanna be here in the moment, living my life to the fullest. I don't want to regret anything anymore. I just want to smile.

So I do, and at that moment, our eyes connect, and my

heart stops. When he looks at me, it becomes hard to breathe. I don't know why he has this effect on me, and why I don't want him to ever stop looking.

He dances to the music and shows off his skills, and I can't stop staring at those abs dripping with sweat. My body swings along to the sound of their killer track, and I realize that I don't need anyone to have a good time. I can be here all by myself, be safe, *and* still enjoy the evening.

When the song is over, the crowd goes mental as the boys thank them and bow out. They walk off stage, high on the enthusiasm and cheers, and I smile at seeing Cole's satisfied face. Heck, from this point of view, I totally understand why girls would call him handsome. He's practically a sex god up on that stage. No wonder they all fawn over him and his music when they see him play.

Suddenly, he points at a girl in the crowd. My smile disappears.

The girl jumps up and down and runs over to the rope, which separates the crowd from the stage and waits until she's let inside by the bouncer. My heart sinks into my shoes the moment he throws his arm around her and walks off backstage with her.

Disappointment sets in, and I reach for my phone, but I realize I never actually got his number. Fuck.

Well, he asked me to come backstage. He didn't forget, did he? Maybe this is all a part of the plan. Maybe they're having a backstage party, and that girl was just invited because they know each other. Who knows.

At least, that's what I tell myself as I walk up to the bouncer, and say, "Cole Travis wants me backstage."

The burly man glares down at me. "Name?"

"Monica Romero," I reply.

It takes him a few seconds, but then he steps aside and pulls the rope down.

I quickly pass without giving him a second look as I don't want to piss him off and end up getting thrown out, or worse. There's a small corridor next to the stage, which leads into the dressing room and guest chambers. Three doors, and I guess each band member has their own room, but which one do I go in?

And am I really welcome?

"Cole?" I mutter.

No response.

I knock on one of the doors, but there's no reply. So I check the doorknob, and to my surprise, the door is unlocked. I open it and step inside. The room smells like an intoxicating mix of vodka and cologne, a scent I recognize all too well. And judging from the black leather clothes hanging over the lounge in the back, this is definitely his changing room.

But where is he?

I walk inside and check out the bathroom, but that's empty too. Except for a few bottles of liquor. Yikes.

Suddenly, the door handle is pushed, and my eyes widen. I immediately go into flight mode and run to the nearest closet in the room and lock myself inside. It's stupid and plain idiotic, but if I get caught in the act of snooping, what will his band members do to me?

Michael already ripped into me for bumping into Cole. I can't imagine what else they've got up their sleeve if they found me here.

Cole must've forgotten he invited me.

And fuck, the mere thought pisses me off ...

But not as much as him slowly backing his way into this room while a girl is tousling his hair and calls him tiger.

Gross.

There's a slit in the closet door, and it provides the only light in this cramped space. I don't want or need to see any of the things about to take place, but what if I have no choice?

I can't leave now. They're right here in the room, while it looks like she's trying to seduce him, and they don't even know that I'm here. If they discover me hiding here, it would be the most awkward, shameful discovery ever.

I peek through the hole to see what they're doing, but my leg itches so much it distracts me. My eyes widen. There's a huge ass spider crawling over me.

I squeal and jump, bumping into the door, which bursts open, with me dropping out like an unwanted guest. As I flick the spider off me, I look up and stare straight at two bewildered people who were still hugging each other.

Fuck.

"Monica?" Cole mutters, narrowing his eyes at me.

I crawl up from the floor and shake off the jitters,

patting down my dress like it's no biggie even though I'm mortified.

"Who is that? What is she doing here?" the girl asks.

"None of your business," I reply.

She gives me a dirty look. "Whatever. Cole, I'm gonna go, I think." She turns and gives him one last shoulder squish before leaving. Cole shuts the door right as I run to it, his hand flat on the wood. I swiftly spin on my heels, but he's right there, a few inches away from me.

"What the hell were you doing in there?" he asks, glaring at me.

I try not to look, I really do, but those muscles are just staring at me, and it's hard not to notice. I force back the shame. "Checking out the spiders. You've got a lot of those."

He looks confused and then shakes his head. "Don't make up bullshit."

My nostrils flare, and I force my eyes to look at him instead of his delicious body. "Fine. I was looking for you, and when you came barging in with that … that …"

"That what?" He playfully raises a brow, a stupid grin on his face.

"*Girl*," I say. "I hid. Happy now?"

I don't care who she is. I search for the door handle with my hand, but when I try to open it, he stops me. With a hand firmly on the door, his arm right beside my body, he blocks the way. "No. Not at all."

Fine. He wants to play this the hard way? He's got it.

"You invited me here, remember?" I say, putting my hands against my side. "What? Cat's got your tongue?"

He smirks and lowers his eyes. A snort follows right after when his head drops between his shoulders. "No ... I didn't forget."

"Then what? Why the hell did you invite me backstage, Cole?" I ask. "When you weren't even here in your room. When you were off somewhere else doing ... God knows what." I choke up. I really don't want to think about what he was doing with that girl, but I can think of a few things.

"Oh ... jealous now, are we?" he muses, the look on his face practically spelling out sin.

My eyes widen, and my lips part, but all I can do is stutter. "Wha—No, of course not."

He laughs in a guttural way that puts all my senses on high alert. "You're funny, you know that?"

"What's so funny?" I ask.

He shakes his head again, the stubborn grin on his face so sexy yet so infuriating at the same time. "Your reaction is better than I thought it would be ..."

I frown, completely confused. "I don't get it. What is going on? Why did you want me to be here if she—"

"She was a distraction," he says, his muscles tensing up as he leans in closer. "For *you*."

My lips part, but I have no idea how to respond. With his free hand, he reaches for my face, his thumb grazing my cheek as he grabs a strand of my hair and tucks it behind my ear. "I wanted to see what you'd do."

That … that was a prank? To get me to make a fool out of myself?

I thought he was finally opening up to me and trying to be a friend, and now he pulls this shit.

Fuck him. "No, fuck that, you don't just get to prank me—"

"Prank *you*?" he interjects, his brows furrowing.

"You're an—"

I can't finish my sentence. Can't even utter the words off my lips.

Because he's covered my mouth with his.

With his hands, he cups my face and slams his lips on mine.

And I stop breathing entirely.

The kiss is earth-shattering, hot, and greedy as if he's wanted to do this since the day he met me but never found the right opportunity. As though he wants to take me right here, right now.

His grip on my face is overpowering, and when his body pushes against mine, I lose it. My knees feel weak, and my heart beats faster and faster as I struggle to cope with what's happening. His lips feel electrifying against mine. Like they could kill me if I didn't stop.

But I can't.

I can't let Cole Travis do this to me.

So I force my brain to kick back into action and bite.

He leaps back, touching his lip. Blood seeps down, and his tongue darts out to lick it up. "You bit me," he says in a way that almost makes it sound unbelievable.

"Asshole," I finally finish my sentence, and I wipe my index finger along my lip.

"I told you not to call me that," he growls, approaching me again.

But I swiftly push down the door handle and open the door before he tries to seduce me.

"That's what you wanted, wasn't it?" he says with an arrogant tone.

"I knew it," I hiss, marching out the door. "Coming here was a mistake."

"Where are you going, Monica?" he calls after me.

He might've thought I was easy, but he's wrong.

I won't become another one of his long list of victories.

And instead of responding to his obvious taunt, I stick up my middle finger and stride out through the hallway, determined not to let that fucker toy with my heart again.

ELEVEN

Cole

I slam the door to my room so I don't hear my dad preach about how I should be more careful with women because they're snakes, and how I shouldn't let my anger out on the mansion because I'm wasting all his hard-earned money. I don't care. After what happened backstage, I need to release this pent-up rage.

Fuck.

I grab the expensive lamp from my nightstand and throw it against the wall, and it shatters into a million pieces.

My dad storms up the stairs and rams on the door, but it's closed.

"Open your fucking door, Cole!"

"I know, I'm fucking sorry, okay?" I reply. "I didn't do

it on purpose."

"I'm done with you breaking things in this house. You'd better respect the roof you live under, or you're out. Got it?"

"Yeah, I got it, Dad. Sorry. I'll get it repaired." I should really stay on my dad's good side. I've seen his bad side when other men tried to negotiate a bad deal for him. It did not end well.

"You're going to pay for the damages. Twice. And don't ever do that again," he yells, punching the door again.

I sigh out loud. "Yeah … I won't."

"No, you won't. And stop getting involved with those fucking whores. They're not worth it," he barks. "The only thing worth it is hard work and money. That's fucking it. Got it?"

"Yeah, yeah, I know," I reply as he stomps down the stairs.

But I didn't get my anger issues from a stranger.

I really need to get out of here fast, but I don't want to spend all the hard-earned cash from our band performances on getting a new place to live. No way. I need to ride this out until we're famous enough that I can do whatever the fuck I want where I want.

Anything to get away from my dad and his schemes.

God, I can't believe I ever looked up to him as a kid.

I grab some pieces of the shattered lamp and throw them in the trash. I should really fix my temper, but it's hard, especially with a girl tempting you and then running off like she has other plans.

Monica ... fucking Monica ...

I knew she was gonna be trouble. But I couldn't help myself. The more someone tells me to stay away, the more I wanna get close, and with both her and Ariane telling me not to, how could I resist?

She's like a walking temptation to me, and I can't get enough. Now that I've had a taste, I need more. More of those lips, those eyes, her touch ... I want it all.

But I chased her away.

A part of me is angry because I had my shot, and I wasted it on a stupid prank, but I needed to see her true feelings, and they shone brightly. Jealousy sparked in her eyes, but it also pushed her away from me. That's the part I hate.

Because some part of me wants to stop me from hunting her.

She'd never survive.

I shake my head and mutter, "Monica, Monica ... what have you gotten yourself into? Playing with the devil."

I lie down on my king-size bed and stare at the painted ceiling, trying to banish her from my head, but it's impossible. I'm still reeling from our encounter, and I can still taste her on my lips, and fuck me, I want more. But I can't. I can't fucking expose her to the wolf in me.

Especially not when she ran off like that, with that look in her eyes ...

That look that I've never seen before, not in any other girl I just kissed... one filled with fear and anguish.

Something about her makes her pull away, and the more I think about it, the more I wanna find out what it is.

Fuck.

I shouldn't fucking do this, shouldn't even be this fucking into her, but when my dick wants something, it's hard to ignore. And this dick is rock solid right now, as I imagined her riding me right there against the wall of the backstage room. My mouth on her lips, her pussy on my cock, her moans loud and clear.

My mind is playing me, and I can't fucking take it anymore, so I rip down my zipper and pull out my hard-on. I jerk myself off to the thought of her lips kissing mine, her tits bouncing up and down as I fuck her against the wall, my balls squeezing tight to release the cum inside her and fill her up.

I come hard and fast, groaning as I cover myself in cum.

Fuck.

This fucking girl … is going to be the death of me.

***

Monica

When I'm home, my mom's right there on the couch watching her favorite show. "Hey, how was the concert?" she asks.

I swallow. "Yeah. Cool."

"Cool?" she repeats, turning her head to me.

"It was fine," I say, shrugging it off. I don't want to give her the complete rundown because she'll vilify me for it. "I'm going to my room."

"Okay. I'll be here if you need me," she says, and I wave it off and swiftly leave.

I don't want to lie to her, but I don't want to worry her either.

I mean … nothing really worrisome happened … nothing extraordinary.

Unless you count a dirty kiss.

Oh man, just thinking about it still makes my heart beat faster. I don't understand why Cole has this effect on me, but he does. Every time I get close to him, something flutters in my stomach, and I feel so heavy and unable to breathe. I never felt that way before, not with any guy.

And when he pressed his lips onto mine, I swear it felt like heaven and hell all wrapped in a tiny package of sin.

If I hadn't stopped him right there, who knows how much further he would've taken it.

How much further I would've driven myself into madness.

This guy would destroy me … if he had the chance.

Maybe not intentionally, but likely. This is not a guy you give into. Not willingly, anyway. And I almost did.

I sigh to myself as I close the door to my room and rest against it.

I can't let myself go like that ever again. Even if it was

… amazing beyond words.

He probably didn't mean a single second of that kiss. I was probably just another one of his prized collections. Something to win over and conquer. Something to boast about to your friends.

Everything about him screams trouble and those kisses? He probably gives them to fifteen different girls per week.

I shake my head and slap my forehead. "Stupid."

I shouldn't have accepted his offer to come to the concert.

I lie down on the bed and bury my head in my pillow, screaming into it just for the sake of it. Boys. Sometimes, I really hate how I'm so fucking attracted to them.

Especially the ones who people told me to stay away from. And still, I didn't listen.

I grab my phone and call my cousin.

"Hi!" Her upbeat voice makes me pull my phone away from my ear.

"Hey," I mutter.

"Mo? Is that you? You sound … wasted," she scoffs. "Did you have too much to drink?"

"No, but I did have a terrible time," I reply, snorting.

"What happened?" she asks, but before I can say a word, she's already talking again, "No, wait, don't tell me you went to that concert where TRIGGER is playing?"

I feel caught cheating. "Well … I dunno, I couldn't not go, I mean—"

"But I thought you didn't *like* concerts?" she interrupts.

"Well, I do, or … I did … before …" I choke on my own words. "I just went because he invited me."

"Who did?" She sounds curious as hell. "Don't tell me you've already got a boyfriend?"

"What? Boyfriend, no!" My cheeks turn red. "Of course not. You warned me about him, and you were right."

Suddenly, she goes silent, and I wonder if I still have a connection or if the line is broken.

"Ariane?" I mumble. "You still there."

"Yeah, yeah …" she mutters. "Who invited you again?"

"Cole," I say. "I thought he was finally gonna be nice. I think the rumors about him are true."

"Rumors? What rumors?" she asks with a heated voice.

"That he was a cheater," I say.

"Yeah, totally," she says. "He cheats on every girl he dates." But every word she utters is snappy as if she's in a hurry. "I can't believe he invited you. And that you went there, oh my God."

I'm a bit flabbergasted she'd question me. "Well, I'm sorry. I just thought—"

"I'm sorry, I have to go, Mom's bothering me, but I'll see you at school, okay?" she says.

The phone beeps against my ear, and I pull it away to stare at it for a second, completely dumbfounded that she hung up on me.

What the hell?

***

Cole

I'm rudely pulled from my daydreams about Monica by a call by none other than fucking Ariane. I contemplate pushing the red button, but for some reason, I don't. Maybe it's because I've already been enough of a dick to the people around me, or maybe I'm bolstered by my encounter with Monica, enough to make me want to give Ariane a piece of my mind.

So I pick up the phone and bark, "What do you want?"

"Listen, you asshole, *stay away* from her."

I frown. What the fuck happened here? "Really? That's why you're calling me? To threaten me?" I laugh. "You've got some nerve."

"I told you not to get close, and you still did it," she hisses. "Why? You wanna get revenge on me so badly?"

"No," I scoff. "Or maybe yes. It depends on when you ask."

"Fuck you," she growls.

"Are you done now?" I ask, contemplating whether I should just hang up on her. It would probably make her fume … and yell at me in public. That would make a nice show.

"She's not your toy, Cole! Don't fucking use her to get to me. I told you to stay away for a *reason*!"

I sit up in my bed. Now it's getting interesting. "What

reason?"

She's suddenly quiet as a bird. "Nothing, it's none of your business, and *she's* none of your business either."

"Oh, she's all of my business now," I retort, my tongue darting out to wet my lips. "Tell me more."

"Fuck you. You're an asshole, and you know it," she says.

"Call me more names. It turns me on," I jest.

"She's not some girl, Cole. She's my cousin. You don't get to use her and throw her away too."

"You don't even know what you're talking about," I say. "What did she tell you?"

"It doesn't matter what she said. You don't get to ruin her, too," she says.

"Ruin? Who said anything about ruin?" I muse. "If anything, you've only gotten me more interested. So tell me … what's the big secret?"

"What?" she mutters. I can clearly hear her getting choked up on the other end of the line.

"You wouldn't be so determined to keep me away from her if it wasn't for something … something you're not telling me …" I add.

"There is no *secret*," she hisses, which makes me believe she's lying because she always hisses when she lies. "Don't get near her again, don't invite her, don't say anything to her, got it?"

"I do whatever the hell I want, and I don't need your fucking permission," I reply. She's getting on my nerves now. "As a matter of fact, you threatened me. You shouldn't have …" A smirk spreads on my lips. "Because now I'm only going to try harder."

"COLE! No!" she yells. "You'll fucking break her heart *and* her body."

"Body? How?"

Her body? How strong does she think I am?

Unless she means something else … I wonder.

"Don't. I don't need to tell you anything. Just stay away, or I swear to God," she growls.

"Tell me what it is, and then maybe I'll listen," I say.

"Over my dead body," she says through gritted teeth.

She hangs up the phone, clearly enraged.

Definitely interesting.

Because nothing in this world can anger Ariane … except for two things.

Not getting enough attention and someone messing with her family.

And one thing's for sure … If Ariane tries to keep something away from me, the more I'm going to latch on to make it mine.

And I definitely want to find out what it is she's protecting.

Monica.

You just got a whole lot more interesting.

TWELVE

Cole

I grab the apple off my tray and eat it in plain sight of maybe fifteen girls that are all staring at me with big blue eyes, sighing as I lick my lips after swallowing. Jesus Christ. Never in my wildest dreams could I have imagined so many thirsty girls waiting in line just to get a taste.

I always thought it'd be the endgame. That this is what I was doing it all for. But really? This apple tastes better than all those girls ever could. None of them capture my attention, and the only girl who actually does isn't here.

I take another bite, throw it down on my tray, and look at my buddies, wondering if we should skip the rest of our classes so we can practice. If I can't get my hands on the only girl I'm interested in right now, at least I can hone my skills.

One last sip of my Coke ends in a coughing fit.

Michael's rolling a fatty right in front of me, right here in the cafeteria. What in the …?

"What the fuck are you doing?" I growl at him, glaring him down.

"What?" he mutters, sticking the joint in his pocket. "It's for later."

"I told you that's not what we do," I bark. When he joined our group last, I explained the rules to him. No alcohol and no drugs. Keep a clean track record to have a better chance of making it. I thought I made that clear, but apparently not clear enough.

"Throw it out," I add.

"Fuck no," he scoffs, looking at Tristan and Benjamin as though they'd support him, but they wisely stay out of it. "What am I supposed to do with it then?"

"Flush it," I answer.

"Why? Give me one good reason," he says.

"Because it's our fucking rules," I say through gritted teeth.

I don't do fucking drugs.

Not here, not anywhere, never.

I don't judge others who take them at a party, but I gotta draw the line when he brings this shit into school. No fucking way am I gonna let him taint our reputation.

"Don't you understand? This is bigger than you. Bigger than that fucking joint," I say. "You're risking our whole fucking band. What if we get caught completely stoned?"

"Relax, it's just some weed." He leans back in his chair and sticks both hands in his pocket as if it's nothing.

"Doesn't matter what it is. Drugs are off the table. When you joined this band, you fucking agreed."

He raises a brow. "Why do you care so much?"

"Because I wanna be fucking rich and famous without the added stigma, that's why. And your bullshit is getting in the way," I retort, cocking my head. "Maybe I was wrong about you. Maybe you're not the right fit for our band."

"Cole, simmer down a little," Tristan intervenes.

"No," I say, folding my arms.

"People are looking," he adds.

"So? Let them look," I say, shrugging while focusing my attention solely on Michael. "Do it, or I'll do it."

We stare each other down. I'm not lying. I don't make empty threats. I'll come over there and snatch them from his pocket and throw them in the garbage myself if I have to. I'm willing to do whatever it takes, and if I have to sacrifice a friendship over it, fine with me.

"Fine," he growls after a while, and he scoots his chair back and stomps toward the bin, where he chucks them away in full view of every girl watching both him and me. He doesn't seem to give two shits, though. Neither do I. The point was made. And I'd rather have them see him throw them out than smoke a blunt in school.

I fucking hate drugs. No matter how small the amount or how insignificant the type. Thanks to my dad, I've seen what they can do to people. No fucking way am I letting that shit anywhere near my band or me.

Michael plops down on his seat again and crosses his arms while leaning away from the table, still glaring incessantly at me. "Happy now?"

I look up at him from my tray. Fuck this. I'm not hungry anymore.

I pick up my tray and get up from my seat.

However, right as I turn around, someone bumps into me.

"WATCH IT!" I yell as two trays bump, and the contents splatter all over us both, then tumble to the floor.

But as I stare with rage at the person in front of me, that anger dissipates as quickly as it appeared.

Fucking Monica Romero.

***

Monica

My new school clothes are completely covered in chocolate milk. And everyone around us laughing.

I'm humiliated and downright angry that this would happen to me so soon, when I'm just getting used to this school and getting to know my new classmates. I wasn't planning on making a fool out of myself, but here I am, thanks to this dude.

When I look up, my eyes widen, and my heart sinks into my shoes.

Cole motherfucking Travis.

I've been deliberately avoiding him for days, and even then, I still bump into him without wanting to. And with a tray chock-full, no less. Both my clothes as well as his are covered in food.

I'm not sure which one of us is more upset.

"Bumping into people, is that your thing or something?" he jokes, throwing the tray on the table he just got up from.

"It was an accident," I growl back.

I'm really not up for his silly games right now. That kiss he gave me is still at the forefront of my mind, hot and center. In fact, I think about it every single minute of the day, but that doesn't mean it still wasn't wrong of him, or that I forgot how much of an asshole he really is.

"You could've watched where you were going," he says. "Look at my shirt."

"You could've seen me coming if you'd looked before getting up," I retort. "I mean, look at my dress."

He cocks his head. "Really, Mo?"

My jaw drops. "You did not just call me that."

"What, Mo?" A devious smirk spreads on his lips. "Angry now? Good. You should be. You wasted both our food and our clothes."

"You were getting up to throw it away!" I reply in shock that he'd go this far for attention.

Everyone's looking at us like we're a giant spectacle.

Even Mel, who I was on my way to before all this went down.

"Doesn't matter," he spits back. "These are school uniforms. They're expensive."

Oh, now he's pretending to care about the school uniform? I don't believe it one bit.

"Fuck the clothes," I growl back, anger taking over. "And fuck you too, asshole."

His nostrils flare, and everyone's looking at us. Or more specifically, they're angrily staring at me, as I was the one at fault. And it makes me question my sanity because I could've sworn he was just doing this to intimidate me, to make me feel small, insignificant. To remind me who's in charge ... who could crush my chances at this school in an instant.

So I slam my lips together, spin on my heels, and throw my tray on top of the bin before marching out the door. I can still feel his stare piercing my back, but I don't care. I'm not gonna stay there and be humiliated in front of the entire school.

But I still have class today. I can't go home and get another shirt. There's only one other solution; clean it with water and pray it comes out.

I rush into the teacher's bathroom and open the faucet, leaning in to carefully hold my shirt underneath the running water. It's definitely gonna be cold, but if I can clean this well enough maybe it won't leave a stain.

Suddenly the door opens, and I jolt up and down from

the surprise.

Especially when my eyes find his. Cole followed me here.

"What are you doing in here?" I bark, turning away from the faucet.

His eyes dart at my wet shirt, which clings to my skin, and I immediately cover it with my hand.

"Did you forget again?" he muses, walking up to me in such an overpowering way that I back up as far as I can until I hit the wall. He leans in, smiling at me with that familiar half-smile of his, before whispering. "Teacher's bathroom pass. And it's unisex."

Fuck. I hate how he says the word 'unisex,' so full of himself, so … raunchy.

"No worries," he says, and he turns toward the faucet, giving me a second to catch my breath. "I didn't forget."

He throws his jacket onto the counter and pulls off his tie. Then he starts unbuttoning his shirt. One by one, each of the buttons come off, making me gulp even harder as more skin is revealed. The fabric slides off his shoulders with ease, but then he turns his head and looks right at me, the penetrative stare boring into my soul.

My cheeks immediately heat as I attempt to look away, but it's hard because he's literally right in my face and those tattoo-covered muscles … boy, they're in a whole different league of their own.

He smiles, shaking his head, and proceeds to wash his shirt under the running water. A few droplets splash onto his perfect skin. When he turns around to face me in all his half-naked glory, I gulp, and I swear to God, he could hear it because that fucking smirk appears again … the one he's given me so many times when he caught me in the act.

"Are you done?" I ask.

He raises a brow. "Are *you*?" He approaches me again. "Because all I know is that you never stop running into me."

"Running into you?" I scoff. "It was an accident. Those happen."

"Not that often," he replies, getting closer and closer again. "So I'm thinking … what if it isn't a coincidence?"

"It is," I growl back. "An unfortunate one too."

"Really? Because your eyes don't say what your mouth is saying, Mo."

"Stop calling me that," I hiss.

He leans in and plants a hand on the wall beside my head, trapping me inside. "Why can't I call you Mo, *Mo*?"

"It's a name reserved for friends," I reply in all seriousness even though he's messing with me. Again.

"Ouch … That hurts, Mo …" He grabs his heart with his free hand. "Almost enough to make me care."

My stomach churns. "Why are you doing this? Do you enjoy taunting me?"

He wets his lip with his tongue. "Maybe … Or maybe I want to find out what makes you …" He taps my chest with one finger. "Tick."

"Why? Why do you care so much?" I ask, my lips shuddering when he leans in so close that I can feel his breath on my skin.

A tepid, angered smile appears on his face, one that makes my heart stop.

"The question is ... why don't *you*?" he whispers, the tension between us almost visible with the naked eye, crackling in the air. He bites his lip, right where I left my mark the last time he tried to kiss me. "You pretend you don't like it when I look at you. You pretend you don't care when you see me play ... but you want me." He brushes along my cheek with the back of his hand in such an addictive way that I almost want to give in. "Admit it ... You loved it when I kissed you ... and you wanted more."

His hand slides down my shirt, down along my nipples, which immediately peak from the attention, and I gasp in response. He's never been this direct, this bold, and it literally takes my breath away when he grabs my waist and pulls me closer to him.

"Tell me I'm wrong ... tell me I'm lying ..." he whispers into my ear, his hand diving underneath my skirt. He's unrelenting as he slides up my thighs and pulls at my panties, tugging them down in one go. His hand cups my pussy, and my eyes almost roll into the back of my head as he starts fondling me without hesitation.

"Tell me then ..." he whispers. "Tell me the truth, and I might just care enough to leave you alone."

My lips part, but my voice chokes up completely from his lips grazing my skin right beneath my ear.

"You can't, can you?" he whispers, and I can hear him

smile.

Suddenly, he pulls his hand away, and my pussy is left throbbing with a need I didn't know I could ever feel. Fuck.

"Fuck you …" I growl as I quickly pull up my panties. He smirks with pleasure, as though he's just won the grand prize.

Right then, the door opens, and a teacher steps inside. She stops the moment she notices Cole standing there, half-naked like some rock god on stage. He doesn't even grant her one look. All his attention is focused solely on me, and I don't know if I should be mortified by her catching us or scared of the consequences of Cole fucking Travis setting his eyes on me.

The teacher swiftly passes Cole and enters a stall, which breaks his attention.

Then the bell rings. He makes a face and shakes his head. "You got off lucky, Mo …" he muses, and he grabs his shirt and throws it over his shoulder. "You won't be so lucky next time." As he turns around to walk off without even putting on his shirt, he still manages to throw me a wink … one that dizzies and confuses me more than ever. Because I swear to God I've never wanted any guy more than I want Cole Travis.

And it's going to destroy me.

THIRTEEN

Monica

"So tell me, Monica. How have you been?" my therapist asks. "Is everything going well at your new school?"

I sigh and lean back in my seat. "I don't know … okay, I guess."

"It must be quite the change," she says.

"Yeah …" I reply. "I mean … everything's new. I have to get used to the new schedule and new classes."

"And what about friends?" she asks.

"I have one good friend right now, Melanie. She's nice." I smile. "She keeps inviting me to stuff, so I don't feel left out."

"That's nice of her," she replies. "You must feel lucky with a friend like that."

"Yeah, I mean, Sam was like that too, but I don't see her as much as I used to nowadays." I choke up a little. I really miss my girl. "But I guess that's a part of changing schools."

"You can still meet up with her if you both want to," she says. "Nothing wrong with that."

I rub my neck. "I know, but I don't really know what to talk about."

"You can talk about your new school and what you do with your friends," she says.

"It's just weird," I say. "But I know, I should talk more with her. She's the only one who knows …" I avert my eyes. "About what happened to me, you know."

"She was there when you needed her," my therapist says. "And she will be as long as you keep her in your life."

"I don't want to push her away," I say.

"Then don't. Meet up. Invite her." She shrugs. "What could happen?"

I nod. "You're right. Maybe we should hang out more."

"It's good to connect the old with the new."

"Because it helps with letting go?" I ask.

"Because it helps you accept what happened to you," she answers, leaning forward. "Talking about it helps."

But that's just it. I don't want to think about it. A part of me wants to run away and never look back. But trauma doesn't work that way.

I sigh again. "I don't think I can move on from it. But I want to. I just want to be normal. I just want to be me. You know? Be the smart-ass, have fun, hang out with boys." I close my eyes, trying to find that happy-go-lucky girl again that I once was, full of energy, no fear, no anger. I hung out with all the boys. I belonged, and I fucked and had fun. Now all I see is threats. Everywhere.

"Think of yourself as a painting that never finishes," she says. "You're never the same you."

"I'm too young to think about all that," I reply.

"You have a right to feel that way, Monica." She nods. "Just make sure you take things slow if you choose to start hanging around boys again."

"I know." I bite the inside of my cheek.

"Is there … a boy you're talking to right now?"

Why does she always notice? Am I such an open book?

"Well … we're not actually talking. Not much anyway." My cheeks glow red hot.

"Do you feel you're ready?" she asks.

I hate those questions. "I don't know. Shouldn't I be? It's been so long."

"That's up to you to decide." She shifts in her seat. "Have you told anyone about him? Your mom or your friends?"

I gulp. "Well … Melanie sort of knows, but not really." I lick my lips. "Then there's Ariane." When she looks confused, I add, "My cousin. She knows him, apparently."

And boy … do I know him too.

I still get sweaty thinking about how he had his hands all up in my skirt until I almost wanted him to fuck me. And all that from a bit of fondling. What is wrong with me?

I shouldn't be thinking about him at all with the stunts he pulled, yet I am, and I can't fucking stop thinking about how good his lips tasted and how I wished he'd kissed me again in the bathroom.

"Monica?" my therapist suddenly pulls me out of my thoughts.

"Huh?"

"I asked if you want to talk about him? If you feel comfortable."

I shake my head. No. Not at all.

"That's fine," she says. "You know you can always come and talk with me when you want, right?"

I nod. "I know, but I'm too confused about my own feelings."

"That's understandable," she replies in her typical therapist manner. "The first time after something so huge can often feel strange or confusing."

"Right," I say. "But the confusing part is that it doesn't feel strange at all."

She cocks her head and leans in. "How so?"

"It just feels … good." I mull it over for a second. "But at the same time, it also doesn't feel good."

"So you're conflicted," she says.

"I can't really explain it. Like, I know he's bad for me, and that I shouldn't get close, or feel any of this, but—"

"But … your feelings are valid. And you're allowed to feel things, even if you think they're wrong."

"But what do I do if the boy is wrong?"

"Is he?" She raises a brow.

"I've been told he is … and … well … he's been kind of …"

"Kind of what?"

My whole face turns red, and I struggle to even say a word at this point.

All I can think about are his wet lips against my skin, his fingers on my thigh.

Fuck.

"I can't do this," I say as I get up. "Can we continue this another time?"

I should leave now before I say or do something I regret.

"Sure. It's okay if you don't want to talk about it. And if you prefer, you can always confide in your friends." She gets up too. "You know I'm always available when you need me."

"Thanks," I say as I hurry out the door.

"Call me when you want another appointment," she adds, right as it shuts.

But I don't know if I want to do that anymore.

I should.

I definitely should.

But with Cole tempting me so much, this little devil inside my heart doesn't want to be constrained by my past anymore. It wants to come back out and play.

As I walk out of the building, I get a text from Mel.

Mel: Bonfire party tonight up at Devil's Bluff Lake in the mountains. Wanna come?

Mo: I'm game

Mel: Cool, pick u up at ur place at 9

Mo: Awesome

I don't even think about it before I hit send.

I'm so tired of being that girl, that meek girl who's got issues, that tentative girl with the past. No more of that. I want to enjoy my teenage years before they're over, and I'm not letting any boy get in the way of that.

***

Cole

Being at home is one of the worst places I could ever be. But since the boys wanted a free day without band practice, I'm all by myself today. School's closed, and there's nowhere else I can study, so I'm stuck here in this huge, expensive mansion.

Not the worst place to be, but the best? Far from it.

When I was a little kid, I thought my parents were cool because they were rich, but I know better now. Not all money is money to be proud of.

I grab a Coke from the fridge to prepare for studying, but on my way to the stairs, my eyes land on my dad and his partners having a heated discussion about funds and packages. One of them slams his hand on the table, and my dad stands up, enraged.

On the table is a whole stack of money, being counted by my mother. But the moment she sees me stare, she stops and immediately gets up.

"Cole? What are you doing?" she asks.

My dad turns toward me, the thunderous look on his face as he realizes I've caught him in the act of a deal makes me tense up, expecting a fight.

But then my mother closes the doors, shutting us both off.

"You know you're not supposed to look," Mom says. "Why are you even here? I thought you'd be with your friends."

"They're busy. I thought I could study here," I reply, completely flabbergasted. "What are you doing? Are you really counting *money* in our home?"

"It's none of your business how we do ours," she says.

"Yeah, it is. I'm your son. I know what you're doing. I know how you make money, and I know it's against the fucking law."

She places her finger on my lips. "Don't ever talk about it. To anyone. You hear me?"

When she removes her finger, I scoff, "So what? You're gonna pretend nothing's happening? That everything's okay?"

She grabs my arm and squeezes hard. "Listen. This is

how we've always done things. This is our family, and you'd better damn well be proud of everything we've accomplished."

That's not fucking okay. "By selling drugs to poor people?"

SLAP!

Her hand stings against my cheek.

Fuck.

"I told you not to fucking eavesdrop on us," she says. "Now listen to me. We worked hard to get where we are. To give you everything you could ever want and an amazing home. You wouldn't be in that expensive high school if it wasn't for your father's hard-earned money."

She scowls at me. "So be happy we allow you to stay here with those ignorant and disrespectful comments about our method of income." Her condescending tone is as harsh to the ears as her hand was to my cheek.

"Go upstairs and wait until I call you for dinner. And don't play any of that horrid music or I'll come and end it myself, you hear me?" she growls, raising a brow. "And don't fucking mention any of this to anyone. Do you understand?"

"Fine," I say, and I turn around and run upstairs before she changes her mind and makes me face my dad.

Because if there's anything I know, it is that he can hit ten times as hard as her.

And there's way too much at stake to risk getting another bruise.

When I get to my room, I slam the door shut and throw my bag in the corner. So much for a quiet day studying. Who would've guessed my parents actually did these illegal things at our own damn home? Not me. I mean, I knew how they earned their money, and I've always known deep down they were dirty ... but bringing the danger into our own house? How long have they been doing this? And why did I never notice?

I run my fingers through my hair and try to shake off the rage, but it's tough because all I can picture is my dad's chauvinistic face barking at me for interrupting him and his trade.

Suddenly, my phone buzzes, and for a split second, the thought of Monica chatting with me crosses my mind. I haven't given her my number yet, but it's easy to come by when I dish it out to fans. It isn't smart for my number to be out there in the world, but it helps with getting laid. And if it helps me get ahold of Monica's phone number, that's an even bigger plus.

Disappointment sets in. It's not her. Guess I'm getting a little too excited at the prospect of her talking to me.

It's my clock, which I have no recollection of setting. There's a bonfire tonight at Devil's Bluff Lake in the mountains, held every year by class seniors. I completely forgot, thanks to my mom and dad. But there's still enough time.

I grab my bag and fill it with swimming trunks, a towel, and some other stuff. Then I open the window and check to see if anyone's watching before I jump out onto the balcony and go down the canopy right beside my window.

Fuck my parents, and fuck dinner. I'll eat some snacks at the lake … a particular snack I'm very hungry for right now, and it starts with the letter M.

FOURTEEN

Monica

When Mel and I are dropped off by a friend at the bonfire, the sun is already on its way down. She immediately joins the crowd, while I'm struck in awe at the beauty in front of me. There's a pristine freshwater lake hidden in a crevice between the mountains, surrounded by luscious trees and moss all around, giving it an earthly vibe. It's like a secret hideout, a romantic escape, but with the bonus of partying teenagers and a fire they built in a stone circle right at the lakefront.

Everyone's dancing to the music blaring through someone's speakers that they put on a stump, most of them holding drinks that were served from a keg in someone's truck. To the left, someone is placing bowls of chips and cookies on a long chopped down log, while a few others are roasting marshmallows in the bonfire, the smell wafting my way, making me smile.

"Want some beer?" Mel yells at me from the sidelines, holding a cup.

I saunter toward the lake, but as I approach, there's a particular group of people drawing my attention. A bunch of girls gawk at four boys standing on a big rock at the edge of the lake.

It's Cole and his band in swimming trunks, getting cheered on by the crowd. One of them, Tristan I think, makes the jump, a cannonball straight into the lake. Everyone screams in excitement, even the people below him who are splashed with water.

Then Cole looks in my direction, almost as if he could sense I was here.

Our eyes connect, and at that moment, images of him sliding his hands down my body reappear at the forefront of my mind. The look in his eyes, filled with fervor and hunger, makes me gulp. Even though I'm wearing a bikini, I've never felt more nude than I do now.

That familiar half-smile on his face forces me to stop and watch as he approaches the edge of the rock. He stares down at the water, just one second, then glances back at me.

He takes a leap and jumps.

More squeals follow as excited girls wait in line to get

some attention from him. But the second he rises out of the water, body glistening in the bonfire, hair slick and thrown back, he immediately looks my way. And no matter how hard I try, I can't take my eyes off him either.

Suddenly, someone grabs my shoulders and pulls me out of my trance. "Here." It's Mel, and she pushes a cup in my hand. "You okay? You look like you've seen a ghost."

"Yeah, why wouldn't I be?" I laugh, trying to shake it off.

"You weren't looking at those TRIGGER boys, were you?" she asks, but a fiendish smile immediately follows. "Fuck, you're one of them now."

I quickly punch her arm in a playful way. "Fuck no. You wish."

She laughs. "Good. I don't wanna lose a new friend to those fuckers so soon already."

"I'm not gonna make any promises, though," I reply, not wanting to lie when I know damn well what's happening between Cole and me.

She narrows her eyes. "You're hiding something." She nudges me with her elbow. "Spill it."

"It's nothing," I say.

"You don't have to lie," she muses. "I know you've got a crush on Cole."

"What?" I gasp, adrenaline shooting through my veins. "I do not."

"It's fine. Half the school does," she says. "Just as long as you don't become one of those screaming groupies, I'm good."

I laugh. "Hell no. That's so not me. If I ever get that desperate, I give you permission to slap me."

Now she's the one to laugh. "I'll hold you to that."

"Good," I say, and I take a sip of my drink, which burns my throat so hard it makes me cough and spill half on the ground. "Jesus."

Mel laughs even harder. "I was wondering what your reaction would be. It's always fun to see."

"Fuck, that was a trap, wasn't it?" I try to swallow back the tears. That was some thick alcoholic juice.

"Nah, they always make it that way for the bonfire. Spice things up, you know." She winks and bumps her hips against mine. "So what do you say we go for a swim?"

"Hell yeah." I put my drink down next to my bag. I'm not supposed to leave it unsupervised, but there's no way I'm taking another sip of that bomb.

I follow her to the lake, which is teeming with people. Everyone's dancing in the water, making out, throwing balls, having fun. I recognize a lot of people from school, who also happen to have classes early in the morning. A lot of people must be here without the permission of their parents, which makes it even more exciting. Old Monica would've jumped at the opportunity, so I want to give this my all and enjoy the evening like I'm supposed to.

And as Mel wades into the water to join the party, I make a running start and jump in so hard the water splashes everywhere. It's invigorating, and seeing everyone laugh and smile is the icing on the cake. This is what I used to love, to be at the center of attention. The good kind. And when the music blares from the speakers, I'm in my element, dancing to the rhythm and jumping up and down in the water.

The night has now covered the land in pitch-black darkness, with only the bonfire lighting the area. There are tension and excitement among the partygoers, and some of them bump into me on and off, causing me to go under quite a few times. I don't like how it feels, like I can't breathe, so I quickly move away from the biggest crowd and watch them dance and bump each other. There are people kissing and swimming, probably fucking too, and I'm not sure I want to be part of that right now.

That's when I spot them. Students … from my *old* school.

They're here? At this party?

Who invited them?

Or did they always go here … and I just never knew?

Questions flood my mind as the memory of everyone looking at me while I walked those hallways with shame fills me with anxiety.

I wanted to leave it all behind, but I can't. No matter how hard I try, my past will always follow me.

With a racing heart, I swim off, not wanting to stick around until someone recognizes me or talks to me. I need to get the hell away from that crowd.

"Monica?" Mel's voice makes me stop and turn around in the water. "Where are you going?"

I stutter, not wanting to tell her the truth. "I, uh ... I'm just going for a swim."

"You okay?" She frowns.

"Yeah, I'm fine," I reply even though I'm not. If I don't, I'm going to have to explain everything, and I don't want to revisit those memories anytime soon. "I just wanna see the rest of the lake."

"Want me to come?" she asks, but someone's already calling out her name.

"No, you go back to the party." I smile. "I'll be fine, I won't be gone for long."

"Okay, but I'm sending out a search party if you're gone for more than an hour."

I laugh. "Thanks. Appreciate it."

She smiles. "Just don't get lost, okay? I have a ride to get us both back home tonight."

"I won't. See you later," I reply. "Have fun!"

She swims back to the crowd while I flounder farther and farther away. No way I'm staying there after what I saw. Especially with some partiers from both schools, tapering off into the bushes while wildly kissing and touching. I'm sure more goes on here than just dancing and drinking, but I don't wanna know or see, that's for sure.

I swim off into the distance to try to calm my agitated heart and mind. Beyond the beach, the lake is so vast, and there are tons of tiny alcoves hidden by thick bushes and trees, as well as magnificent rock formations scattered all around. I just wanna admire the beauty of this place. And even though the music in the background makes it anything but serene, it's peaceful to swim around nonetheless. I've found a new appreciation for being all by myself, and I don't mind at all, considering where I am.

"Going somewhere?"

I almost gulp in some water. Fuck.

On a big rock that leans over the water to my right, Cole is casually sitting there with a smile on his face.

How long has he been spying on me?

"Didn't mean to scare you," he replies, his muscles flexing as he moves closer to the edge.

"I wasn't scared," I reply.

He snorts and stands up, towering over me. "Sure about that?"

"Definitely," I lie, but I'm not about to let him have this petty victory.

He wants to make me feel small. Insignificant. Bullied.

"Is that why you almost drowned when you heard me?" he muses.

My jaw drops. "Drowned?" I scoff. "You wish. You're pathetic, Cole."

"That's a word I don't hear a lot." He runs his fingers through his smooth, black hair, water dripping down the bird wings tattoo on his buff chest. It almost looks like he came walking right out of a photo shoot. That's how handsome he is. And he knows, judging from that arrogant grin.

"You know what I do hear a lot?" he says. "That people

think you're a scaredy-cat."

"A scaredy-cat?" I frown. Where the hell did he hear that? I shake my head. He's just trying to get to me. "You're just making stuff up now."

"I'm not." He approaches the edge even farther. "You think changing schools will stop gossip from reaching others? Girls talk. And they told me you've changed."

Okay, enough. I don't need to hear him talk about how other girls spill the beans to him because he's so popular, and girls want to get close to him.

I try to swim on, but I can't escape his voice.

"You can swim away, but you can't run from the truth, Mo," he says. "You're running away from who you are."

"You don't know shit about me," I retort.

"I know you used to love parties. And boys."

That makes me stop.

I turn and look at him. He's taunting me, tempting me to come to him. And I'm *this* close.

"I told you …" He cocks his head, strands of tousled black hair tumbling over his darkened eyes. "People talk."

"Who?" I growl.

But then I realize … it must've been someone at the party. Someone who recognized me.

His brow rises, and a familiar smirk appears on his face. "I could tell you … or …"

"Or what?" I make a face. "I don't negotiate with extortionists."

"It's not a negotiation," he says, lowering his eyes at me.

I gulp. I don't know what this guy is planning, but it can't be good.

"Truth or dare," he says, and he licks his lips in such a mischievous way that it makes my heart palpitate, and I don't know if it's in a good way or a bad way.

"Why would I?" I reply.

He grabs the tree branch hanging over his head and says, "Because you want to."

His light green eyes flicker with passion, as though he relishes the game of tricking me.

My nostrils flare. This guy has balls.

But if I say no … I'll only prove what these people from my old school said about me. I'll only give Cole more reasons to talk about me to his friends. To everyone who would listen. He could ruin my reputation within seconds. And that would mean a quick game-over for my new start.

"Do I really have a choice?" I raise a brow at him.

He knows damn well the power he holds, and he loves using it to his advantage.

"Guess they were right about that too …" he says.

"About what?"

"That you weren't afraid to back down, even when you should." He releases the branch and sits down on the rock only to slide down into the water, without ever taking his eyes off me. "Even when you know it's going to end badly for you."

I swallow hard. I don't know where he got this information or how anyone would ever know me so well …

unless it was Sam. No, no fucking way would she ever spill the beans on me, let alone attend a party like this. That isn't like her, but then who did Cole talk to?

He wades through the water, coming closer and closer until my heart beats in my throat and my lungs feel constricted. Even in the darkness, his eyes still glimmer provocatively, and it feels as though he's fucking me with his eyes. It makes me cower underneath the water until it covers my chin, as though it'll hide the fact that my body is leaning toward his.

"Truth or dare, Monica …" he repeats. "What's it going to be?"

"Only if I go first," I retort, staying put despite his sexy body towering over mine.

"Bold," he replies. "But I'll play. Truth."

"Who told you all those things about me?" I ask.

He smiles. "Wrong question to ask … But fine, if you really care that much, her name was Jenny."

My eyes widen. Jenny. As in best-friend-of-Layla-the-bitch-Jenny? That same Jenny who bullied Sam and did despicable things? That Jenny?

"Looks like you two know each other," he says.

And if I fucking know those whores from Falcon Elite Prep.

If I ever see their faces again, I'd probably punch them so hard someone would have to call an ambulance. They deserve every inch of pain for what they did to Sam … for what they did to me.

"She doesn't know *anything* about me," I say through gritted teeth.

"Enemies?" His eyes narrow. "Good to know."

"Forget it," I say. I don't want to give him even an inch of power over me, but I guess it's already too late for that. "Is she here?" I ask because if she is, I'm gonna give her a piece of my mind.

He raises a finger. "My turn." The smirk that follows is insufferable. "Truth or dare, Mo?"

I sigh out loud and fold my arms. Guess I'll have to postpone my search for Jenny. "Fine. Dare."

He seems disappointed. "People say you're too afraid to try something new. So I challenge you to jump off that ledge."

I snort. "What? That rock you were standing on? Easy."

He points up at a much, much larger one. "That one."

My whole body turns frigid just from the height. Fuck. Am I going to do it or am I going to be a chicken, just like Jenny told him I was?

Fuck Jenny. She might've been there watching me when Layla did all that shit to Sam and me, but she does not *know* me. And whatever the fuck he heard coming from her mouth is a blatant fucking lie.

So I push past him and march out of the water, heading straight for that rock. I climb all the way to the top and look down at him, smiling right there in the water. It's really fucking high.

"Are you scared?" he yells.

I shake my head. I wasn't ever scared of anything, way back when ... back before all this happened ...

I want to remember what it feels like. What it is not to fear a single thing in this world. To feel invincible and on top of the world.

So I scream out loud, "Here I fucking come!"

And I take a run and jump out into the nether.

It's quick but fast, so fast I can barely breathe, and then I hit the water feet first. The cold water rouses my senses, and the rush of adrenaline that follows feels so damn good.

Cole cheers me with a few claps. "Knew you had it in you."

"Oh, shut up," I reply, splashing some water at him.

But it doesn't faze him. Instead, he wades closer and closer until we're right in front of each other again, my heart still beating out of my chest.

"Truth or dare," I say, as my eyes struggle not to follow all the tiny beads of water trickling down his tattooed chest.

"Truth," he replies, his voice as serious as the look on his face.

"Why do you bully me?" I ask.

He lowers his head to meet mine. "Because I need you to hate me."

I gasp. "But ... why?"

That familiar smirk pops right back up onto his face. "One question, Mo."

Fuck. I wish I'd asked a better one.

"Truth or dare."

"Truth." I don't think I'm gonna like this, but I'm not up for another one of his dares.

"You felt something when I kissed you, didn't you?"

My heart swells.

Fuck.

I had not expected that.

Don't get lost. Monica. It's not real. None of it is. He's a player. Someone who toys with hearts and minds. Someone who likes to win just for the sake of it.

"No," I reply, trying to shake off this dread.

The look on his face is dead serious now. "Don't lie to me. That's not how this game works."

"Prove it," I retort, glaring right back at him. "Prove I'm lying."

His hand reaches for my face. I don't flinch, the mere touch of his hand on my skin enough to make me freeze. His palm cups my cheek, and I melt into him as his thumb brushes my lips, pulling one down as he slides farther and farther.

"Is that a dare?" he asks with a husky voice.

I don't know how to answer without stuttering. My mind is going in circles, trying to tell me how bad this is, that I shouldn't get close. But all I want is for him to kiss me.

And when I nod, I've sealed my own fate.

Because with his hands, he grabs my face and smashes his lips onto mine.

FIFTEEN

Cole

I kiss her hard and fast, unable to stop myself from going further.

I tried. Fuck knows I tried so damn hard not to get close to the only girl I'm not supposed to have. The girl who's irrevocably connected to the one person I hate the most. The same person who warned me to stay away.

But I *can't*. I can't fucking stay away from this girl, even though I should.

Even though I'll probably wreck her …

I don't care anymore.

I fucking wanted, no needed to kiss her right now, so I'm taking what's mine.

She's yearned for this as much as I have. I can taste it on her lips, feel it in her body that's pressed against mine. Our connection was obvious from the start, but we both knew we were bad for each other. I take and take and take until I had my fill. I use girls like I use the fame, for self-gratification, and she knows.

It's why I pushed her around, why I needed her to hate me.

Because if she lets me in ... I'll destroy her.

I'll turn her into a weak, fumbling, driveling girl, just like all the others, until there's nothing left but ruin when I'm done.

But this girl ... this girl is different.

I don't just want to be greedy. I want to give her everything I have. And that's not something I've ever felt before.

My mouth can't stop latching onto hers in desperation, almost as if it would kill me not to. I don't know what it is about her that makes me so frenzied, so hungry for a taste. Maybe it's the newness, or maybe it's because she's forbidden.

Or maybe my lips can uncover the truth beneath her lies.

Because no matter how much I desire to claim her as mine and have my way with her, another part of me still wants to know what makes her tick.

Her eyes shut slowly as I kiss her deeply, my tongue swiftly sliding in to claim her fully. I don't care if she thinks this is wrong; I know she wants it. She doesn't fight back, doesn't push me away, doesn't even flinch as I ravage her and leave nothing unscathed.

My hand curls around her waist to pull her closer against me, the cold water brushing her skin, creating goose bumps all around. Or maybe that's because of me …

A smirk forms on my mouth, and I unlock my lips from hers to gaze at her from underneath my lashes. "Liar."

"What?" Her eyes burst open.

"You felt something …" My tongue darts out as her eyes widen, and the realization of her own attraction to me shocks her to her core. "Truth or dare … Mo."

Her lip twitches as she rubs her thumb along the edge, almost as if to wipe off my mark. But my kisses leave more than just a stain on her lips, and she knows.

"Dare …"

The word slips from her lips before she realizes it.

Before she understands the consequences of her words.

And she covers her hand with her mouth, almost as if to push the word back inside.

But I heard.

I definitely heard.

And I'm fucking ready to convince her.

***

Monica

I didn't know what I said until it'd already slipped off my tongue.

Dare.

The word reverberates over and over in my mind.

I didn't mean to say it.

But my mind was absent.

Completely stunned by what he just did.

He kissed me, right then and there, each one of them scorching hot. Demanding. Greedy. Hot. As if his life depended on it, and I craved them all.

But my heart is betraying me now.

Cole doesn't like me.

Cole doesn't want me.

He wants to own the thought of me, like some prize he can put on a pedestal and show off to his bandmates. And I *know* this … so then why is it so hard to push him away? To ignore his advances and let him go?

I don't want to be another one of his victims, yet I'm falling harder and harder for his game of cat and mouse … and I don't know if I'm prepared to find out what happens when the tug and play ends.

He's using me, trying to get to me … but why? What's so special about me?

That I'm the new girl? One he's never had?

Or is it something else?

Something he knows about … that I didn't tell him?

"I dare you …" A wicked smile spreads on his lips. "Not to come."

There's a sparkle in his eyes that makes me shudder, as he lowers his body farther and farther until he disappears beneath the water. It's so dark that I can't see where he is, only that he's gone.

And for some reason, that disappoints me.

Fuck.

I hate what he's done to me, that he's made me so desperate for more with just a simple, all-consuming kiss.

Suddenly, his head pokes up out of the water again near a small alcove, underneath a bunch of hanging trees. He looks at me with a mischievous grin, then goes under again.

Am I supposed to follow him or not? But then why did he dare me not to?

I wade toward him, curious as to what he's planning. Even though I shouldn't get close, I can't stop myself from approaching anyway. He's a bad boy, but I still want to know why he plays these games with me. Why it specifically had to be me.

But as I look underneath the leaves dipping into the water, there's no one there. "Cole?"

Why would he lead me away from the middle of the lake toward a tiny alcove out of view from the party, only to disappear? It makes no sense.

Suddenly, two hands appear from behind. One wraps around my waist, and the other covers my mouth right as I scream.

"Shh … Don't want the others to hear us now, do we?" Cole whispers into my ear.

I shake my head as he lowers his hand a little. "I thought you were gone."

He smiles against my ear, his lips grazing my skin. "You think I'd leave you like that? All hungry and desperate for more?"

My heart rate shoots up into the stratosphere as he pulls me against his rock-hard body, his pants tented with need.

"I wasn't—"

"Shh …" he interrupts, his hand sliding around my throat. "No more lies, Mo … You asked for a dare. Here's your dare …"

His hand slides down my waist, all the way to my bikini, and slips down inside. I gasp, my mouth wide open, but no sound comes out as he squeezes my throat slightly. His fingers spread my pussy, and he slides between with ease.

He's done this before, and still, it doesn't stop my body from turning mush in his arms. He was right when he said I was hungry for more, but I won't ever admit that. I won't. I can't. He's the bad guy, the guy I should run away from as fast as I can.

"We both know this is what you really want," he murmurs, planting a sweet, sinful kiss right below my ear. "Secretly, you've been dreaming about having my lips all over you and my fingers inside you."

He shoves two fingers inside, and I hold my breath,

afraid I'll moan out loud if I don't. He thrusts in and out and circles my clit between, causing delicious shockwaves all through my body.

"You think I didn't see you practically fawning over me at band practice? You've been yearning for me from the first day we met," he murmurs, and his tongue dips out to draw a line from my ear down my shoulder as if to mark me as prey. "And I tell you now I've been waiting until you finally gave in."

"Fuck …" I growl as he increases his pace.

I hate him for doing this, hate him for knowing exactly what I want and giving it to me, even though I *know* we shouldn't. He *knows* he shouldn't, and still, he does it just for the sake of it. Just to be able to say … I won.

"Why would you do this?" I murmur, almost unable to catch my breath as he fingers me so swiftly and without reservation.

"I told you … you should've listened to your friends when they warned you about me."

Too late.

I already made the plunge.

I should've stopped when I still had a chance, when I could still resist.

But with one hand all over my body, touching me in places I didn't know I wanted to be touched, I'm losing myself. His hand brushes along my breasts until my nipples are peaked, and he slides my bikini aside to free them. A guttural, animalistic groan emanates from his mouth, the sound setting me ablaze.

Fuck. I never knew I could fall this hard for any guy.

Until Cole fucking Travis came along and turned my whole world upside down.

"See? You're gushing wet," he groans in my ear, tugging on my nipple. "Your lies won't work on me."

"It's not lies," I hiss, almost unable to control myself because he's hitting that sweet spot.

He keeps rubbing me until I'm about to burst, and I don't think I can stop it from happening.

One hand wraps around my neck, squeezing as he tilts my head to allow himself more of a view of my breasts. His cock is fully erect, poking against my ass, begging to join the fun, and my eyes almost roll into the back of my head.

God, I hate that he does what he does so well that it almost makes me want to beg for more.

"I hate you," I hiss.

"Good … That makes this all the more fun," he groans, and he continues flicking me right up until I hit that edge. "Come on then, Monica. Show me what it looks like when you fall apart."

"Fuck," I growl, not wanting to give him that part of me.

But it's too late.

Too fucking late to stop the tsunami from rolling over me with sweet, delectable waves. My body cramps and convulses against him, pussy tightening as he thrusts in and out.

A victorious grin pushes against my ear. "You lost, Mo."

"What?" I'm panting as he pulls his fingers out of my bikini panties.

With arrogant swagger, he says, "You lost the dare."

The blissful intoxication I drifted in shatters and turns to dust.

I whisk myself out of his arms and adjust my bikini before turning to face him. "That's what you did this for? A dare?"

He playfully licks his lips. "I told you *not* to come …"

That's what he meant?

I thought he was talking about following him. Never in my mind did I think it meant … *this*. Him, touching my pussy, kissing me under the moonlight, only to make me come for a stupid game. All this, just to mess with my head. I can't believe it.

Fire erupts in my belly. "You can't be real. You … you did this to me just to win some stupid game?"

He stares at me without saying a word.

I shake my head. "I knew it." I should've listened to that voice inside my head telling me not to play along, not to even give him an inch of my time. But I did it anyway … and why? Because deep down, I'm as desperate as he said I was.

"You're a fucking asshole, Cole Travis," I say, tears staining my eyes.

His nose twitches with rage the moment I say the word *asshole*. "Don't."

"What? Say you're an *asshole*?" I'm furious, so I scream out loud, "Cole Travis is a fucking asshole!"

I hope everyone heard. It seems like it, judging from the laughter coming from somewhere on the other end of the lake. And Cole's flaring nostrils prove it.

"Forget it. Forget this ever happened," I add, and I turn around and try to swim off, wishing I could forget all the sinful things he did to me and how much I liked it.

"You don't know what you've done, Mo," he says through gritted teeth.

My eyes narrow as I pause in the middle of the water. Was that a threat?

But before I can ask, he's already vanished.

Disappeared underneath the dark waters of the lake … just like my cold, melted heart.

SIXTEEN

Monica

I haven't seen Cole again tonight.

Not that I wanted to.

I'd probably be mortified if I saw him dancing with other girls after what he did to me. He made me feel weak, vulnerable, and I let him willingly.

I should've put up a fight, should've shoved him away, should've …

But it's too late now.

I can't take back what I did, can't undo that stupid game of his.

Cole Travis marked me, just like all his other prized wins.

Fuck him.

He wanted me to hate him? He has his wish.

"Monica? You haven't said a word, are you okay?" Mel asks while we're in the car together.

I waded all the way through the lake only to tell her I wanted to go home. I couldn't stand to stick around another minute. If she hadn't said sure, I probably would've left without her. With a taxi or by foot, just as long as I could escape the scene of the crime.

My body is still frigid from the water, and I'm shivering in place. I quickly dried myself off before we jumped into the car, but it's not enough to rinse off the shame.

"Monica?" Mel grabs my arm and pulls me out of my thoughts.

"Huh? Uh … yeah … I'm fine," I lie, not wanting to make this a bigger deal than it already is.

"Are you sure? Because you don't look like it," she says.

I look out the window, wishing I could erase what happened from my mind, but I can't stop thinking about his hands and lips all over my body and how good it made me feel … and how hard I came crashing down when I realized it was all a game to him.

"No," I say, shaking my head. It's the first time I've been honest with her.

"What happened?" she asks. "Did someone hurt you?"

"Cole," I say through gritted teeth.

She grabs me and turns me around to face her. "Did he do something to you?"

I mull it over for a second. I'm not sure I want to tell her.

"You can trust me," she says. "I promise I won't tell a soul."

"Honest?" I say. "I didn't actually stop him. That's the problem."

She cocks her head and sighs. "Oh, Monica …"

I clutch my towel closer. "I should've trusted you. You warned me about him. And I still fell for it."

"It's not your fault. It's just what he does." She puts her arm around me. "Don't beat yourself up over him."

"I know … it's just … hard. Hard to forget about him when he makes it so difficult," I scoff.

She laughs. "Yeah, you're not the first to say that."

"He's had many, hasn't he?" I ask.

"Oh yeah." She rolls her eyes. "By the dozen. Usually, they don't last more than a month."

I snort. "I didn't even last a day."

"Aw, come here." She hugs me tight. "Fuck that guy. He's not worth the trouble."

"I know, especially with my baggage," I reply.

"Baggage?" She looks up at me.

Shit, I forgot, I never told her.

I rub my lips together. "Ah, it's nothing." I shrug it off.

Not sure I want to spill the beans to her, even though I came close. This is something I need to deal with on my own. Mel has nothing to do with my problems.

"Hey, I can punch him for you, if you want," she jests.

I laugh. "You don't have to do that for me, but I appreciate the thought."

"Hey, you might be the new girl, but you're also my friend, Mo." She smiles. "I don't like seeing my friends get hurt."

"You're a good friend," I reply. "Actually, the only friend I have right now." I snort.

"C'mon, you can't be that lonely?" She raises a brow.

"Well, there's always Sam, but she's somewhere out there partying with people from my old school, I guess." I shrug.

"She's your bestie, right?" she asks. "Why don't you invite her to join us sometimes?" She grabs her phone and hands it to me. "Here, add her number. I'll add her to the group convo."

"What? You sure?" I mutter in disbelief.

"Yeah, of course." She grins. "The more, the merrier. And if she's anything like you, I'm sure it'll be fun." She winks.

. Well, I guess this miserable night might just have one silver lining.

***

Cole

I'm tuning my guitar, but every single time I play a note,

I'm reminded of the fact that I'm gonna have to play these songs again. The same songs that I played while Monica was looking at me. And I can't get those eyes out of my mind. That body that curved so beautifully into the palm of my hand, those lips that yearned for more, that wet, aching pussy begging to be relieved.

Fuck.

I've never had this before, not with any girl, and it's infuriating. She's just a fucking girl, someone I got intrigued by because of Ariane's protectiveness, nothing more.

I shake my head, trying to forget about her, but the harder I try, the stickier her image becomes. Just like the rage-fueled hatred seated in her eyes when she realized I won the dare.

I've always liked winning, especially girls. They fall for me in droves, and I enjoy the attention. Seducing comes easy to me, but something about this girl makes it not as easy to let go as it was with all the others. Normally, I would've moved on already ... but right now, all I can think about is her, and it's driving me insane.

I growl out loud and put my guitar aside. What the fuck is wrong with me?

Tristan walks into the room with a beaming smile on his face. "Dude. Check this out." He holds up a closed envelope. "Found it in the PO box."

"What is it? More fan mail?" I ask, expecting a lot of gushy messages.

"No, idiot. It's an invitation." He smacks the envelope

down on a table in front of me. "From DAP Studios."

My eyes widen. DAP Studios. That's only the most prestigious recording agency in the state. We sent them a sample of our work a few months ago but never heard anything back. I always thought we were rejected and that we wouldn't hear about it anymore.

"Holy shit," I reply, getting up to pick up the envelope.

"I know," Tristan says with a grin on his face. "Open it."

I pick it up, but then I realize the rest of the band isn't here. "We should wait for the others."

"Benji, sure …" He frowns. "But since when do you care about Michael?"

I shrug. "We're a band. I don't like him, and I don't have to, but I can at least be a man about it."

He makes a ridiculous face. "I'm impressed."

I throw him a playful punch. "Oh, shut up."

"No, I'm serious. I know it's been hard ever since … well, you know." His eyes travel away from mine, and suddenly, the air feels thick with unspoken words.

He knows I miss Jayden. He was our number one guitarist, and I could never match his solos. But sometimes, the pressure of being in a famous band gets too much, and it got to him in the worst kind of ways. Drugs killed him … and his death was a wake-up call to me.

"I miss him too," Tristan says, and he places a hand on my shoulder.

I nod in response, but as I look up, there she is,

marching down the hallways.

Monica Romero, the only girl who manages to catch my eye not once but twice.

She doesn't look my way even though we both know she only passes through this hallway to watch me play. Today she pays no attention, not a single glance, and for some reason, that makes me want to shout out to her. It's infuriating, and I don't know why.

Fuck.

"Cole?" Tristan mutters, narrowing his eyes at me. "What was that?"

By the time he turns around to see what I'm looking at, she's already long gone. "Nothing," I reply, and I tap my foot to deal with the urge to run after her.

"*Nothing?*" He shakes his head. "No, I recognize that look."

"What look?" I gaze up at him in feigned ignorance.

"*That* look," he retorts. "You're lying."

"I'm not—"

"It was a girl, wasn't it?" he says, his jaw dropping. "That's why you've been acting out so much lately."

"No, I'm just tense because of the new setup, that's all."

I brush it off as if it's Michael's fault, but Tristan's right.

He laughs and bites his lip like it excites him to see me get worked up over a girl. "Who is it?"

"No one," I reply, making a face.

"Oh, c'mon." He rolls his eyes. "You've got chicks following you for days. There must be one who's distracting you so much."

God, I hate it when he digs. "It's not some chick, just … it's not important."

Fuck. I may have said too much because he's completely silent and judging me with a simple look.

"Wow," he mutters. "She must be really good for you to be protecting her like that."

"*Protecting*?" I step closer. "I'm not protecting anyone. She means *nothing* to me."

"Right …" He throws his bag over his shoulder. "You tell yourself that. As long as she doesn't get in the way of that." He points at the envelope.

"It won't," I say.

But he's already turned around and thrown his finger in the air as he walks off out the door.

"Fuck …" I growl, staring at the envelope right in front of me.

A lot is hinging on this one letter.

If they wrote us back, that means something. Something important that we've been working for our whole lives.

Tristan is right.

Nothing can get in the way.

Not even finding out about the secrets of Monica Romero.

***

Monica

I was so not looking forward to my first class without Mel but with Cole. But here I am, walking right into the death trap. Unfortunately for me, he's beaten me to it, as I spot him sitting in his usual seat at the back of the room, a moody look on his face as he stares out the window.

I try to be quiet, but the teacher immediately says, "Monica! Do you have that paper for me?"

I completely forgot. "Oh, right," I mutter, digging into my bag. "Here it is." I place it on her desk. "Sorry for the late turn in."

"It's fine," she replies. "As long as you tell me up front."

"Of course," I say, nodding awkwardly.

The whole class must think she's playing favorites, but my mom talked to her about my … problems, and now the teacher is willing to give me more time to get my stuff done because of the therapist appointments I have. Or had … at least … because I wasn't planning to attend anymore.

But maybe that judgment call was too early.

As I look around for a seat, the only available one is right next to Cole.

And the deadly look in his eyes, like I'm the world's worst person to come and sit next to him, makes me gulp.

I wasn't planning on going anywhere near him anytime soon, but I guess I have no choice in the matter if I want to attend this class.

Every step I take in his direction seems to make the look on his face worse and worse, almost as if he's warning me not to get close or he'll do something to me. Fuck.

Clutching my bag, I sit down and lean as far away from him as I possibly can while being as quiet as possible. The teacher has already started class, so there's no time to get comfortable in this uncomfortable situation.

"What are you doing here?" he suddenly barks.

It takes me a few seconds to form a good response to that blatant attack. "Attending class like I'm supposed to." I look his way. "You?"

"Thinking about bailing," he retorts.

There's an edge to his voice. Almost as if he's taken a personal dislike to me.

Is it because I called him an asshole? Maybe. Did he deserve it? Hell yes.

"You want to ruin your education?" I shrug. "Go ahead."

"Better than spending the next hour in your vicinity."

I throw him a dirty look. "Wow, that's a low blow, Travis. Even for you."

He raises a brow. "Travis? We're on a last name basis now? Okay, *Romero*."

I stick up my middle finger. "I'm not interested in a conversation with you."

"You sure seem awfully bothered by me, though," he retorts.

"Not at all." I flip open my book and try to read, but his

constant rage-filled gaze makes it hard. I plant my fist on the table and glare at him. "What do you want?"

"From you? Nothing. Absolutely *nothing*," he replies with a husky voice that pushes all my buttons. Again.

"Then why are you looking at me like that?" I ask, trying not to get upset, but he's making it hard.

He leans on his fist. "It's hard to look elsewhere when you're constantly in my face."

"I'm not," I scoff.

"Always following me around, landing right in my lap …"

Landing in his lap? God, the fucking nerve of this guy.

"That's not true, and you know it," I say, trying not to break the pencil in my hand.

"Right … of course, it isn't," he retorts.

I return my attention to the book and tell myself not to look at him.

However, when he starts poking me in the side, it gets really, really hard not to scream.

"Stop it," I say through gritted teeth.

"Why would I?" he replies, still poking me.

I grab the pen he's holding and throw it away. "I didn't do *anything* to deserve this, and you know it."

A devious brow rises. "Oh, really? And what about that night at the lake?"

My cheeks turn red, and my pupils dilate. I cannot believe he brought that up in class.

"We had a conversation," I retort.

"You call that a *conversation*?" he taunts.

"Shut up," I growl under my breath.

"Make me," he retorts.

I wish he didn't bring it up, I wish I could bury it forever and never think about it again, but he makes it impossible.

"You still think about it, don't you?" he muses, his hand inching closer and closer like a spider sneaking across the table. "You think about me touching you … kissing you …"

I shudder in my seat, trying to pretend it all played out in my head instead of reality, but it's damn hard when he confronts me like this.

He pulls at his shirt. "I can't blame you."

"Oh my God …" I roll my eyes. "You're so full of yourself."

"What? You think I don't know what I do?" He cocks his head.

"No, enlighten me," I reply.

"I could tell you about how much I enjoy bringing girls to their knees …" he says, his voice so husky it reminds me of him whispering dirty things into my ear in the water, and it makes the goose bumps appear on my arms. "Or I could just torture you by not giving a shit."

I slam my pencil onto the desk. "You like this, don't you? You like to see me squirm. You're just a fucking bully."

"A bully? That's the first time I've heard that," he replies in an aloof way that shows how little he takes me seriously.

"Maybe it's the first time a girl actually fights back," I

bark. I can't stay here. I tried, I really fucking tried, but he's so obnoxious I can't finish this class. I simply can't.

"Fuck you, Cole Travis. You wanted me to hate you? You have your fucking wish," I say through gritted teeth, and I grab my bag, stuff my books and pens inside, and march off, with literally everyone's eyes pointing lasers at my back.

But I don't care. Let them look. Let them know Cole Travis isn't the idol they think he is.

SEVENTEEN

Monica

"So … tell me all about your new school. What's it like being the new girl?" Sam asks me while sliding a cold spoon of ice cream into her mouth. "And this Melanie girl, is she a good friend?"

"Definitely," I reply. "She's saved me from bad situations multiple times."

"Bad situations?" She leans in. "Tell me more."

"Oh, you know … boys." I take a spoonful of ice cream and shove it in my mouth.

"Boys?" Her eyes widen. "Shut up. You're not already dating, are you?" She laughs when I shrug. "Oh my God, Mo. Really?"

"I'm not … I just have boy trouble," I reply. "You

know how it goes."

"I thought you'd sworn off all boys," she says, taking another bite.

"I did, and I still do." I shove my spoon back into my giant ice cream cup. "But this one just can't stop annoying me."

"Annoying?" She narrows her eyes. "Don't tell me you're being bullied. Is this the same guy you talked about on the phone?"

I nod and rub my lips together. "He just can't seem to get enough."

"Fuck that shit." She slams her spoon down. "What's his name? I'm gonna go look him up on Facebook."

"Fuck no," I say, my cheeks turning redder by the second. "I'd rather die."

She frowns at me. "C'mon."

"I mean, no offense, I love you, but I'm too ashamed to show you the truth."

She makes a face, and a grin creeps up on her face. "Now, I really need to know."

"What? He's a nobody," I say.

It's a lie, but I can't tell her the truth … That a fucking famous singer in a rock band has his sights set on me, and not in a good way.

"A nobody, huh? A bully that can't stop chasing you?" She wiggles her brows. "Yeah, I don't buy it. This guy's getting to you, and you're not giving me the juice."

Her eyes travel off to my phone, which lies in front of

me on the table. We both lunge at it, but she manages to snatch it up before I do.

"Ha!" she squeals.

"Sam, fuck off, give it back!" I yell at her while she pushes me away and searches through my contacts and Facebook friends.

"Where is he? I need to see him. Do you have his number?" she asks.

"No!" I try to snatch it back, but she keeps avoiding me with that nimble body of hers. "You don't wanna mess with this dude, trust me."

"That only makes me more intrigued," she replies. "C'mon, show him to me."

"Why? He's an asshole," I retort.

"Maybe I'm gonna give him an earful," she says, folding her arms while hiding the phone underneath.

I hold up my hand. "Please don't. I don't want to be more embarrassed than I already am."

"I won't embarrass you, promise."

"Sam …" I sigh. "This is my new school. I'm *still* the new girl. I can't be making enemies right now."

The look on her face softens. "I just wanna help …" She sighs and then hands the phone back to me. "I don't like to see you get hurt."

"I know." I smile. "You're the best bestie a girl can wish for." I beckon her to come to me, and we hug each other tight. "But I need to deal with this on my own."

"You sure you're ready? After everything that

happened," she mutters.

I suck in a breath but choke on it a little. "Yeah," I reply even though I'm not at all certain of myself. "I have to move on, right?"

"Well, you don't have to if you don't want to." She cocks her head. "I mean, no one's forcing you."

I roll my eyes. "Could you sound anything more like my therapist?"

She laughs and punches my shoulder in a playful manner. "You know what I mean."

"Yeah …" I lower my head. "I know. I've been burned one too many times."

She places a hand on my shoulder. "You know best what you need. And you'll figure this out. And if you need me, I'm always there. You know that."

"I know," I say.

"And if you need Nate and me to punch someone, we'll be there too," she adds. Making a fist, she slams it against her other hand, making me laugh. "Oh! Fuck!" She points at the ice cream. "It's melting!"

"Shit," I hiss, and we both sit down to gobble it down before it's ruined, and we look ridiculous doing it. So ridiculous, we both burst out into laughter with full mouths and full hearts.

***

Later that week

"Are you sure you wanna go?" my mom asks. "Last chance."

I roll my eyes. She's asked me so many times my ears are starting to bleed. "Yes, Mom, I wanna go on this school trip."

"Promise me you'll stay away from the boys' rooms," she says, tapping my chest. "They're liars and cheaters and—"

"Mom!" I say with widened eyes. "Please."

"I know, but I'm scared …" She grabs my shoulders and sighs. "I don't want you to get hurt. It feels so … soon."

"I'm okay," I say. "And it's gonna be fine."

"Stay out of trouble," she says, looking into my eyes. "I know you want to, but you're not ready yet."

I raise a brow. "That's not up to you to decide."

"I know, but you know what your therapist said," she says.

"My therapist wants me to go at my own pace, which is exactly what I'm doing," I reply. "Relax, Mom. I've got this. Trust me."

"Okay." She smiles and then pulls me in for a hug. "Oh, Monica. I don't want to worry so much anymore."

"Then don't," I say. "I'm over it."

People always say that saying it out loud makes you believe your own words, so I hope it works.

"If you say so, I'll believe you," she says, then she pats

me on the shoulders one more time. "Go on then. Don't wanna be late."

"Thanks, Mom." I throw my bag over my shoulder and fish my car keys from my pocket.

"But if any of them give you any trouble, you call me, and I'll pick you up right away, no questions asked. Got it?" she shouts as I'm about to head out the door.

"Got it, but it won't be necessary!" I shout back as the door closes behind me.

I'm so glad I got out of there before she made me give a full rundown of all the activities we plan on doing. I don't even know, to be honest, I haven't checked. I just saw that we were going to some big lodge with cabins in the woods up in the mountains and figured it'd be an amazing distraction from the previous fiasco at the lake. Besides, Mel invited me to be her bunkbed buddy, so there's no harm, right?

Cole probably won't even be there, as I checked TRIGGER's schedule before I signed up, and they definitely have a show the day after we leave. No way they're going to go back and forth like that.

So with a placated heart, I hop into my car and drive to school, where a bus is already waiting on the parking lot. I quickly grab my bag and run toward the last teacher standing outside.

"You're late, Miss Romero."

"I know, I'm sorry," I say, trying to catch my breath. "My mom was holding me up."

The man doesn't seem impressed. "We're about to leave." He cocks his head at the door. "Get in and find a seat."

"Thanks," I say, and I hop in and breathe a sigh of relief.

But that sigh is silently suffocated by my own esophagus.

Cole Travis is sitting right there, on a seat in the back. Next to the only free seat by the window.

Fuck.

He eyes me with a slanted head, and he touches the tip of his nose before grinning at his band buddies who are right there in the back with him. When I grip the chair, he narrows his eyes at me, almost as if to dare me to come and sit down next to him.

He knows I hate him, and he knows I'm about this close to running out and telling the teacher I've changed my mind. But I can do this. I told myself I got this. I told my mother. I can't back down now.

So I march forward, clutching my bag, not giving him an inch of my resolve. The look in his eyes is brutal. It's as though he wants to either kill me or fuck the living shit out of me. I'm not sure which is closer to the truth, and it makes my heart palpitate.

It still won't stop me from sliding along his thick, muscular legs to sit my ass right down next to his.

I put my bag underneath the seat and look the other way toward the window. But even then it's impossible to escape

Cole's blistering gaze.

"Thanks for shoving your ass in my face," he says. "I enjoyed that."

My face turns ungodly red, but I try to hide it behind a curtain of hair. He's just teasing me because in his sick, twisted fantasy, it's some enjoyable form of passing the time.

"Who said you could sit there?" he growls.

"I have a right to a seat, just like you," I retort. "And since you conveniently left this only spot open, I took it. Guess no one else wanted to sit next to you, huh?"

"Bold move," he replies, laughing it off as if my comment doesn't even faze him. "And you thought that was a good idea?"

I shrug. "I'm going on this trip, whether you like it or not."

Cole snorts. "Again you thought that was a good idea?" His tongue quickly darts out to lick his lip, and it still manages to catch my attention, despite the fact that I'm doing my very best not to look.

"As a matter of fact, yes," I retort. "Because I *assumed* you weren't going to be there."

A short but unmistakable laugh leaves his mouth as he shakes his head. "You assume too much, Mo."

"Really? Then that performance you and TRIGGER were supposed to have tomorrow suddenly vanished into thin air?" I reply, folding my arms.

He laughs. "Yeah ... except it got canceled at the last minute."

Well, fuck.

He leans back in his seat and gazes at me with a puzzled but amused look on his face. "I'm impressed. You actually checked out our schedule?"

My body turns stone cold, and my face probably shows it too.

"Interesting," he adds, making it even harder for me to recover from my embarrassment. "Anything else you want to admit to? Or is that all the stalking you did?"

"Jesus." I make a face at him. "I am *not* stalking you. Please, as if I don't have anything better to do."

"Like what?" he leans forward, gazing at me with that same devious look that predicts trouble. "Tell me … I'd love to know."

***

Cole

"As if I'd ever tell you," she replies, obviously upset that I hit a chord.

She knows as well as I do she's thought about me. After the way I touched her, it'd be hard not to.

I lean in so close my lips are almost on her ear. "Let me guess, you can't because it's too inappropriate for the rest of the class to hear."

She gulps. She knows what I'm insinuating, and the

thought has probably crossed her mind several times. But she won't admit that to me, of course. Not yet.

"You wish, Cole Travis," she spits back. "Stop messing with me."

I cock my head. "Now why would I do that?"

"You just love it, don't you?" she rebukes, leaning away from me with disdain. "Everything is a game to you."

She's right. I love this game. I love seeing her break. And I love picking up the pieces that fall. Because it's interesting. Exciting. New.

Girls normally fall at their feet for me, but not her.

She refuses to give in, doesn't lose her resolve when I try so hard to make her yield.

Maybe that's what makes me come back for more again and again, despite knowing it's bad for both of us. But I just can't stop myself.

I need more.

I need to know what makes her who she is.

"Tell me the truth then," I say. "Tell me you don't like me. That you don't want me. And I'll stay out of your way."

She blows out a breath, but it takes her a while to form a response. "I don't know what you want from me."

"That's not an answer to what I asked, and you know it," I reply, gazing at her. "You can't say it, can you?"

She makes a face, smothering her lips together in that cute, angry way she always does. Like she wants to punch the shit out of someone but won't because she can't. Which is exactly how I feel when I'm around her.

"Fine. Yes. I felt something that night at the lake. Happy now?" she retorts, clearly on edge. "Go on, add me to your long list of conquests. I don't fucking care anymore."

I frown. Is that why she pushed me away that night? Why she called me an asshole? Or is there more?

"Is that what you think about me?" I ask.

"It's what everyone told me," she says with a serious face. "And you've proven it too."

"How? What did they tell you?" I reply. "Where's the proof?"

She stutters. "I ... well ... all those *other* girls ..."

"What *other* girls?" I reply. "The ones that tell you what ... that I collect girls like prizes? And you believe them?"

"Oh, stop feigning innocence. You know damn well what you do. You treat girls like your personal playthings," she says, her fists balling. "But I'm not going to be one of them. Not anymore. I won't let you ruin my heart, Cole."

She grabs her earplugs and phone, plugs them in, and stuffs them into her ear, blocking me out. I continue to stare at her, wondering how long she's going to keep this up.

At least I got closer to the truth. She may not like it, but she loved what I did to her at the lake. She hides her needs behind a veil of lies, but I see right through it.

I pluck her earbuds from her ear and say, "You can hide all you want, but that won't keep me from finding out the truth."

"What truth?" she says with furrowed brows.

I shift in my seat and bite my lip. "You're hiding

something."

Her lips part, but nothing follows, except the look on her face, which turns darker and darker by the second. "Who told you that?"

I cock my head. "I don't spill my sources. It's bad for publicity."

Her nostrils flare. I've never seen her this upset, not even after I told her I won the dare. Her body stiffens as the harshness settles on her face unlike ever before.

Whatever it is I asked from her made her crack.

"Screw you, Cole. This conversation is over."

She stuffs her plugs back into her ear and looks the other way, determined not to give me any time of the day.

But she's given me more than enough. She gave me a clue.

That I was right.

She *is* hiding something.

And that's only gotten me more convinced to find out exactly what it is.

EIGHTEEN

Monica

When we get to the location, Cole and his buddies didn't want to get out, so I jumped out of my seat and slid out without saying a word. I wasn't going to stay there one more minute with his wolfish eyes on me.

His questions came in hard and fast, and I did not expect to get that triggered by them, but I did. He has no right to ask me about anything, let alone my "secrets." I don't know who told him what, if it was Jenny or some other gossipy bitch from my old school, but one thing's for sure … he's fishing, and I don't want to wait until he's baited me into telling him the truth.

"Monica!" Mel calls, waving at me from the parking lot.

I clutch my bag close and go to her. "Hey. Sorry for

being late. My mom gave me an earful of advice I didn't need."

She laughs. "Don't worry about it," she says. "I was gonna save you a seat, but the teachers forced us to fill up the bus. Literally, all the spots were taken …" She rolls her eyes. "Well, except for next to Cole's."

"I swear, he left that open specifically for me," I reply, rolling my eyes.

"You think?" She blinks at me a couple of times. "I mean, I hate to say it out loud, but you two really have something going on there."

I gasp. "Nooooo, nothing's going on."

I really don't want her to know about the lake thing, even though she technically knows, I'm not about to spill the beans on the whole story.

"He's trying to get to you," she says, placing a hand on my arm. "Don't let him. This playboy thing is just his jam. He likes the fangirls. I mean, look." She points at the front of the main lodge where the registry is. There are a bunch of people collected all around Cole and his buddies, all asking for autographs. Girls fawn over him like he's some kind of god, and it makes the bile rise in my throat.

"See? He loves it," she says.

"Tell me about it."

She nudges me with her elbow. "Just forget about him. Don't let him hurt you again."

"Right …"

"And chin up, we're here, we're not gonna let him spoil

all our fun." She winks, making me smile. "C'mon. Let's go pick our bunkbed."

***

Cole

After a long and boring day out in the woods, we finally get back to the cabin and throw ourselves down on our beds. Tristan managed to secure us a four-person cabin, so we don't have to deal with fans while trying to sleep. I mean, it's happened before, and it's not a pleasant experience, save from the few times I jumped into bed with some of them. I used to love it when girls randomly slipped into my bed, but right now, I'm only interested in that girl being Monica.

But I'm not here to play games. I'm here because our gig got canceled, and Tristan wanted to use this time to practice in front of a crowd and hopefully get ready for our big meeting. Because I'm opening the envelope right now with the boys looking over my shoulders, eager to read every single word.

We read through it all at once, but three words are enough to make us all go bonkers. "Invitation to an audition …"

Tristan and Benjamin bro-hug and dance together while Michael throws a fist up in the air. "Fuck yeah!" They hug me and force me to get up, so we all jump together and butt-heads.

"We're the real deal, fellas," Benjamin says.

"Honest to God, I thought we'd never make it," Tristan says. "But it's all thanks to you." He looks at me now.

"No ... we did this together ..." I say, looking at each one of them in the eyes. "And we'll finish this together too. TO TRIGGER!" I roar, and the boys roar with me.

***

Monica

I'm on my way from the girls' common room to the cabin where I'm staying when loud screaming makes me jump up and down on the stone path. I almost shrieked from the scare. I wonder what the hell it is. It came from the cabin next to me. Maybe someone needs help?

I approach the cabin, making sure no one sees me as we're not allowed to go anywhere near the men's cabins according to school rules, but I can't help it. I need to know if someone's in danger, you never know.

So I walk up the wooden staircase, which creaks under my weight. I hold my breath and lean toward the door, listening in. A bunch of dudes is cheering, making loud, grizzly bear-like noises. It sounds like they're excited about something and want to celebrate. But more importantly ... they sound like Cole's band buddies.

Then one of them says his name, and I know for sure. Shit. I can't fucking believe it.

A few seconds later, the door bursts open, and I barely manage to scramble to the side before it hits me in the face. Two boys, Tristan and Benjamin, come out, drunk on euphoria or something else, I don't know, but I've never seen them this happy.

But as they leave and walk their way up the path toward the main lodge where all the fun takes place, they left open the door. And a light inside reveals there are still two boys left.

Cole and Michael. And for some reason, I can't stop peeking through the small slit that's left. Even if it's probably going to end badly for me, I need to know what Cole's up to. If he's planning to do something to bully me or worse … take me down along with him.

***

Cole

A few seconds earlier

"Fuck yes, time to get a fucking drink and party!" Benjamin boasts, bumping chests with Tristan. "C'mon."

They try to pull me along, but I'm still busy reading the letter. "Cole? You coming?"

"Nah, I'm good," I reply.

"Aw, c'mon. You're the biggest star," Benji says. "The girls are waiting for you out there."

"I just wanna celebrate in private. That cool?" I reply, sitting down on the couch.

"Whatever, bro," Benji says, shaking his head. He throws an arm around Tristan, who's still looking at me like he doesn't know which side to pick. But I'd rather not throw myself into a bunch of fangirls right now. I've had enough of that for a while.

"You go on. Have fun." I wave them off, and they both leave the room.

Only Michael is left, who is suspiciously silent, even though he's normally the one to party the hardest. The youngest member of our band, but also the one who craves the attention the most. And right now, he's not acting like his usual self, because he's hovering over his bedside stand with his back toward me without saying a word. And I don't trust it one bit.

"Michael?" I mumble. "Aren't you gonna party with Tristan and Benji?"

He looks up and sniffs. Hard. Then he runs his finger along his nose. "Yeah. Of course. I just … needed a sec."

I narrow my eyes and get up from the seat. "To do what exactly?" I peer over his shoulder at the nightstand only for him to snatch a tiny bag that was there … A bag filled with some kind of white powder.

I immediately pounce on him and grab him by the

collar. "What the fuck are you doing, Michael?"

"Relax." He holds up his hands. "It's just some coke. No biggie."

"*Just some coke?*" Rage fuels my bones, and I tighten my grip. "Do you have any idea what the fuck you're doing?"

"You should take some. It might take the edge off," he says, raising a brow. "Lord knows you need it the most."

I punch him right in the face.

He falls on the hardwood floor with a big, fat red mark on his nose. Blood pours out.

"Jesus Christ, Cole! What the fuck!" he growls, wiping the blood from underneath his nose. "What'd you do that for?"

"I told you not to fucking do drugs while you're a part of our band," I say through gritted teeth. "Do you have any idea how fucking dangerous it is to bring that shit here?"

He makes a face and leans up on his elbows. "Who gives a shit? It's just coke. We're not the only kids who—"

"I DON'T FUCKING CARE!" I'm boiling over now, but it's for a good reason.

I know where he got those drugs. I'd recognize those baggies anywhere.

The mere thought of my family's drug empire creeping its way into my blood, sweat, and tears just to spoil everything I've worked so damn hard for is too much.

I hold out my hand. "Give me the fucking bag."

"What? Why?"

"Do it!" I growl. "Or I swear to God, not playing for us

will be the last thing on your mind."

He gulps and fishes the baggie from his pocket. "You're a fucking lunatic."

I ignore that last comment and bring it straight to the toilet, where I flush it down whole. Good fucking riddance. Then I focus my attention on him.

"This is the last time, do you hear me? The last fucking time," I growl as he gets up from the floor. "No more free passes. This is your last shot."

He looks at me with disdain in his eyes. "Or what? You're gonna kick me from the band? As if the others would let you."

"Watch me," I hiss. "Don't for a second think I wouldn't. I created this band, and I have the power to disband it too. You want that on your conscience?"

He seems agitated, but not as much as when he looks over at the door. I imagine it's because he wants to leave to escape this harrowing situation so he can party with the boys and forget this ever happened.

But when my eyes follow his, I know right then and there why the look on his face turned lethal. And mine do too ... because Monica fucking Romero is peeking through the crack in the door.

NINETEEN

Monica

My eyes widen in shock.

Fuck.

I got caught watching, and Cole's eyes are churning with rage.

Then Michael steps in front, blocking my view.

The look on his face is beyond any Cole has ever given me, filled with murderous intent.

"You sneaky bitch!" Michael yells.

Before I know it, the door flings open, and he grabs my arm and drags me inside, slamming the door shut. I scream, but he covers my mouth with his hand. "Don't you fucking dare."

"Monica?" Cole growls. "What the hell are you doing

here?"

"Snooping on us, that's for sure," Michael fills in, glaring at me with a smug face that reminds me of a bulldog. "Fucking girls. They're all the same."

I try to free myself, but his grip is powerful.

"Ah, ah, little girl. You should've thought of that before you tried to listen in to our conversation," he growls.

Tears spring into my eyes.

"Michael ..." Cole intervenes while leaning against the cabinet near the door. "Let her speak."

Michael's nostrils flare. "Isn't this the same one who bumped into you in the hallway?"

When Michael looks at him, Cole doesn't even flinch, almost as if he's reluctant to admit it.

"Yeah, she is. I recognize you," Michael says with a vicious grin. "You're that fan girl who just can't get enough, can you?"

He ogles my nightgown, and he slowly lowers his hand from my mouth only to move it to my thigh.

"Get your hands off me," I growl, crossing my legs so he can't feel me up.

"Michael," Cole barks.

"What? I'm just having some fun. What's the problem?" he retorts.

"She doesn't want you," Cole says, approaching us. "She's here for me."

Michael narrows his eyes. "Oh, really now? All the fan girls are just for you?" Michael's clearly looking for a fight, just like before, and I'm on his radar somehow. "Taking all the fun for yourself," he mopes.

This dude's got issues, and Cole knows, judging from the darkened look on his face.

"Tell us then. Why *are* you here?" Michael asks, still firmly gripping my arm. "Huh?"

I make a face at him. "I heard yelling, and I thought someone needed help. Obviously, you don't."

He smiles, but it turns into a roaring laughter right away. "Oh, you've got to be kidding me. That's your excuse?" He turns his head to Cole. "This girl is full of shit."

"I swear, Cole, it's the truth," I reply, hoping he'll believe me.

But Cole doesn't budge. The tension between us is grim.

"Now, what did you see?" Michael asks in a way that makes me think he doesn't care about hurting me. He just wants to protect his tiny ego. "Tell me *all* of it."

"Nothing."

"Don't lie to me," Michael hisses so close to my face that it makes me close my eyes. "Or I swear to God …"

"Stop," Cole growls. "Let her go."

The tension between us breaks, and he turns his rage on Cole. "Why? You know what she saw," Michael spits back. "And you know what happens if she tells others. We can't let her leave."

When Cole doesn't respond and merely stares at him with folded arms, Michael finally releases me from his grip. I immediately rub my sore arm and take a few steps away from him. I briefly glance at the door, but he's keeping a close eye on me. No way he'd let me escape without blocking the exit.

"Tell us the truth," Michael says.

"Or what?"

He snorts. "Girl, you don't want to mess with me. You don't know what's at stake here."

"Your band?" I retort as I manage to muster up some courage. "Or the drugs?"

Michael raises a brow. "See? Now we're getting somewhere."

"I was just watching because I heard a noise. That's all," I say. "You guys do whatever the fuck you want. It's not my business, and I don't care."

I try to turn around, hoping I can leave like Cole said, but he's right there blocking the way.

"Get out of my way," I say.

"Can't do that," Cole replies with a stern voice.

"You said I could leave," I hiss.

When I try to move past him, he moves backward too, blocking the door with an arm. He inches closer, and murmurs, "I said he had to let you go. I never said you could leave."

My pupils dilate. They're gonna keep me as a prisoner?

"You can't be serious," I say, my voice sounding more strangled by the second.

"I don't think you've met my boy then," Michael says. "He's dead serious."

I gulp as Cole refuses to budge. I glance over my shoulder at Michael, who's stepping closer and closer. Fuck.

"Come on now. You didn't think you'd be off the hook that easily?"

"What do you want, Cole?" I ask, trying to ignore the looming threat in my back. "Tell me, because I'm curious. I thought you were better than this."

His face scrunches up as he clenches his teeth and looks up at Michael then back at me.

"What? Cat got your tongue?" I ask. "I didn't think this was your ammo, trapping girls in cabins, doing illegal shit."

"You don't know us," Michael says. "And I'm not in the mood to play games with silly fangirls."

"I'm not a fucking fan girl," I retort at him while looking over my shoulder. He's closer than ever, trying to intimidate me. But it won't work on me ... not unless his name is Cole Travis.

"And you ..." I point at Cole's chest, trying to stay strong. "You've already treated me like shit. What else do you want to do? Huh? Think you can break me?"

Michael approaches from behind like some wolf stalking its prey, and I don't like it one bit.

"I'm not against showing someone what to do and what not to do ... there should be a punishment for eavesdropping, right?" Michael muses, and I can hear his belt buckle ring.

My eyes widen, and a single tear rolls down my cheek as I realize what's about to go down.

Fuck. No fucking way.

Suddenly, Cole grabs my waist in a sudden bout of rage and spins me on my heels. He pulls me close, my back against his thick chest, his arm across my body, head leaning against my shoulder. I gasp in complete shock, my heart pounding in my chest.

"She's mine." His familiar husky voice makes me gasp for air.

He and Michael glare at each other in some kind of epic stare down until Michael finally throws in the towel. "Fine. Whatever." He tilts his head and points at me. "But I want you to make sure she doesn't get away with this. She can't walk out of here if she's gonna spill the beans."

"I won't," I say. "I don't have a reason to—"

"Oh, believe me, people have plenty of reasons to take us down. I'm not about to let it happen," Michael says, biting his bottom lip. "And I don't trust your word."

"Then what do you want me to say?" I ask. "You want me to beg? Jesus."

"Maybe." Michael shrugs, licking his lips at the prospect. "But I'll let Cole take care of you." Michael glares at him again. "Seeing as he was so eager. Right, Cole?"

Cole doesn't budge. If anything, his muscles only grow tighter around my chest, and heat comes off his body, forcing me to remember just how close he is.

If his eyes had lasers, he would probably burn a hole through Michael right about now.

"I'll be outside then, waiting," he tells Cole. "You know

what you have to do."

Right as he passes us, Cole grabs Michael's shirt with a fist and stops him in his tracks. "Don't ever tell me what to do." Michael gulps in response, and Cole releases him from his grip. "You owe me."

Michael doesn't respond, but judging from the look in his eyes, I'm sure he got the message.

Then he leaves, but not before throwing me a final look.

I can't hear him go down the steps, though, which means he's right behind the door, waiting for us to come outside. But after what? What is Cole supposed to do?

When I lean away to look at Cole, he doesn't seem his usual self. The smug smile that's usually on his face is gone, replaced by a scornful scowl.

"You have no idea what you've done," he growls, looking at me from underneath his eyelashes.

I take a step back away from his hot, muscular body, but he grabs my wrist and stops me from moving away farther.

"What's going on? Why was he doing drugs?"

"Did you hear everything we said?" he asks, completely ignoring my question.

I nod slowly.

"Pity." He lowers his eyes.

"But I swear, I won't tell anyone. I just …"

"You couldn't control yourself." He scoffs and then snorts. "Where have I heard that before?"

"I was telling the truth, Cole. I did hear a noise and thought someone needed help," I say. "But that's obviously not necessary."

I try to pass him, but he still blocks the door.

"You think I can let you go now?" He cocks his head, strands of black, tousled hair tumbling over his eyes, the look on his face dead serious, scary even. "I told you your friends were right about me. They didn't even know the half of it." His tongue quickly darts out to wet his lips. "You're the one that's going to need help when I'm done with you."

His words make me swallow. Hard.

What the hell is he planning?

"Look, I gave you my word," I reiterate.

"That doesn't mean anything," he spits.

I jerk free from his grip. "What else do you want? I can't give you anything else."

A devilish smirk forms on his lips. "Yes ... Yes, you can." The carnal look he gives me makes goose bumps scatter on my skin.

I've seen that look before ... when we were in the lake, and he was about to kiss me. Everything comes flooding back in; his lips on mine, his hands on my body, all over me, touching me in places I didn't know I already wanted to be touched.

At that moment, I wanted nothing more than for him to take what he wanted.

And he threw it right back in my face.

"What do you want, Cole?" I ask. "If my word isn't enough, then what is?"

He licks the roof of his mouth with a devilish grin on his

face. "You know *exactly* what I want."

I suck in a breath. "You want my body," I say, my voice fluctuating in tone, "as insurance."

He takes a step in my direction, and the weight of his power comes down on me. Not just the power of his presence or his popularity … but his physical prowess too. For a moment, his eyes taper off to an envelope lying on the small table in the corner, and his fists clench.

My heartbeat shoots through the roof.

For a second, I contemplate if I should run. Run from him … run from the inevitable clash.

But I've already tried that before, and it didn't work.

This is what they all warned me about and why they told me to stay away.

Because if Cole Travis wants something, whether it's now or later, he's going to get it, no matter what.

TWENTY

Cole

She thought she could spy on us.

That she could step in the wolf's den and not be bitten.

She should've thought twice before coming to my domain. Now she gives me no choice.

"You shouldn't have come here, Monica ..." I growl, eyeing her down as I step closer and closer while she backs away until a wall hits her back.

"So what? You want me to get on my knees? Suck you off?" she hisses, her hands against the wall as if she's afraid of what might happen if she touches me instead. "That's what you want? You want to *use* me?"

Use her?

That's an odd way to put having my dick in your mouth.

Any other girl would've been drooling at the thought, no matter the circumstance. If I flick my finger, any number of them would happily throw themselves at my feet, even if I threatened them with consequences.

But not her. Definitely not her ...

Which is why I've gotten so obsessed with her.

I cock my head and plant a hand on the wall beside her head, the sound making her jolt up and down. "You have sensitive information on us, so now I'm going to need the same thing from you."

My hand inches to her face, but she recoils, her head turned, her lips shuddering, and her body tensing up. She didn't respond to my touch that way last time. What changed?

She looks at me from the corner of her eyes with fear.

Is she scared of me?

I lean in closer, trying to get a read on her, but it's hard. For some reason, she's shut me out, even though she was so open to me before. Back at the lake, I'm sure she would've been more than willing to get on her knees or let me fuck her until I came inside her.

But now ... now all she exudes is disdain.

A single tear that forms in her eye confirms my suspicion.

As it rolls down her cheeks, I frown and pick up the tear with my thumb. Still, she stands tall and proud. I've never seen her this courageous. And it makes me smile. I can admire a girl who, despite all odds being stacked against her, still refuses to budge.

"If you tell me you're not gonna get on your knees for me," I murmur, sliding aside her hair with my fingers. "I'm going to need you to give me something else."

Her chest rises and falls as she gasps.

She and I both know there's no other way out of this.

If she runs off with what she knows, she could destroy us. Me.

And I won't let that happen.

This band and its reputation are everything, and I cannot let *anyone* jeopardize that. Not even her.

My fingers slide down her chest, which rises and falls faster than before.

"Don't be scared," I whisper. "I won't hurt you."

She stares at me, her eyes seeping with hatred, hate for her own fear, hate for me … hate for what she feels when I touch her. I can tell from the way her body flinches every time my hand slides across her body, every time my lips come close to her skin.

I lean away and look at the beauty that stands before me.

Her eyes close, almost as if she's expecting me to hurt her.

When both my hands touch the bare skin right near her chest, her eyes burst open, and she sucks in a breath.

I don't take my eyes off hers, and neither does she, as I slide my hands down across her tits and into her nightgown.

RIP!

The top tears open like it was easy, the fabric parting to reveal more of her skin. The mere sight of her naked skin rouses me and makes the devil inside me hungry for more. And I don't stop ... I keep tearing through her nightgown until it's completely ripped all the way to her belly button. Until the fabric falls off her shoulders and her ample tits are revealed.

Her nipples peak from the cold, and my mouth waters at the thought of sucking them until she moans out loud. And my eyes can't help but consume every inch of her flesh like a goddamn animal. She's beautiful, naked, and vulnerable, like an empty canvas waiting to be painted on.

A smug grin spreads on my face. "So many secrets ... I can't wait to uncover."

She stays in place, head tilted proudly upward, as she glares down at me with scorn. Beads of sweat roll down between her crevice, and I pick one up with my index finger and bring it to my lips. My tongue darts out to lick it off, and she can't stop watching my every move, her lips parting right as my tongue slides off the tip.

I know she wants it. She only needs to ask.

But that part ... we'll get to it later.

I part her nightgown farther until it completely falls off and onto the floor. What's left is Monica in purple undies with frills near her thighs. So innocent ... yet so sinful. Almost as if she's trying to hide that part about her that's begging to be released.

And I want nothing more than to loop my fingers into

each of those frills and tear them loose, one by one.

I step closer until I tower over her, her eyes following mine wherever I go. I know she wants to see me. The *real* me. In all its corrupt, ugly glory.

My finger slips underneath her panties, right where her pussy is, and she swallows hard.

RIP!

The flimsy panties tumble to the floor, her resolve faltering by the second. And I lean in so close that our lips almost touch.

At that moment, I want nothing more than to own her.

I want her so much that I can't stop myself from planting my lips on hers and stealing a kiss. A desperate, greedy, insatiable kiss. One that makes me want to groan and shove her against the wall and do wicked, dirty things to her body until she screams my name.

I fucking want her to be mine, but she can't.

She can't be mine …

Because I would break whatever barrier she's built around her heart and smash everything to pieces.

My lips tear away from hers. I can almost taste the fear.

Fear … of *me*. Of what I've done, what I've become … what I could do to her.

And as her eyes water, mine narrow and my nostrils flare.

Every time I look at her, something animalistic inside me wants to take over.

Something dangerous. Something that's already ruining

her…inch by inch.

As much as this had to happen, I don't want to murder what's left of her self-worth.

So I step back, fish my phone from my pocket, and snap a picture of her. Her eyes flash from the light, and she closes them briefly, only to rub them harshly.

"What are you—Did you just take a picture of me?" she asks, making a face.

I can't deny it. But now she'll know why I did what I just did. "Proof."

The look on her face turns from pure angst to complete rage, a beautiful painting of emotions slathered across her face. All because of me.

"Of what?" she retorts, clutching her own body. "That you're a despicable human being?"

I hate that she talks about me like that, that I'm not even worth being called an asshole anymore. No, I've morphed into something worse.

With my teeth grinding against each other, I turn away and grab a white shirt lying on the table. I throw it at her and look away. "Put that on and go."

"What?" she mumbles as if she's still in shock about what happened. "So that's it?"

I don't respond.

She quickly puts on the shirt and stares at me for a few seconds. "A picture? That's all this was for?" She almost chokes on her own words.

I point at the door. She has to leave before I do

something I'll regret. I don't want to take her, not like this. I'm not a fucking monster.

"Don't say a word about this," I add.

We briefly exchange looks. She knows this isn't a game. This is serious.

She'd better accept this one chance before it's too late.

"So you're actually gonna let me leave?" she asks. "Just like that?"

From the corner of my eyes, I spot her glancing at my fists and the fingers that ripped her innocence away. And for a moment, I wish I could tear out my own stupid, bleeding heart.

"OUT!" I bark.

It's enough to shake terror into her, and she immediately rushes off. She slams open the door and hurries out the cabin, rushing down the wooden steps with Michael's keen eyes on her back.

I didn't want to scream, but I had to. For her sake. For mine.

When she's gone, Michael turns his head toward me and raises his brows.

"Do I need to follow her?"

If he even tries, I swear to God, I'll kill him right there on the spot.

I smash my lips together and hold up the phone.

He smiles. It's a tepid, distasteful smile that makes me want to rip it off his face.

But at least he won't try anything on her now.

I already did that.

Like the beast I am, I tore right through her soul.

But better it be me ... than him.

***

Monica

Without thinking, without even looking, I run straight back through the woods on my bare feet to my cabin. When I'm inside, I slam the door shut and push myself up against it, breathing out loud. My hair is stuck to my face, sweat dripping down as I struggle to maintain my composure.

What just happened was evil and nothing I would have ever expected from Cole Travis. And from the way he looked at me when he was done, I almost feel as though he didn't either.

And all that just for some stupid picture.

A picture he holds over my head, in case I talk.

Fuck.

I wish I'd never went to look, wish I never even cared about someone yelling, wish I never saw them do drugs and flush them down the toilet.

Fuck!

I punch the door behind me and sink down against the wood, tears forming in my eyes.

"Fucking asshole!" I yell. "Why the fuck did you have to

do that?"

I don't know why I'm talking to him when he isn't even here, but I have to let it out somehow. I should've known when he told me to believe my friends. This is why he wanted me to hate him. Why he was such a bully.

He saw the weakness in me and used it for his own gain ... to my demise.

And it pisses me off.

I should've kicked him in the balls when I had the chance. I should have sucker-punched him in the nose for trying to pull that shit on me.

Instead, I stood frozen to the floor, and I let him touch me like I was some kind of doll to play with.

Grinding my teeth, I look down at myself, wondering what the hell I was thinking when I let him do all those things to me. He keeps claiming my mouth and my body as though I've always belonged to him.

But I'm not some toy he can play with. And he'll regret ever taking that picture.

"Monica?" Mel sits up in her bed, her eyes barely open. "What happened?"

Shit. She was sleeping already. "Sorry, I didn't mean to wake you."

"Where were you?" she mutters, completely out of it.

"Um ... on my way back ..." I tuck my hair behind my ear. "I had to make an extra bathroom stop."

"Oh ..." she replies sleepily. Then she frowns. "Why are you wearing a men's shirt?"

My eyes widen as I look down at my clothes and realize what I'm wearing. Shit.

I quickly get up from the floor, take it off, and throw it in the trash.

"Whoa," Mel says. "Let your freak flag fly I guess."

I snag a new pajama from my suitcase and put it on, staring at the shirt in the trash can.

I want to light it on fire.

"Did … something happen?" she asks, clutching her duvet.

"Boys …" I growl.

She throws off her duvet. "Did Cole do something again?"

I lower my eyes and ball my fists. I don't fucking care what he does anymore. I'm not a weak, pathetic little girl, despite whatever he thinks. I've been through far more than he'll ever be capable of giving me. So if he wants a war, he can fucking get one.

Mel slips out of her bed and approaches me while I keep staring at that shirt, thinking about all the things I'm going to do to get even with Cole fucking Travis and his band members. Or should I say gang?

Mel places a hand on my shoulder, pulling me from my thoughts. "Are you okay? If you need me to call someone—"

"I'm fine," I reply, maybe a little too direct, judging from the look on her face. I smile gently. "Thank you."

It's a little white lie, one I tell often. I've done it so many times it comes naturally to me.

But I'm done being the victim. I'm tired of giving and giving and not getting anywhere. My life is worth something, and I'll be damned if I let some playboy ruin it.

I've already been destroyed once, but I kept my shattered heart intact with every bit of tape I could find. No fucking way will Cole Travis ever find a way to unravel the coils around my heart.

And one thing's for sure … I will make him pay for what he did.

TWENTY-ONE

Monica

The rest of the trip was surprisingly uneventful, mostly because I stayed the hell out of Cole's way. He and his band were basically glued to their groupies, so they didn't even notice me during most of the outings, which I don't mind at all, even though I'd expected Cole to continue pestering me over what I'd seen. I guess he thinks he's safe now that he took a picture.

Oh, how wrong he is. He thinks he can bully others into submission, but I have some tricks up my sleeve too, and he's not going to like them. He doesn't know how far I'm willing to go to get my point across. And to get that picture deleted.

My reputation is at stake here, and you do not want to

mess with a woman who's already been scorned.

Cole fucking Travis doesn't know who he's playing with. But he'll find out soon enough.

I wait for the right moment, a normal day at school, a few days after the trip, when everyone's calmed down again and going about their normal routine. That's when I strike.

Cole's standing near his locker with a bunch of groupies surrounding him. After their new song came out a few days ago, they've been following him around the school even more than normal. It's sickening, especially considering he's not just handing out autographs. Every time I watch a girl grope him or peck him on the cheeks, bile rises in my throat.

No fucking way will I ever turn into one of those people who beg for attention from a rock star just because they're famous.

But Cole knows how to use it to his advantage, how to turn it into power. It's how he controls everything around him, from the band's image to his school grades by sucking up to the teacher ... even me.

Not anymore.

With a smirk on my face, I wait until Cole's distracted by one of his fans. I sneak into the crowd unseen and slip past until I reach his locker. It's still slightly opened, as they all bombarded him when he was taking out his books for his next class, and it's the opportunity I've been waiting for.

I shove the canister inside and attach the pull wire to the little door, then close it shut. Slithering away, I snicker to myself and wait on a bench at the end of the hallway with my bag clutched closely to my shoulder. A few minutes pass, and when the bell rings the fans dissipate and go to their classes. Cole spins on his heels to open his locker again. But instead of a book tumbling out, the canister sprays him with black paint until he's completely covered.

I snort and let out the laughter while Cole backs away from the locker, looking confused as hell. People in the hallway laugh and snort at him. Then he turns my way, and I stop laughing … but the smug smirk never leaves my face.

The way he looks at me is the same as when he saw me snooping, but now I'm the one on the winning end of the game. And he doesn't like it … not one bit.

I lick my lips in pleasure and stick up a middle finger before walking into the teacher's bathroom. I don't care if he follows me or not. What is he going to do to me? He's already got me under his thumb by using my nudes as a way to blackmail me. Might as well enjoy this revenge while I still can.

As I apply some red lipstick, the door slams open and in marches Cole, covered in black paint from head to toe. He glares at me through the mirror, eyes narrowed, muscles tightened, as if he's contemplating whether to shove me around or to release the picture. I continue applying my lipstick until I have puckered up, kissable lips that scream sex. Lips that will make him wish he never fucked with me. Because he may think he owns my body, but these lips are off-limits.

He doesn't say a word.

Instead, he saunters to the sink, his eyes still blazing right at me. He opens the faucet and throws me a look. Then he takes off his shirt in one fell swoop and throws it in the sink. I work up my mascara and fix my hair, which has gotten all messed up from laughing so hard.

"You enjoyed that a lot, didn't you?" Clutching the sink, he cocks his head. "It's fine if you don't want to admit it. I don't care."

He chucks his shirt under the faucet and splashes his face with some water too.

"Whatever it is that you're doing," he says, water dripping off his handsome face. "Keep doing it. Keeps me on edge."

I narrow my eyes at him. He's playing me, but I can't help but bite. "I'm not doing anything in particular. Except for my makeup, of course." I shrug and apply some more blush.

"Of course …" he repeats in a mocking fashion. His body turns my way, and his muscles tense with each move, almost begging me to look. "You're trying to get back at me. I get it."

"You don't get shit," I hiss, turning my head toward him. "Give me that picture."

He raises a brow, and a devious smirk appears on his face. "This look on your face …" His hand inches closer, his fingers almost grazing my cheek. "That's what I do it for."

I lean back and hiss, "I'm not your fucking toy, Cole."

"You think this is all a game?" he asks, while the water is

still gushing over his shirt, but he pays no attention to it. "That I'm only in this to bully you for fun?"

"You're an asshole, and you know it," I spit, clutching the sink with one hand while putting the other on my side. "You just love bullying me."

"Again with the *asshole* …" He scoffs, shaking his head. Then his dark, devilish eyes home in on me. "Keep saying it and you'll only push me harder … and harder."

Every time he says that word, he takes a step closer, and I can't help but notice he bites his lip while doing so.

Fuck.

Don't get distracted by his fucking looks, Monica. It's all in your head.

"You got what you deserved," I retort. "And there's more where that came from."

A smug grin softens his face. "You keep doing that. Keep messing with me, and before you know it, you won't be able to stop," he says, leaning in so close he could practically kiss me right then and there. But I won't allow it. "And I'll be right there … to pick up the pieces." He taps me on the forehead, so I slap away his hand.

"If you're not gonna give me the picture, then delete it. Or shit like this will keep happening, and it'll only get worse," I growl, not backing down.

He cocks his head at me, mere inches away from me. "Threatening me now?"

It's almost as if me threatening him is more of a threat to me.

And I don't know why but the mere thought of what else he could do to me makes me gulp.

"You think that picture is the only thing I can take from you?" His tongue darts out to wet his lips, and it's so infuriatingly sexy that I want to scream. "Monica … you should know by now who you're dealing with."

His breath smells like menthol sweets and hot summer nights, and it almost draws me in.

Fuck.

I shove him away before he gets the chance to do it again. "Yeah, I know damn well who I'm dealing with," I growl back. "You think you're the only boy who has tried to ruin me? Wrong."

His eyes flicker with interest. "Another boy? Now I'm curious."

"Like I'd tell you." I pass by him. "And I'm far from finished with you."

He smirks at me as he turns around to watch me walk. "Keep running, Mo. Someday I'll catch you."

"In your dreams." I give him the finger while marching out the door.

He might think this is all fun and games, but he doesn't know how far I'm willing to go to get my point across. If I can't hurt his reputation, I'm going to have to tackle the one thing that matters to him the most; his band.

And I know just what to do.

***

Cole

With or without a clean shirt, I'm going to my fucking band practice. They can drag my ass out of school for not sticking to the dress code, but I won't leave voluntarily. No fucking way, especially not when Miss Sassy Pants Mo gets to continue her classes as if nothing ever happened.

Of course no one saw it was her. Who would pay attention to a girl going through my locker while fifteen others were all begging me for an autograph? No one.

She's sneaky ... and I'm surprised she actually took action.

If it wasn't for that damn picture, I would've reported her to the dean. But of course, she knows I can't. Instead of that picture being my safeguard against getting in trouble with my band, she's using it as blackmail to bully me into submission.

Smart ... but infuriating. So infuriating it almost makes me want to corner her and fuck her tight little ass until she begs for mercy. That might teach her not to mess with me.

Then again ... I don't think she'd mind. Even if she says she doesn't want me, I don't believe a word from her mouth, and we both know that's not the truth. She just denies it because she loves to hate me. I guess my plan for her to hate my guts was successful ...

But now I'm starting to question why I ever wanted it in

the first place.

Is protecting her from me worth it when I'm still the one hurting her the most?

Sighing, I scratch my head and walk into the band practice room, hoping to take my mind off things. But what I see in there, slobbering all over the table, has the hairs on the back of my neck standing up straight.

Ariane is all over Michael, kissing him like she wants to show him how she's going to suck his dick later.

Fuck that shit.

"What the fuck are you doing?" I growl.

They stop kissing as if caught by surprise and look my way. "Oh, I didn't see you there," Ariane says with a giggle. She quickly wipes the red lipstick stain off Michael's lips. "Not that I care."

I throw her a look. "What are you trying to do, huh? Work your way up to all the band members?" I growl, folding my arms. "Suck their dick and hope you get famous too?"

"Oh, please." She jumps off the table and puts her hands against her side. "Like I'd ever be that pathetic."

"You already are," I bark.

"Aww … poor Cole. Did I hurt your feelings?" She raises her brows in a mocking manner.

"No, just my eyes," I snarl.

"Calm down, Cole," Michael intervenes as he gets off the table too. "It's no big deal."

"You're the one to talk with these sloppy seconds," I

spit back.

"Hey, fuck you," Michael growls.

"Yeah, Cole. Simmer down," Ariane says. "Don't want to get in a fight with your own band member, now do we?"

I march to her but come to a full stop right before I do something I regret. "Don't fuck with me, Ariane."

"Or what?" she hisses, glaring up at me with that same fucked-up glare she used to give me. "You gonna punish me?"

"Stay. Away."

"What? From you?" She cocks her head. "I think I was already doing that. In fact, I'm hooking up with Michael, and there's nothing you can do to stop it." She shrugs. "So peace out and stop being such an asshole, will you?"

I avert my gaze and focus on Michael. "You have no idea what you're messing with, dude."

He scowls. "What the hell is up with you? You've been acting all strange ever since …"

"Since *what*?" Ariane asks, looking at us both.

"Since that fucking girl came to our school," Michael continues.

Ariane focuses her attention back on me, but her eyes are fiery this time. "*That* girl …"

"Yeah, you know … what's her name …" Michael flicks his fingers and rubs his forehead. "Monica!"

"Monica," Ariane repeats, but her voice has darkened quite a bit. "Tell me more, Michael."

I glare at Michael, sending him practical death threats

with my eyes.

Still, he ignores my warning signals. "She was snooping on us on that trip when I did some coke, so Cole here had to shut her up."

"Oh, is that so? And how did you do that, Cole?" Ariane cocks her head at me, clearly mocking me.

I make a fist with my hand to stop the rage from culminating in a fight. "I did what I had to do."

She narrows her eyes at me. "And what was that, exactly?" She pokes me with her index finger, but I swat it away.

"Enough with your fucking games," I growl.

"I could say the same to you," she replies.

"Hey, do you two need a room or what?" Michael interjects. "'Cause it sure seems like you've got some beef."

"I'm fine if she leaves," I growl, keeping my deadly stare on Ariane.

"No," she retorts. "Why would I?" She marches back to Michael and puts her hand through his looped arm, then pecks him on the cheek. "He's my new boyfriend."

My eyes both widen and narrow in a split second, and I swallow. "Whatever."

"What? You don't approve?" Michael asks.

"You do whatever the fuck you want," I say. "As long as it doesn't get in the way of our band."

"Right, because that's all you care about," Ariane scoffs.

I snort and shake my head. "Why are you so obsessed with me?"

"I'm not," she says through gritted teeth.

"Sure seems like it," I spit back as she comes marching at me.

She presses her fingertip against my chest again, "Stay the fuck away from Monica."

I lean in, a vicious smile on my face. "Or what?"

"You're gonna regret you ever lived."

A devious grin forms on my face. "Yeah … you think that."

I pass by her and go up to the stage to prepare for practice.

"I ruined your reputation once, I can do it again," she barks from the back of the room.

I slowly spin on my heels and cock my head at her. "Try me. See if I care."

Her eyes were fiery before, but now they're blazing to the point where she might explode, and I can almost see the steam coming from her ears.

"Fuck you, Cole. I will fucking find out what you did to Monica, and when I do, you will be sorry you ever existed," she snarls, and she storms out the room and slams the door shut without even saying goodbye to her new lover.

"Wow. That was explosive," Michael says. "What a …"

"Maniac?" I fill in.

He laughs. "Well, I wasn't gonna say that, but …"

"It's the truth, though," I reply.

"I was gonna ask you, but you were too busy with that other chick, so I figured I'd tell you later. But you're okay with it, right?" Michael asks. "I mean, no hard feelings."

"I don't fucking care," I retort, maybe a little too harsh, but it gets the point across. "Don't ever bring her here again. Got it?"

"Sheesh," he says, scowling. "Taking out your shit on me today or something?" He eyes me up and down. "And what happened to your shirt anyway?"

I close my eyes and take a long, deep breath. "Accident."

He frowns at me as he grabs his guitar and steps onto the stage. "Yeah, sure looks like an accident."

He's obviously fishing, but I'm not gonna give him the satisfaction of knowing it was Monica. Especially not knowing what he is capable of. "Can we just fucking start?"

"Fine," he says, and he fishes his cell phone from his pocket. "I'll text the rest and tell them to get their asses down here ASAP."

TWENTY-TWO

Monica

On my way to the club where TRIGGER's going to play tonight, I get a call.

When I pick up, a voice immediately blares through the phone. "Did Cole hurt you?"

"Whoa …" I mutter. "Ariane? Why are you calling me?"

"I just wanna know. I was gonna talk to you in person, but when I went to your house after class, your mom said you weren't there, so I thought I'd call."

"I don't …" I stammer, completely taken by surprise.

I get that she's concerned about me, but how did she find out? Who told her? Cole?

"Don't make it difficult," she says. "Either he did something to you, or he didn't. Which is it?"

"Y-yes," I reply while crossing the street.

"I knew it!" she screams, almost causing me to step out in front of the traffic. "I'm going to kill that son of a bitch."

"No," I say, and I come to a screeching halt. "Please. Don't. I know you're trying to protect me, but it won't help."

"Of course it will, after he's dead, he won't hurt you anymore," she retorts, and I'm not even sure if she's joking at this point or not. "He needs to be punished."

"I'm already taking care of him myself," I reply, hoping she won't do anything stupid that might get us both in trouble.

"What?" she snaps. "What are you doing?"

"Just … stuff." I swallow. "Look, I gotta go. I have to be somewhere in a few minutes, and I can't be late."

I hang up the phone before she asks what it is exactly that he did. Because I don't want to talk about it, let alone explain it in great detail, which Ariane always asks about. She's a sucker for gossip, and all the more when she can embellish with juicy details whenever she talks to her friends.

I'm not dumb. I know how she works. She's one of the popular girls, the ones who talk shit to get their way. Power doesn't just come in sheer force—it comes from underhanded gossip and deals too—and she knows all too well how to wield that kind of power.

My phone buzzes with texts that I'm not going to answer. I know who it is, and I know nothing will stop me from what I'm about to do.

I walk into the club in my sky-high black heels and little red dress with slanted shoulder straps and look around. Eagerly waiting girls, gushing over TRIGGER while the curtains are still drawn, fill the space. A bulky man approaches me and asks for my ticket. I hand it to him, and he lets me pass.

I search the bar area until I find what I'm looking for.

"Mel!" I say, and she swivels around on her seat with a beaming smile on her face.

"You're here!" She sounds so cheerful even though she knows damn well what we're about to do. "I'm so fucking excited. When do we start?" She grabs my arm and pulls me up to a seat. "Do I still have time to gulp down my drink?" She slurps on her straw.

"Make it quick," I say with a wink, "'cause we're starting right now."

She squeals and sips on her straw until the glass is empty. "Whoa … Dizzy."

I laugh. "But it's not even alcoholic."

"It's cold!" she spits back. "But not as cold as this icy bitch will get in a minute." She bumps into me with her elbow. "So what's the plan again?"

I point at the guard to the right side of the stage. "You're going to distract him so I can slip past."

"Right." She nods. "And then?"

"Then I do my thing," I reply.

"Which is what?" She raises a brow. "C'mon, Mo,

you've been dangling this revenge plan in front of me for ages now. I need details."

I sigh. "Let's just say … this won't be one of his greatest performances."

Her eyes widen, and something sparkles in her eyes. "Oh … you're gonna mess with the band? Nice." She raises her hand, and we high five. "That's my girl."

"Shhh …" I put a finger against my lip. "I don't want this to get out before I'm done."

She makes a gesture that her lips are sealed. "I won't talk … unless it's that guard, of course. I'll spin him around my finger and pretend I'm a floozy." She hops off the stool and flaunts her stuff. "What do you think? Can I pull this off?" She shows off her leopard print skirt and cropped top coupled with a cute bow in her hair.

"If you can't, no one can," I say, and she smiles. "Feel free to start whenever. I'll be waiting in the crowd."

She nods and walks off toward the guard. I slip off my seat after checking to see if anyone's paying attention before disappearing into the gossiping, eagerly waiting crowd. The tension is high here. Everyone's waiting for TRIGGER to come out and give them a show that'll make their ears pop. And I can't help but grin knowing what's going to happen once these people don't get what they paid for, and what Cole's reaction is going to be once people start recording on their cell phones. I hope they film an epic meltdown that'll follow him and his cronies for the rest of his life.

Don't mess with Monica. That was once a statement I

lived by, and I'm finally starting to feel like my old self again. And I guess I have that twisted asshole to thank for that.

I wait in the crowd while Mel does her thing. She approaches the guard and sweet talks him, twirling her hair with her finger, touching his arm, playing with his emotions like she's done this plenty of times before. I didn't know she was this well-versed in the flirting game. Within seconds, she manages to lure him away from the hallway he was protecting, and they face the wall together while she keeps distracting him. I'm impressed.

I swiftly pass through the crowd and slip along the stage only to come face-to-face with Mel. We briefly make eye contact only for her to wave me off with a finger before returning her focus to the beefed-up guy in front of her.

Without much trouble, I manage to bypass the guard and run into the hallway when she's got him looking away. I don't go into Cole's room; instead, I hop into a 'SERVICE ONLY' room that's full of mops, buckets, and cleaning supplies. There, I wait until Cole comes out and goes into the bathroom, which is straight across from his changing room.

That's my shot.

Bursting out, I reach his door, opening it silently, then closing it again without making a sound. I look around and move as fast as I can. In the corner, on top of the table, lies his guitar case.

Bingo.

I immediately open it up. It's a beautiful guitar, one he

always carries with him, so this is my only chance. Such a shame, though, it's a damn nice guitar.

I fish a knife from my pocket and grab a string.

"Here goes nothing," I whisper to myself, and I cut the first one off, and then another one for good measures.

Suddenly, the toilet in the other room flushes, and panic fills my veins as quickly as the water rushes through the bowl. I have to get out of here before I'm caught in the act.

But there's no time because the moment I close the case, someone's already grabbing the door handle.

Cole!

My body freezes, and my mind goes numb. What do I do? If he finds me here, everything will have been for nothing. I have to hide.

I look around to find a closet in the back. It's my only option.

Fuck, not again.

I run to it and hop inside, slamming the doors shut behind me ... right as Cole saunters inside.

My whole body tenses the moment I spot him strutting around with mere boxer shorts on. His muscular body covered with tattoos stands out among all others, and even after all the things he did to me, I still can't stop ogling him.

I wish I wasn't this attracted to him. That watching him strut his stuff did nothing to me. That the kiss he gave me in the lake meant nothing to me. But they do, and I hate myself for it. I let myself fall for the trap that is Cole Travis, and I've paid the price.

Now it's time for him to pay his.

I swallow as he picks up his clothes, his signature leather jacket and pants, which were spread out on a chair, and he puts them on. With some setting spray and a comb, he does his hair in the mirror and grins smugly at himself.

Sure, Cole. You enjoy the foreplay ... while it lasts.

Because as soon as you go out there on stage, your world will come crashing down.

Just as you did to mine.

Suddenly, he walks straight toward me and the closet I'm hiding in.

My eyes widen, and my breath falters, so I hold it in.

He pauses right in front of the tiny sliver that allows me to spy on him. His phone buzzes, and he picks it up.

"Yeah? Okay. Be right out."

He puts it back in his pocket and picks up the guitar case, and I breathe a sigh of relief.

The crowd in the front room begins to chant, and a voice blares through a microphone. "Ladies and gentlemen … TRIGGER!"

Screaming ensues.

The door opens and closes.

The air around me is silent. Empty.

And I can breathe again.

I close my eyes for a second to allow the calm to wash over me.

A deranged smile forms on my lips.

I did it. I fucking did it.

I laugh and smash open the door, laughing my way out. I'm so struck by how well this massive operation—that could've been filled with major fuckups—went that I can't stop laughing. So I grab the chair to keep myself from falling down and laughing even harder. I'm just so amazed it actually worked.

The crowd begins to boo, loudly. Right then, a roar emanates from the room beyond. I glare at the door.

That was … definitely Cole.

He must've seen what happened to his guitar, which means the concert can't happen. And he'll be back in this room within seconds.

Shit.

I shouldn't be here. Why am I still here? I should've run straight the fuck out, but I couldn't help myself and had to gloat over the situation as if that would help me get out.

I hope it's not too late.

I run to the door and turn the knob, but as I open it wide, someone in a black leather jacket stands in front of me, blocking the way. And when my eyes travel up to meet his, I cower beneath his towering figure.

"Cole."

As I take a step back, my lips quiver in fear as I realize all the things that are probably going to happen to me now … and that I'm not prepared.

TWENTY-THREE

Cole

Three minutes of complete and utter embarrassment. That's all it took for me to completely lose my shit right there on stage. Everyone saw—my band members, my fans, and hell, even this event's crew. Many of them were shocked, but most were laughing right in my face, and it fucking hurt.

My personal reputation might not be that great, but performance is everything to me, and tonight I couldn't do shit. Not with this broken ass guitar with the strings cut … by none other than fucking Monica Romero.

Because the second I stormed into my changing room and saw her staring straight at me, I knew she did it. No one else would carry so much grudge as to try to ruin my concert. No … this was a sophisticated plan. And I want to know *all* the details.

When I step toward her, the door slams shut behind me. She silently mocks me with a scowl. It's almost as if she wants to say, *What are you going to do?*

And that's exactly what I'm thinking too.

What *am* I going to do with her?

Especially with her wearing that tiny bright red dress that barely covers her ample thighs that make me want to bite into them.

Instead, I bite my lip and stare her down. "I should've known you'd stoop this low."

"You get what you wish for," she hisses.

What I wished for? Damn, she's got some spunk saying that to my face.

"So you admit that you destroyed my guitar?" I lift it up for her to see.

She raises a brow at me, but it's all I need. And in my rage, I chuck the guitar away. She jolts up and down from the scare.

"I thought that—"

"That guitar meant something to me?" I interject. "Damn right. And you ruined my performance tonight."

She straightens up again as if she's proud she managed to hurt me a little. "You brought that on yourself."

Those beautiful red lips are a sinful distraction to our conversation, making it hard to focus. I step closer, and she steps back as though we're stuck in an eternal dance of push and pull. "I brought *you* here?" I growl. "Because as far as I know, I didn't invite anyone into the back."

She swallows as if she got caught in the act.

"Sneaked past the guard? Got a friend to help you out?" I cock my head, still walking closer while she keeps backing away. "You do realize I could get you kicked out of here for good, right?"

"I don't care," she retorts. "Do it if it makes you feel better."

My nostrils flare. It might be a small pinch of retribution, but it wouldn't make a difference. Not to this situation.

"Did it feel good?" I ask, my tongue darting out to wet my bottom lip. "Sneaking in here just to vandalize my guitar?"

Her eyes glimmer with pride. "Damn right … And I'd do it again if I had to, just to make a point."

I lower my head as I keep stepping forward while she steps back. "And what point was that?"

"That you messed with the wrong girl," she says through gritted teeth.

A smirk forms on my face. I can't help it. She just makes me laugh. "You're funny."

"What?" she mutters, clearly confused.

I shake my head and snort. "I'm amazed …" I look her directly in the eyes. "That you thought this would stop me from getting closer to you."

Her pupils dilate, and her lips part as if she wants to say

words she doesn't dare to speak out loud. After a few seconds, she regains her courage. "Why?"

"Why not?" I retort.

When she can't back away any farther, I plant a hand beside her against the wall.

"Don't you ever get tired of bullying?" she asks as I tower over her.

"Bullying?" I snort, shaking my head. "You throw that word around a lot, but I'm starting to doubt you even know what it means."

"Like hell, I don't. That's what you do," she says, glaring up at me. "You twist things. You tease me, play me like I'm some kind of dumbass." She tries to shove me away, but it's no use because I'm much stronger than her.

I could move ... but I'm not interested in letting her off that easy. Not after the stunt she just pulled.

"Monica ... oh, Monica ... you should've thought about the consequences before doing what you just did," I say, grabbing her chin to make her look at me. "You come in here to try to ruin me, my reputation, my band, and you think I'd let you off the hook? You should've run when you had the chance."

She makes a face. "I came here to give you a taste of your own medicine, and you know damn well you deserved it."

I guess she's right on that part.

"If you wanted attention, all you had to do was ask," I say, raising a brow.

"I don't. You degrade me. Push me to my limits. You even took a picture of my body. Why?"

"You know why," I retort, trying to make her see.

"To protect your reputation?" She scoffs. "Like it's that amazing."

I cock my head. "Now, that's a low blow."

"You could've asked me not to tell anyone," she hisses.

I narrow my eyes. "And trust you on your word?"

Her brows furrow. "And I'm supposed to trust *you* with a picture of my body?"

We stare at each other for a moment, but I can't come up with a good comeback. Damn. She really got me there.

"I guess we should work on that," I jest.

"*Work on that?*" She sounds offended now, and she folds her arms in defense. "You think it's all fun and games, don't you? I'm not amused."

A few tears well up in her eyes again, the same kind that trickled down her cheeks back in the cabin, and they immediately bring me back to that moment … when I turned into a monster. And I did it all just to protect my band … the same band she just thrashed into the ground.

If that isn't poetic, I don't know what is.

"You think you can mess with me, but I don't play nice," she snarls. "I'm not a fucking victim. I bite back. And you're finally catching on."

Grinding my teeth, I stare at the girl in front of me, clearly hurting because of all the things I did to her. It wounds my fucking soul, and I don't fucking understand why.

I never used to care. Not for anyone, not even for myself.

And here she is, breaking open the parts of me I thought were forbidden.

A tear rolls down her cheek, and I instinctively reach for it and brush it aside with my thumb.

She just stands there in complete shock, her mouth opening as my thumb slides down her lip, while my eyes find it impossible to look away from all the pain I've caused this beautiful girl who deserves better. Better than *me*.

"Do you hate me so much?" she growls.

Hate?

Hate *her*?

I couldn't. Not ever.

And that's exactly the problem. I needed her to hate me, so I wouldn't have a reason to come close. But she refuses to give up on me, keeps fighting back. And it finally begins to dawn on me why.

The more I push … the more she pulls.

It was inevitable from the beginning.

No matter how much I told myself to stay away, to focus on my band, to keep myself from getting involved with someone related to the one person in this world who I hate the most.

But this girl … this girl is far from anyone I could ever hate.

And it's about time she knows.

"You've got it all wrong, Monica Romero," I say. My hand slides down to her chin, and I tip it up with my index finger. "I don't hate you. I hate what you do to me. I hate … that you make me *want* you."

Without thinking, I grab her face with both hands and kiss her hard.

I can't stop myself. I have to claim her. After that stunt she just pulled, I need this from her to make it right. Because every damn time I kiss her, the turmoil inside my heart momentarily ceases to exist.

It's something I never knew I needed until she came into my life.

It's why I've found it so hard to stay away even though I should.

But I can't do it anymore. I just fucking can't.

I fucking crave her. Her mouth is like sweet, sinful sex on a midsummer day at the beach. Like a glass of expensive liquor after a night singing my lungs out. Like something I shouldn't ever want but *need* more than anything else.

Her.

It's always been her.

The day she set foot in Black Mountain Academy, she was already mine.

So I finally take what belongs to me and kiss her until I can't breathe anymore. When I pause, I lean away from her swollen, reddened lips momentarily to look into her eyes and see the truth reflected in them: The same hunger that swept over me mere moments ago.

A half-smile perks up my lips.

Her jaw tightens, and her eyes smolder with fierceness.

SLAP!

Out of nowhere, a hand lands right on my cheek. The sting comes before I realize what happened, and my hand instinctively reaches for the spot on my cheeks.

She looks mad, completely unhinged, as though she wants to kick and punch her way out.

And I wait to see what she's going to do … if another slap will follow. The pause seems eternal, as if time is ticking slower than ever, while her eyes search mine for answers to the questions burning deep inside her heart.

But we both know they won't be answered … not without her learning to let go.

Her hand reaches for my face.

I close my eyes, expecting another blow.

Instead, she wraps her arms around my neck and pulls me in for a deep, heavenly kiss.

TWENTY-FOUR

Monica

I slapped him.

I slapped fucking Cole Travis right in the face.

And then I kissed him.

I'm fucking kissing him right now, and I can't stop. I don't *want* to stop. He tastes so good, like sin and spice all wrapped into a devilishly sexy package, and I can't fucking stop wanting him.

My lips instinctively went back to his, even after slapping him. Even after my heart realized what he had done was wrong. That he kissed me just to make me forgive him. Just to throw me off.

But I can't fight the attraction, can't stop from wanting my lips on his, even when it's going to be the death of me.

Because I know, deep down, that this boy is a killer.

Not a murderer of people but a murderer of hearts.

And my heart is on the line right fucking now, and I'm not even doing anything to stop him from claiming it as his. And I don't understand why.

Why am I doing this?

Why am I letting Cole fucking Travis seduce me with his soul-green eyes, gorgeous tousled black hair, and those perfectly chiseled abs hiding behind that leather jacket?

And why does it come so easy?

I thought I was over him, that I was done being his plaything, that I was able to resist temptation after the shame he put me through. He's a bad boy, a player, a bully someone can hate. And I thought I needed that in order to get over him.

But all those things I thought I needed pale in comparison to how good his kisses feel on my mouth … on my neck … on my chest. And the more he gives me, the more of them I want to keep.

I'm addicted. Like a sinner on drugs, I need his kisses like I need air to breathe. The same air he steals every time he plants his lips on mine and claims them as though I always belonged to him.

"Finally, you give in," he groans against my lips, making me all hot and bothered.

How am I supposed to resist when he says things like that? I'm so fucking confused by my own emotions, but the whiplash from his are putting me through the wringer, and I can't get a fucking grip.

My lips unlatch from him to stutter, "But I thought … You didn't … I wasn't …"

He places a finger on my mouth, and says, "Stop talking. Stop thinking. Just fucking kiss me."

When his fingers slide down, and his mouth smashes back onto mine, I lose myself in the moment … to him.

I was always lost to him.

From day one, the moment I saw him play, I knew … it was gonna be him.

It was only a matter of time until I lost my heart to this boy …

A boy I shouldn't have, *can't* have, but a boy whose heart I want nonetheless.

And right now, he wants me too, even if it means nothing to him, even if he only wants my body, right now is all that matters.

Even if I wanted to, I can't fucking stop, and neither can he.

He's got his hands all over my body, touching me in places that only turn me on more. His lips turn my mind to mush as his fingers curl around my dress, pushing it up until my panties are exposed. He cups my pussy and makes me clench my legs.

"Fuck … I want you, Monica," he murmurs against my lips. "Don't ever say I hate you again."

"But I do," I mutter, trying to resist temptation, but it's too fucking hard when he touches me in all the right places.

"I fucking hate you."

"You say that, but you don't mean it. Just like me," he whispers from underneath those beautiful dark lashes. "And I'm done fighting you just to get you to stay away from me."

That familiar smirk makes my heart flutter with greed.

I'm already lost to him, whether I want to admit it or not.

He's got me right where he wants me. Trapped between his thick, muscular arms and the wall behind me, I'm longing for his every touch, quaking with need. And without thinking about it, I reach for his pants and unzip them.

He stops kissing me and looks at me intensely for a moment, almost as if he's gauging my reaction. With his index finger, he briefly caresses my cheek, and my body instinctively leans in to his as he leans in to press a kiss against my collarbone.

"You shouldn't have come here," he groans.

Suddenly, he grabs my thighs and lifts me up against the wall, kissing me hard and fast. My arms wrap around his neck as he plants his lips all over mine, leaving red stains of my own lipstick like some sort of victory mark.

He smirks against my skin. "Oh, Monica … You fucked me up so badly. It's time to return the fucking favor."

I don't know whether he means the guitar or his heart.

Either way, I can't stop him. It's far too late for that as his hands are already shoved up my dress and he's pressing his bulge against my pussy. I love how he feels against my body, how he grows thicker with every kiss he gives me, every moan that leaves my mouth.

But the closer he gets to pulling down his pants, the more my legs tense up, and my arms tighten around his neck.

He leans away, looks at me again, and something flickers in his eyes.

"You confuse me so fucking much, do you know that?" he mutters.

My lips part, but I don't know how to respond or what he even means.

Cole pushes me up against the wall and gives me greedy kisses again, all along my chest. He tugs down my dress far enough until my bra is visible, and then he pulls that down too. The grunts that emanate from his throat set me on fire, and when he grabs my breast and kisses that too, I almost explode.

Yet when his body leans into mine, my legs still want to clench together, even when I tell them in my mind not to.

He inches away again and narrows his eyes.

Just one second.

Then he pulls me away from the wall, still carrying me in his arms with his lips on my skin every other second. "You ruin me, Monica. Fucking ruin me," he murmurs. "Now lie down and let me give you all the attention you so desperately need."

Fuck. I hate how he makes it sound as if I'm so pathetic.

But the look in his eyes is anything but someone who feels sorry. Not for me. Not for him. Not for anyone else.

That look … Pure and utter hunger for more.

And it's so damn sexy that I just go along with it, as he throws me down on the velvety couch and kneels at the edge. He nudges up my skirt and tugs at my panties, tearing them off only to throw them in a corner somewhere. I don't know because I can't fucking look away from his hungry eyes as they home in on my body, my pussy.

He bites his bottom lip, then his tongue flicks out to wet that too. And then he dives in like there's no tomorrow. I gasp, my body arching from the sheer pleasure of feeling his tongue right there on my clit.

He cups my ass with both hands while toying with me in a way that feels like he's known my body for ages. All the nooks and crannies, all the delicious little spots, he knows just where to hit them right.

Closing my eyes, I struggle to breathe as my heart rate shoots up into the stratosphere. I feel guilty, heinous, for enjoying something so wrong, so evil, yet it feels so damn good that I want more.

More. More!

"Fuck!"

The word slips out before I realize it, and that goddamn infuriating grin spreads across his face again. His tongue dips out, and with the tip, he touches my pussy, his hands moving to my thighs to keep me spread. And I know right then that he's enjoying every fucking step of the unraveling of Monica Romero.

"Don't be so greedy, Mo," he murmurs, planting a kiss

on my pussy before he continues to suck me.

I wish I could answer—that I could tell him to fuck off and let me be. That I could get up from this fucking couch and tell him to his face that he's an asshole for seducing me yet again when I had no fight left in me and had already used up my defenses against him.

That I could stop myself from feeling so guilty for wanting a guy who's unattainable and out of bounds.

That I could force my body not to enjoy every inch of pleasure he's giving me right now.

Because damn, he knows how to make me squirm.

"Oh, God," I moan as he keeps licking me to the point I can barely hold on.

"Cole will do," he quips, grinning against my skin.

"Shut up," I retort, trying not to get upset when everything started feeling so good.

"Only if you come for me," he whispers.

My eyes widen as I look up at him diving between my legs. Did my ears really hear that right? Did he ask me to come?

He keeps licking me and swirling around in my pussy, and I'm finding it hard to breathe, let alone respond to his words. My eyes almost roll into the back of my head from sheer pleasure, and my whole body is heating up.

"Do it ... Let me see you come," he murmurs, digging his fingers into my thighs as though he's salivating from the mere thought of me falling apart.

My hands clutch the couch, fingers digging in deep as I

grow desperate for more. My mind has completely lost all form of reason, and lust has taken over. All I can think of is his tongue on me, his hands wrapped around my thighs, and the delicious shocks zapping through my body.

"Look at me," he groans, his tongue still swiveling back and forth.

But when I do, the sheer hunger in his eyes sends me off the edge.

Ecstasy overflows my body, and I fall apart right then and there, causing me to quake underneath him while he laps me up.

My body is still in complete overdrive when he plants slow, delectable kisses all over my thighs, lavishly licking me like a lion.

"How's that for punishment?" he murmurs.

My eyes widen, and as the orgasm subsides, it finally dawns on me what just happened. What I just let him do to me.

I scoot up on the couch and crawl away from him, shaking my head. "I … You …"

"What?" He raises a bold brow. "Cat got your tongue again?"

My face scrunches up. He caught me again and fucked me up with his tongue like it was easy to him. And for what? Just to mark me down as one of his conquests? Payment for destroying his guitar?

"Fuck you," I snarl in anger, and I get up from the couch and pat down my dress.

He frowns, looking confused as hell. "That's not a nice way to say thank you."

"You tricked me," I growl.

"Tricked you?" He snorts. "You were the one who destroyed my guitar for attention, remember?"

"I didn't do it for attention!" I yell back.

I try not to let it get to me, but it's hard, knowing that he's managed to make me come twice now without me being able to resist. And that he did it just so he could punish me. To show me that I'm not in control of my own body.

I can't believe I gave in so easily and that I've now become part of the long list of girls that fawned over him.

Pathetic.

I march for the door.

"Where are you going?" he asks, standing up straight, his clearly tented boxer shorts still visible underneath those zipped down pants.

I gulp but force myself to remain focused. "I'm not one of your conquests, Cole." My heart can't handle this. "I'm not a toy to some rock star. I can't fucking do this."

"But you're not—"

Suddenly, the door bursts open, and Tristan steps inside. He stops abruptly the moment he spots me standing there in the middle of the room.

"Oh, boy ..." he mutters, raising a brow at me, then at Cole, who is still standing there with a boner in his pants like he doesn't even care. "I did not expect to see ... *that.*"

My cheeks turn strawberry red, and I tuck my hair behind my ear, feeling exposed. "Me neither," I retort.

"Dude, I just wanted to give you time to cool off. Not so you could bang girls," Tristan says, passing me by. "And what the fuck happened with your guitar? Why the fuck did you not see this before the concert?"

I glance at Cole over my shoulder, hoping, praying he won't tell a soul.

Because if those boys realize it was me … if Michael finds out … he might do something much, much worse than Cole ever could.

And for some reason, I feel like he gets that too because the way he looks at me makes me stop in my tracks. His jaw clenches, his eyes flashing disappointment.

"It just fucking happened. And it doesn't fucking matter anymore," Cole rasps at Tristan, but he never takes his eyes off me.

A sigh leaves my mouth, but my heart is anything but calm. As I storm out the door, the storm in my heart rages on.

TWENTY-FIVE

Cole

I throw the broken guitar on the table in front of my dad's stack of money. "I need a new one."

He looks up at me as though I've lost my mind. "What the hell did you do to that?"

Well … Monica Romero cut through some strings, but then I threw it in a corner in my rage and broke the rest of it. So I guess I have both of us to blame … or just myself, considering I pushed her to her limits.

"Doesn't matter. It broke. I need a new one," I reply.

He snorts. "And you're gonna work for it, I suppose?"

My nose twitches. "How much?"

"Twenty-five."

"Dollars?" I frown. No way he'd settle for that.

"Twenty-five hundred," he says.

I almost choke on my own tongue. "Fuck, no."

I'm not gonna sell twenty-five hundred dollars' worth of drugs. No fucking way.

"Fine, you don't wanna work for me?" He leans back in his chair. "You're a big famous celebrity now, aren't you? You can play some concerts."

"I can't play without a guitar," I growl.

"Well then, guess you'll have to use your savings," he jests.

"That's literally all we have, and it would all be gone then." I grind my teeth. "Can't you help us a little bit?"

He cocks his head and shrugs. "Depends on whether you're finally going to help our family business too."

My eyes narrow, and I grab the broken guitar and march off. "Forget it."

He scoots his chair back and gets up. "Wait a minute."

"For what?" I bark, pausing to hear what he has to say.

"Don't you talk to me like that." He points his finger at me as though it adds more weight to his words. "I'm your father, show some damn respect."

"You mean the same respect you give my high school classmates when you get them addicted to coke and meth?" I growl.

He slams his fist on the table. "Don't you fucking dare look down on me and my business."

"Whatever. I don't want any part in it," I reply, and I quickly walk off before he has more to say. I guess the time when he'd help me get on my feet are over. I'm on my own now.

"You want to earn money? The right way?" my father barks as he walks after me.

I pause halfway across the stairs while he stares up at me from the bottom.

He sighs out loud. "Your mother and I are going on a trip. We're leaving in a few hours. Clean the house and hire a new maid and gardener *today*. The old ones quit."

Of course they quit. Once they find out how my father earns the money they get paid with, they always do. No one wants to get anywhere near that, and he knows. I'm surprised the cops haven't landed on his doorstep yet, but it's only a matter of time.

"I'll give you fifteen hundred. You can fork up the rest yourself," he adds.

I mull it over for a second. If this means I get to keep part of my savings, I'm still out of this house quicker than I would be if I didn't accept his deal. "Fine," I reply. "Anything else?"

"Yeah ... This place better be squeaky clean when your mother and I get back."

I sigh and walk farther upstairs. "Yeah, yeah, got it."

"No maid will clean the entire house in a day, Cole! Better get on your knees and do the work yourself!"

"I heard you!" I retort, slamming my door shut before he tries to order me around.

God, I wish I didn't have the emotional range of a bull

on steroids, but here we are. Sometimes I let out my rage in a bad way and only end up hurting myself in the process.

I caress my guitar. "Should've treated you better."

We've been through so much together, but I guess every journey comes to an end. I just never expected it to be by my own doing.

But what surprises me the most is how quickly I overcame that anger the moment I realized Monica only did it to get back at me. I guess it's true what they say about scorned women ... never get in their way.

I learned the hard way.

And boy ... was it hard. Hard to stay the fuck away from her.

Damn. It's only been a few days since the concert, but I can't get her out of my mind. Every time I look into her eyes, I want to grab her and kiss her until she's breathless, until her body vibrates against mine, until she begs me to touch her. But I never wait until she does. I always pounce like a lion on its prey. It's like I can't get enough.

There's something about that girl ... something that makes me forget everything I was doing, everything I ever knew, and all I can think about is making her mine.

And I know she feels that same electricity pulling us together. The attraction between us is undeniable, so the only question is, why are we both fighting it?

It's almost as if I'm afraid to get closer, afraid to fuck her up if I do.

But why do I care so much?

Has she already gotten under my skin?

I throw my guitar on the bed beside me and grab my phone. There's no other way to find out what it is that I'm feeling than to get close again. That primal hunger that I felt when she wrapped her legs around my waist and I wanted to shove my cock into her wet pussy and lick up her juices until she came ... that's something I've never felt before.

Lust? Yes. But this need that pulses deep down in my heart? That's new.

Maybe that's the reason I've been pushing her away for so long, why I kept her at arm's length, why I teased her until she had enough.

If she didn't hate me, would I be able to handle it?

Because she isn't just a fan I sleep with.

She never was.

I swallow and close my eyes. I told myself I would let nothing distract me from my goal, not even girls. They were merely toys to fuck, then discard when I was finished with them.

But for some reason, I can't do the same with Monica, and that pisses me off.

And now I've even managed to piss her off as well.

I shake my head to myself and fish my phone from my pocket. I need to practice and earn some of that money for my new guitar, but my parents are gone, so who will notice whether I clean the house now ... or tomorrow?

So I text my band.

Cole: House is empty tonight. Wanna come over?
Tristan: Fuck yeah
Benji: Course.
Michael: Party time!
Cole: It has to stay clean
Tristan: We can do that
Michael: Sure, we can help clean up after
Benji: Totally
Cole: Not sure, guys…
Michael: Oh, c'mon!
Benji: Live a little, Cole
Tristan: Fine by me
Cole: Fine. As long as we clean up together. Keep it small
Michael: I'll bring the goods
Tristan: Great! I'll be there
Benji: Me 2
Cole: Tonight, and don't come b4 dinner
Tristan: Got it. You're gonna love it
Cole: If you say so
Tristan: You need this, bro
Michael: Definitely

I close the app and sigh to myself, rubbing my forehead. Oh, boy. This is gonna be a mess. I can already tell from that conversation. But at least it'll be a fun night, and I won't be by myself in this house.

Besides, Tristan is right. I need some time to myself.

Some amusement without rules or judgment. Nothing but relaxation, some music …

And no Monica Romero to turn my head upside down.

***

Monica

"Sooooo … Tell me how it went," Mel says as she scoots closer to me on the bench outside school. We just finished all our classes, but we haven't had the time to talk about the thing that went down at TRIGGER's concert yet. After I'd fled the backstage room, the guard immediately pushed me out the door and forced me to stay outside.

I couldn't find Mel anywhere, so I figured she'd gone home already, seeing as I was held up backstage for God knows how long by Cole's twisted little big tongue.

"I couldn't find you anywhere," she says, "and the guard was getting suspicious, so I had to leave."

"You don't have to explain," I say. "Besides, I was the one who stayed way too long."

"Spill it. Tell me, how did he react?" she asks with a certain giddiness in her voice that's hard to miss.

"Well …" My cheeks turn completely red even though I try so damn hard to keep it together. "Let's just say it didn't go the way I planned."

"But he was raging off stage," she says. "I saw him

explode right there on the stage. It was magnificent."

"Yeah, that part was amazing," I say, my eyes trailing off. "But what came after …"

She raises a brow at me and leans in closer. "Tell me."

"We kissed," I mutter, biting my lip. "And he did some more … things." I clear my throat.

Mel squeals. "Oh my God, you're kidding, right? Nooooo!"

I bury my face in my hands. "Why is this so embarrassing?"

She grabs my arm. "Don't be ashamed. I mean, you do you."

"Yeah, but you warned me about him," I say. "And I totally didn't listen. Even though I know I definitely should have."

"But you can't help who you fall in love with," she says.

My eyes widen. "*Love*?" I'm mortified and stumble over my words. "No, no, this was not *love*. Whatever the hell it was, I don't know, but it was definitely *not* that."

"Not-love is fine too." She shrugs. "I don't judge." She grabs a chocolate chip cookie from her bag and holds one out for me too. "Want one?"

"Thanks," I say, and I take it and immediately shove it in my mouth.

She laughs at the way I eat, but I can't help it. Stress makes me hungry.

"Hangry?" she asks.

"Very," I reply, which makes her laugh even more.

"That's what boys cause," she jokes.

"Tell me about it," I say, grunting with annoyance.

"Sounds like you two have something special," she says. "You just gotta figure out what it is."

"Nooooo, I'm not figuring out anything," I say, almost choking on the crumbs. "He's an asshole bully."

"Apparently," she says, still mocking me a little with her eyes. "And something else too."

"What else?" I retort, folding my arms.

She throws me a look and purses her lips. "Nothing."

"Oh, shut up." I shove her a little.

She laughs again. "It's just funny. I can't help it."

"But it's not. You know he's a douche."

"Yeah, and I warned you about that too," she says.

"Know-it-all." I scoff.

"That's my second name." She winks.

"Sounds about right."

"Hey, ladies. Enjoying the afternoon sun?"

We both turn around as someone casts shade on us. Or more specifically … Ariane.

"No need to invite me to join. I just came to drop this off." She hands me and Mel a piece of paper. "Special invitation to a special party. Hosted tonight!" She claps her hands. "I'm so excited."

"Um … thanks?" Mel says.

"You're welcome." Ariane's beaming smile almost feels like an attack. "I expect you'll both attend then?"

"I don't really do parties," Mel replies.

"Sure, you do. You were at TRIGGER's concert plenty of times," Ariane retorts.

This shuts Melanie up, but not me. How the hell does Ariane know?

"Surprised? I have a few friends who go there too, and they always tell me who else is there," she says, flicking her hair back. "I like to be in the know, you know?"

"Right." Mel frowns.

She clearly doesn't trust Ariane.

And now I'm starting to wonder what else Ariane knows about us.

"You'll be there tonight, right, cousin?" She looks my way.

"Um …"

"Please?" She raises her brows and pouts at me in that same cutesy manner that I'm sure has convinced plenty of dudes to do things they'll regret later. "You could use the distraction."

I sigh. After that last concert I attended, I sure could use a distraction as long as it has nothing to do with Cole.

"Fine," I reply. "As long as Cole's not going to be there."

"Cole?" She makes a face at me and then folds her arms. "Is there something you wanna tell me?"

My lips part, but I decide not to tell her. "Nope. Nothing in particular."

She looks at me in a weird way for a second before she says, "Well, you'll have me, and I'll kick anyone's butt if they get close to you." She winks.

"Thanks," I reply, feeling creeped out by this whole conversation.

I mean, I always knew she was weird, but she's never been this creepy. Ever since I've been going to Black Mountain Academy, something's changed about her. Or maybe you really don't know who your family is until you see them in a different light.

"Well, all right then. I'll pick you up tonight at eight, okay?" she says.

"Cool," I reply, then turn my head away again.

Mel keeps looking at her until she finally turns around and leaves.

"Thought she'd never leave," Mel mutters.

I snort and barely manage to keep it together.

"And you two are related?" she adds.

It only makes me snort-laugh harder.

***

When it's eight o'clock, Ariane's right there on my front porch, waiting for me.

"Be home on time!" my mom calls out from the kitchen. "And don't get near any boys!"

"Got it, Mom," I say, rolling my eyes while Ariane giggles.

"I'll keep an eye on her, don't you worry, ma'am!" Ariane shouts at her.

"Thanks, lovely!" Mom yells back.

I throw Ariane a look, but she completely ignores it. "C'mon, let's skip before she asks anything else."

"Thanks," I say, marching out and throwing the door closed behind me. "I'm so done with being watched."

"I can only imagine," Ariane replies. "It must've been tough for you, with everything that happened."

"To be honest, I just wanna move on," I say as she opens her car door.

I really don't want to talk about this stuff with her. It's already bad enough that my mom told her.

"Oh, really?" She looks up. "I thought you were still going to therapy and stuff."

"No, I'm done with that," I say, opening my car door too.

"Hmm … you sure about that, hun?" She hums to herself, but I don't wait for her to ask more and immediately sit down.

"So where is this party?" I ask, trying to shift the conversation.

"Up in the hills. You know where all the ultra-rich peeps live. It's a huge mansion." She sits down too and shuts her car door. "Owned by some Mafia guys."

"Mafia guys?" My eyes widen.

She laughs. "Relax. I'm just messing with you."

I sigh out loud and put on my seat belt.

"They're on vacation," she adds, which almost makes my eyeballs pop out.

"So you weren't joking?" I ask.

Right then, she hits the gas. "Nope. But they're out of town, and the house is empty. Perfect for a party. Now let's go!"

I have to hold my titties while she drives. And I thought I was a bad driver, but Ariane literally takes the cake. In fact, I'd bet she'd hit that with her car if it stood in her way. Crossing my fingers, I hope we don't come upon anyone in a crosswalk or meet any lost animals on the way because I swear to God, she'd knock them all over like they were pins in a bowling alley.

When we finally get there, the sheer size of the house makes my jaw drop.

"Told you it was big," Ariane jests, bumping her elbow against mine. "Wait until you see the inside."

"You've been here before?" I say, gawking at the gates that slowly open toward the stretch of land ahead. A sprawling garden is filled with exotic plants and trees, and a giant fountain sits in the middle where the road converges with an actual private parking lot and a garage filled with old-timers.

Jesus Christ. This must be some rich motherfucker.

I mean, my parents are rich but not this rich.

"Sometimes," Ariane muses. "Not often, though. I don't know the actual owners."

I frown. Weird.

"Not that it matters," she says, parking the car before adjusting her boobs in her dress. "You coming?"

We get out of the car, and while Ariane puts on her heels, I admire the huge building in front of me that's booming with music and people. I've never been to such a big party, and I've been at quite a few back when I was still at Falcon Elite Prep. But this ... this surely is something else.

"C'mon!" Ariane hooks her arm through mine and drags me toward the front door, which is wide open and teeming with people flooding in and out.

The music blasts ahead and almost blows me out the door right as we step inside. It's so damn loud that I can't even hear Ariane when she speaks to me, which I'm not sure is a bad thing. Everyone's dancing and drinking. There are even a bunch of dudes throwing beach balls across the crowd. There's a keg in the corner that someone is pouring drinks from while people surrounding it are chanting, "Chug, chug, chug!"

All the rooms in the house are filled with people, even the kitchen where plenty of chips and cups are set up. But I'm amazed at how big this place is because I've only just stepped inside and have probably only seen about five percent.

"Mo!" Ariane calls, and when I turn my head, she beckons me to come. "Here!"

She holds two drinks and pushes one into my hand. "Drink up."

"Thanks," I reply. Even though I'm not sure what's in this, I still take a sip. It's chock-full of some syrup and definitely alcohol because it burns going down my throat.

"Good, huh?" she says.

I just nod. So far, I haven't seen anyone I know yet, no one from school, not even Ariane's friends. Which begs the question ... how did she come up with those pamphlets?

"Where is everyone?" I ask.

"Oh, this is a special-guests-only party, so no classmates," she says, adjusting her boobs again. "Except us, of course."

"Okay, but how did you get those pamphlets then?"

She frowns. "You have a lot of questions tonight, don't you?"

"Sorry." I shrug. "I'm just curious."

Michael suddenly appears behind her and wraps his arms around his waist. "Michael!" She gasps, smiling when he plants a thick, wet kiss on her naked shoulder.

"You look horny, babe."

Ick.

"*Michael* asked me to make them," Ariane tells me, completely ignoring what he said.

I narrow my eyes. *Michael*, the guy from Cole's band, asked *her* to make the pamphlets? So this is *his* party?

"This is your house?" I ask Michael while he's dry humping her.

He looks up at me. "No. I wish it was."

"Then whose is it?" I say, clutching my drink.

"You ask too many questions, Mo," Ariane says while Michael continues to rub up against her. "Just enjoy the evening. Live a little." She winks. "There are plenty of boys here."

I lick my lips and shake my head. She's not telling me something, which means it's important.

"Ariane," I say sternly.

"What?" she mutters, focusing on Michael. "I'm going to dance. You should do the same. That's why we're here, remember?"

I sigh out loud and walk off. I'm really not in the mood for her cryptic bullshit right now. I'm not even sure I want to be here anymore now that I know TRIGGER is involved. Even if it's just Michael or Tristan is close enough to make me run for the hills. But I came here to relax and party, not to panic and sweat. Maybe Cole won't be here. Maybe he's out partying somewhere else, maybe he's busy, maybe he's ...

Right there.

Slouched with parted legs on the big, blue couch in the darkened living room.

With a drink in his left hand and that same girl who was laughing at me when I bumped into Cole in the hallways, Lindy, twirling his hair on the right.

Well, fuck me right off the face of this earth.

TWENTY-SIX

Monica

The cup I was holding is crushed underneath the weight of my hand, turning into a fist.

I immediately turn around and go into the crowd. I'm fuming. Livid. I don't know why he has this effect on me, and I fucking hate it.

So I grab the nearest boy I can find and start dancing with him. The guy doesn't seem to mind as I'm bouncing around his body and wrap my arms around his neck. But my eyes can't help travel toward Cole's … and revel in how furiously they stare back.

My whole body is heating up, either from dancing or from the way he looks at me because damn, he can't take his eyes off me. Serves him right for adding me to his long list of prized conquests. He wants to play? Well, so can I. And he definitely doesn't like what he sees.

A smirk forms on my lips. Too fucking bad.

I dance like nothing's bothering me even though I can feel his eyes bore into my skin. The boy I'm with smells like liquor and drugs, two of my biggest vices, but I try to ignore it as best as I can. Because I need this. That's what I told myself. What Ariane told me.

I've moved on.

But the boy suddenly gets his hands on my waist in a way that I don't like, and I try to push him away.

"What's the problem, girl?" he says. "I'm just trying to get friendly."

"Don't," I say. "Just dance. That's it."

When I try to continue, he keeps touching my breasts and hips. "C'mon, girl. You started it. Now let me get a taste," he whispers in my ear.

"Get off!" I hiss, untangling myself in the middle of a crowd full of people who are bumping into me, forcing me straight back into his arms.

Suddenly, someone rips his arms away from my body.

"She said beat it." Cole's familiar growl makes me turn around in shock.

The boy glares at him for a second, only to taper off like a coward when Cole's muscles tense up. When he's gone, Cole turns his attention to me. "Stop doing that."

"Doing what?" I make a face.

"Whatever the fuck that was," he says through gritted

teeth. "*That*." He points in the direction the boy just went.

"Dancing with someone?" I scoff. "It's a fucking party. Of course I'll dance."

"Don't," he growls. "Don't fucking do this."

"Oh what, I'm not allowed to party?" I raise a brow. "I'll do whatever the fuck I want, thanks."

"You were throwing yourself at him," he says, inching closer.

"So what if I was?" I fold my arms.

"You know how boys work," he says under his breath, looking around to see if anyone's heard him.

"So? I told him not to," I say.

"And he wasn't listening," he retorts.

"That's my problem," I reply, pursing my lips. "Not yours."

"I *made* it my problem when he put his hands on you," he snarls back, closing in on me.

"Yeah, I can see that." I cock my head and ogle the girl behind him. "But aren't you supposed to entertain your own damn girlfriend?"

His brows furrow, and he briefly glances back at the girl sitting on the couch, throwing air-kisses at him. "*Her*?" He makes a tsk sound. "I don't give a damn about her."

"Stop pretending, Cole. I see what you're doing," I say. "It won't work on me."

"I'm not doing anything, Lindy just sat next to me and started flirting with me. Big deal." He narrows his eyes, and a hint of a smile pops onto his face. "Are you jealous?"

I almost choke on my saliva right then and there. "You wish."

He snorts and shakes his head. "Whatever you want, Mo …"

I've had enough of him making fun of me. "Don't." I point my finger at his chest. "I don't need your pity."

"You know what you do need?" he retorts. "You need to leave."

"Why?"

He leans in with my finger still pressed against his chest. "This is dangerous."

Because of that dude? I've been through worse. "I didn't ask for your help."

He grabs my finger. "You don't have to ask. Not with me."

The looks we exchange are so electric the air fills with static lightning.

"Whatever you want, Cole …" I jerk free of his grip. "I don't like this party anyway."

"Good. Leave," he hisses a little too easily.

Fuck. Does he want me out of here so badly? What's his problem? Why does he want to fuck me one second, but then hate me the next? I can't get a grip on him, and that's what's so infuriating.

"Wow, what a friendly conversation."

Ariane suddenly bumps into me, breaking the spell between us.

"Oh, excuse me … Am I interrupting something?" she

asks sarcastically, gazing at both him and me.

His face darkens. "Stay out of this."

"No, I don't think I will," Ariane says, defiantly folding her arms.

"What are you even doing here?" he growls at her. "Who invited you?"

She pulls Michael from the crowd and shows him off like he's some kind of prize. "*He* did."

"Hey, Cole," Michael says, but he's barely walking straight. "Want some?" He shoves a red cup into Cole's hand, but Cole completely ignores him.

"No fucking wonder … So *you* invited all these people?" Cole directs all his anger toward Michael.

"What? You asked everyone over, remember?" Michael shrugs.

But it's a big deal. A very big deal.

Because if Cole asked everyone over … that means this is *his* house.

"Whatever." Cole shakes his head.

"What were you two talking about anyway?" Michael asked.

"Nothing," we both reply.

"Awesome," Michael jokes.

"Fuck no," Ariane replies.

I frown and look at her. Why is she so upset at me having a conversation with Cole?

"You were trying something on her again, weren't you?" Ariane asks Cole.

"Stay out of this," Cole spits back.

"No, I fucking won't. Whatever it is you had to say to her, you can say to me." Ariane steps between us. "She's my fucking cousin, and you've messed with enough girls already. You don't need to ruin another one."

"Oh, *I* ruin things?" Cole spits back at Ariane, making a scene.

"Okay, I'm out of here." Michael scoffs, rolling his eyes, and he disappears back into the crowd.

Cole isn't done yet, though. "Fuck you, Ariane. You play the fucking victim in front of everyone!"

The victim? What is he talking about?

"Shut up!" she yells, her face turning red. "I told you to stay away from her, and you wouldn't listen!"

"Wait, hold up," I say, completely confused by what the hell is going down here. "Back up… You did what now?"

"Oh, you hadn't heard?" Cole snaps. "She's been threatening me to stay away from you."

My eyes widen, and I lean away from Ariane, who doesn't seem remotely surprised by this statement.

"Is that true?" I ask Ariane.

She turns to me and grabs my hand. "Mo, I was just trying to protect you."

Cole snorts and laughs while shaking his head. "Oh, this is rich."

I'm so damn confused by this revelation that I don't know what to do. Even if she was only trying to do good, it doesn't feel right. None of it does.

So I pull my hand away from hers and shake my head. "I didn't ask you to do that."

"I know, and I'm sorry, okay? But you were vulnerable."

"*Vulnerable?*" I repeat, tears welling up in my eyes. I can't believe she'd say that to my face in front of everyone.

"Yeah, with what happened to you at Falcon Elite Prep, I figured—"

"Stop," I interject, swallowing my tears. "Just stop."

"I …" she mutters.

"You heard her." Cole scoffs.

"Shut the fuck up," Ariane snarls at him.

"I can't deal with this," I say, and I turn around and walk away before I do something I'll regret. Because right now, I want nothing more than to slap the ever-living shit out of both of them, but I am not stooping to that level. Not in front of everyone at this party.

So I find the nearest exit into the backyard and sneak out. Away from the noise, away from the people, away from everything until I can finally fucking breathe again.

But no matter how hard I try, I can't catch my breath.

Not as I stumble into the woods beyond the house or as I sit down on a stump and wait for a moment while I stare at the moon above.

CRACK!

A twig snaps in half, but it makes me jolt up and down.

"Who's there?" I ask.

No one replies.

Two seconds later, three boys pop out from the bushes.

They're drunk and walking like idiots. One of them falls over a rock while the other two laugh and drink more booze. And when they look up, they spot me.

I sit there and stare at them.

It's only then that I realize ... Michael is one of the boys.

He clutches his red cup closer to his chest the moment he spots me, a flicker shimmering in his eyes. My nails dig into the wood.

"Hey, isn't that ...?" he murmurs.

I get up from the stump and bite my lip. "Leave me alone."

He tilts his head, wearing a dirty smile on his face. "Yeah, it is. It's you. You're that girl. Cole's."

That girl. Cole's.

Is that how I'm known now?

My stomach twists into knots as the three boys walk closer and closer.

"Hey, why aren't you in there with him?" Michael asks. "Don't you like him?"

"That's none of your business," I say, my hands forming fists.

"Aww ... you're pretty," one of the other ones says. "Wanna dance?"

"No, thanks. I'd rather be left alone," I say, and I walk off away from them toward the trees.

"C'mon! Don't walk away now. We're just trying to have fun!" the other one says. I recognize him now as the guy I just danced with back at the house. Shit.

"Don't leave now," Michael taunts.

"Go back to Ariane," I yell at him.

He laughs. "Why would I? She doesn't care about me. She only came because of Cole."

That makes me stop in my tracks.

"How do they know each other?" I ask as I turn my head to him.

He raises a brow, and a filthy smirk appears on his face. "Yeah … you'd like to know that, wouldn't you?" He licks his lips and then ogles me in a way that reminds me of the night I try so desperately to forget. "What are you willing to do to find out?"

"Never mind," I say, and I quickly turn around and keep walking.

"Hold on, where are you going now?" one of the others says. He catches up with me and grabs my arm.

"Let go!" I hiss, jerking free.

He's momentarily taken aback by my aggressive move, but I've learned not to get close. Especially not to drunk boys … or ones who have done drugs. Because I can definitely smell them on his breath.

"You're too pretty. Hasn't anyone told you that?" he murmurs, making me want to vomit with the way he's breathing in my face. "What's a pretty girl like you doing out here all by yourself?"

"Trying to get away from you," I spit.

The look on his face changes. Monstrous.

Unlike anything I've ever seen.

"Fuck you," he retorts, his voice threatening, vile.

I quickly move away and start walking in the opposite direction again.

"You know, I think you're a catch," Michael says. "Cole doesn't know what he's got."

I don't reply. I keep walking and ignore them because saying anything is just baiting them to act.

"And I think you know that," Michael adds. "Why else would you show up at our cabin?"

They keep stalking me, and I'm getting more and more anxious as my adrenaline starts to spike.

"You wanted a taste, didn't you?" he asks. "You were practically begging for it."

The other boys laugh and grunt. "Maybe she's still asking for it," one of them says.

I wish they'd just shut up and go, but they won't leave me alone … and they keep chasing me farther into the woods.

Suddenly, one of them grabs my arm. "C'mon. Give me a kiss. Lemme see what's made Cole this horny."

I slap him. Hard.

Fuck.

He touches his cheek and releases my arm. When I start walking again, he growls, "Grab her."

Panic seeps in, and I run as hard as I can.

When I look over my shoulder, my face scrunches up at the sight of them chasing after me like goddamn hunting dogs, and I scream.

I run even faster than before, my heart racing in my throat.

Their footsteps crackle behind me as they run across the fallen leaves, a reminder of their nearby presence.

I'm being hunted down by drunk, drugged-out boys who want to do things to me that I can't and don't want to think about.

Tears well up in my eyes, but I keep going, so I can get as far away from them as possible. I don't think. I just run.

But when one of them grabs ahold of my waist and pulls me down, I scream.

He quickly covers my mouth with his hand, wrestling me down onto the dirt. I cry and fight him off, but it's no use. Another one sits down on top of me. A belt buckle is pulled.

No. No. NO!

This can't happen again!

"You know you want it," the boy whispers into my ear.

I squeal, tears flowing freely down my cheeks.

Suddenly, something pushes the boy off me.

WHACK!

Punches fly left and right, but I don't know what's going on. I'm still on my belly, my face covered in dirt and leaves. Then the other boy flies off me too.

I quickly crawl up to my feet and stumble away, barely able to stand. My body is shaking vigorously as I turn cold to the bone, and my muscles freeze from terror. Right in front of me is a tree, split in half by lightning, with a small hollow alcove in its trunk. I hide inside, shivering like a straw.

I can't look. Can't watch. Can't do anything but turn away my eyes from the world, just like I did once before ... the night I was ruined forever.

But this time, someone's out there fighting for me.

Fighting against my demons.

Destroying all who dare cross his path.

Cole.

TWENTY-SEVEN

Cole

The moment her scream echoed through the woods, I knew it was her.

Monica.

Not one second did I hesitate before I rushed outside. I didn't care who was in my way. I shoved them aside.

Not even Ariane could stop me, and fuck knows she tried her hardest.

But no filth that spills from her mouth can stop me from going to find my fucking girl.

Something … or someone … made her scream, and it wasn't me.

Whoever it was, they're gonna pay.

"Cole! Where are you going?" Ariane calls out after me,

but I ignore her.

I've only got one mission, and that's to find Monica.

The sounds came from the woods just beyond the house, my father's personal pine forest where he goes to clear his guilty conscience. With clenched fists, I run past the trees, following the sound of voices.

Three of them to be exact, coaxing her to stay and do something fun.

Fun? I'll give them some fucking fun.

Right then, another squeal follows. All my senses perk up.

Rage overcomes me as I storm toward her and find her lying there, on the ground, with two guys on top of her, one of them pulling down his jeans while the other holds her down. And Michael is right there, sipping at his cup while he watches them do it.

Traitor.

Without thinking, I pounce down on the guy who's on top of her and sucker punch him right in the face. He falls to the ground while I tackle the other one. From the corner of my eye, I spot Monica crawl away.

"Cole!" Michael yells, briefly distracting me.

I'm fighting with two assholes, punching them the second they get off the ground, so I can't fucking take a second to look. Both of them attack me back with lackluster punches and dead-weight kicks. They're completely intoxicated and loaded up on drugs too, judging from the smell.

Still, two versus one is hard to take on, and I have trouble winning the fight. Every punch they manage to land hurts like a motherfucker, and I quickly have a bloody nose and mouth. But I don't stop. I *won't* stop. Not until they're punished ... not until she's safe.

"What the fuck are you doing?" one of them growls at me.

"YOU DARE TO FUCKING TOUCH HER?!" I scream. "You think I'm gonna let you get away with that?" I punch the one who asked me that so hard blood pours from his nose. "WRONG!"

"COLE!" Michael yells. "They were just messing with her."

I kick the other one in the face so hard it knocks him out flat onto the ground. I spit onto his body for good measure and then punch the other one with the bleeding nose again until he's on his knees, begging for mercy.

"Okay, okay! I got it!" he says, almost falling down completely. "I'm sorry!"

"SORRY DOESN'T FUCKING CUT IT!" I scream.

Adrenaline rushes through my veins, pushing me to act, almost forcing me to push myself to my limits. To theirs. Because I want nothing more than to kill them right here on the spot.

Maybe I should. They fucking deserve it for what they tried to do to her.

No one, and I mean no one, touches her.

"She's yours. We got it," Michael says.

"You fucking know that's not what this is about," I hiss, sweat dripping from my face as I point at him. "You and your fucking buddies chased her out here. You knew damn well what the fuck you were doing."

"They're drunk and stupid," he tries to explain.

"I DON'T FUCKING CARE!" I'm fuming to the point of turning red.

"Calm the fuck down, bro," he says. "Nothing happened."

"It almost did. Did you hear her screams?" I snarl back. "Fuck you, Michael. Fuck you." I spit on the ground in front of him. "You're a fucking disgrace."

"You're one to talk," he retorts. "You fucking teased her to begin with. And I'm not supposed to enjoy it too?"

"What I do is none of your fucking business," I say, getting all up in his face now.

"Look at what you did to them," he says, pointing at his buddies as they can barely get off the ground, but I don't fucking care. Not anymore.

"They had it coming. Shouldn't have done what they did."

His nostrils flare. "What now? What are you gonna do then? Punch me too?"

"I'm thinking about it," I growl, but I've lost a lot of energy fighting those bastards.

"Do it then. Show me what kind of a man you are," he says through gritted teeth.

He'd never call me out like that if I hadn't wasted all my

punches on those guys.

I'd win a fair fight, and he knows that. That's why he chooses to taunt me now.

But I won't fucking fall for it.

"At least I'm not the kind who chases screaming girls into the forest and lets his buddies have their way with her," I bark.

We stare at each other for a moment, and I can almost feel the tension crackling.

He's daring me … daring me to act.

But I won't stoop to his level and let him destroy me.

"I should call the cops on you for beating them up," he growls.

"Fuck you," I hiss. "Call the cops, then. Do it. You can't, can you?"

His jaw tightens, but he doesn't respond.

Instead, he turns around and walks off into the woods, taking a sip of his drink as if none of this meant anything to him.

"Thought so." I wipe the sweat off my forehead. "You know what? You're out!" I yell after him. "Out of the fucking band. You hear me? I don't wanna see your fuck face ever again!"

He doesn't say another word, but I know he heard me. Everyone on the goddamn grounds could probably hear me, so there will be gossip going around, and within minutes literally, everyone who follows our band online will know.

But I don't care.

All I care about right now is protecting her.

Monica.

But where is she?

I spin on my heels and look around, but she's nowhere to be found.

I take a step in the direction she crawled toward, but my knee caves underneath me, and I go to the ground. My muscles feel tight, and only now do I realize those punches hurt quite a bit. So much that I find it hard to get up. And I stay here with my knees buried in the soil so I can catch my breath. When I look up, I finally spot her, hiding in a tiny alcove of a tree split in half.

My lungs suck in the biggest breath they have ever taken.

I force myself to get up and brush away the pain. When I walk to her, every noise makes her jolt up and down. Every step I take causes her to turn inward toward the tree, into herself, and I realize I gotta take it slow.

She's shivering, not from the cold, but from the suffering she's endured.

Suffering I took part in.

Guilt floods my bones as I kneel in front of her and wait. I wish I could say what was on my heart right now, but it feels so heavy. She's unraveling before me, and there's nothing I can do to stop the bleeding in her heart.

I try to reach out, but the moment my hand touches her arm, she freezes completely.

"They tried to … to …" she mutters, tears swelling in

her eyes. "It almost happened again, just like before."

Before?

"Did they try to do that to you before?" I ask, frowning, getting angry again from the mere thought of their filthy hands on her body.

She shakes her head, but the tears keep rolling down her cheeks even though she's barely breathing.

I don't dare get any closer.

She's wounded, but not from the fight … it's her mind.

This isn't the Monica I recognize.

This is the Monica she's been trying to hide.

And it finally dawns on me what it meant when Monica was so closed off, why she changed schools, and why Ariane pushed me to stay away from her, telling me that I would only damage her further.

She was already hurt … by someone else.

Just like before.

That's what all of this was about.

The secret she's been trying to keep buried all along.

The thing that kept me from getting close.

Someone completely and utterly destroyed her … And it wasn't me.

But I made it worse.

Michael and his friends made it worse.

Fuck.

I grab her hand and squeeze. "I'm not going to hurt you."

She looks up at me, the pain in her eyes seeping into my

soul, cutting me open like an old wound. And she leaps into my arms, wrapping her hands around my neck as if she's never letting go. The guttural wails that emanate from deep down within her body wreck me, and I kneel onto the ground with her in my arms, just breathing in and out, hoping that I can provide a little bit of solace to the turmoil going on inside her head.

I wish I could take it all away from her.

That I could destroy that part of her and erase it from its very existence.

Because no amount of searching and digging was worth what I discovered.

This beautiful, funny girl was completely wrecked by someone who didn't deserve her.

"I'm sorry," I whisper.

It only makes her cry harder. I don't know what to say or do to make things better, but I won't give up. Not now. Not ever.

We sit here for minutes, maybe hours, I don't even care. I will be right here by her side for as long as she needs me. Until the stars fade and the moon falls from the sky. I'll suck up the pain and sorrow until the memories grow dim, and the gaps in my heart are filled with the shards she's discarded from hers.

TWENTY-EIGHT

Cole

When she's stopped crying, I pick her up from the ground and cradle her in my arms. She's exhausted from the struggle, and her eyes can barely stay open. If I hadn't gotten up, she probably would've fallen asleep right there in the woods against my chest.

But after what she's been through, I can't let her give up. If she can't walk, then I will do the walking for her.

I carry her all the way back through the woods toward my home and walk up the steps. All the guests outside are staring at me. Guests I didn't fucking invite and didn't want to be here. Somehow word got around … thanks to that fucknut Michael. I knew telling them I was home alone was a mistake. But that's what you get for wanting a good time.

Stares and whispers behind your back from people who thought this would be an amazing party.

Well, I have some bad news for them.

"Party's over," I growl right at them as I walk inside.

The music is still blaring from the speakers, so I march toward it and snarl at someone standing next to it. "Turn it off."

He glares at me for a second as if to dare me to act, but he can see the bruises on my face. I don't fucking mess around.

The music is turned off, and everyone turns to look.

Tristan comes toward me with a confused look on his face. "Cole? What the …?" he mutters when he sees Monica in my arms.

I clutch her closer, feeling fiercely protective over her. "The party is over. Done. Finished," I say. "Go home."

Benjamin joins in from behind Tristan. "Dude, you're covered in bruises. What the fuck."

Tristan frowns. "What happened?" He pulls out his phone. "Michael messaged me, told me you kicked him out of the band."

"Not now," I growl, and I look over at the people staring at us. "Did you hear me? The party is over."

Everyone tapers off with disappointed looks on their faces, but I don't give a fuck.

I never asked for this party to begin with, and somehow, it got started anyway. Once the people began to flood in, there was no stopping it. I went along with it for the sake of it even though there were too much booze and drugs, and some girls were all up in my face trying to get my attention despite me telling them I wasn't interested.

And I let it happen because Tristan asked me to enjoy the evening.

No more.

"Dude, why?" Benjamin asks.

"This is why," I growl, gazing down at Monica and the frightened look on her face.

Tristan tries to take a closer look, but I shield her from him. "It's done. Go home," I say. "I'll clean up this fucking mess in the morning."

Tristan swallows and steps back. "Sorry, dude. I didn't know shit was gonna happen."

I ignore him and pass by all the people leaving the house, so I can go up the stairs. Tristan's and Benjamin's stares penetrate my back like laser beams, but I pay no attention to them.

Right now, all I care about is keeping her safe.

Here, with me.

The noise downstairs is growing weaker and weaker, but I no longer care as I walk into my room and shut the door behind us with my foot. I place her down on my bed and sit down beside her, watching her breathe slowly through her nose. She sinks into my pillow, and within seconds, she's out, exhausted as she was. She looks so calm while she's sleeping. Such a stark contrast to how she looked when she was sobbing in my arms.

I lie down beside her and stare at her for a moment, just to center myself. A loose strand of hair has stuck to her face from all the crying, and I gently nudge it aside. The dark of night can't hide the beauty of her face … nor the fragility hiding underneath.

I saw something today that wasn't meant to happen, something that scarred her more than it scarred me, but it still left a mark on my soul. I can't fathom the effects it had on her. She didn't deserve any of that, yet it happened to her anyway.

And on my goddamn watch too.

My hand forms a fist as I grind my teeth, feeling guilty over what happened.

I should've been there sooner. Should've ignored Ariane, should've followed Monica out of the house when I had the chance.

I should've done so many things but didn't … because I was scared of the consequences.

Scared of what it might mean when I let her get close.

Of what it would do to me when I opened my heart.

And she fought me so damn hard every step of the way.

My hand hovers over her cheek, but I don't dare touch her.

It was easy to make her hate me. Easy to let it consume me whole.

And now we're both paying the price.

***

Monica

A bright morning sun wakes me up from a deep and nightmare-fueled sleep. I only remember bits and pieces from the night before, but my brain is flooded with images and memories as though it snapped out of a trance.

Alcohol, music, dancing, fights … and three boys chasing me through the woods until they pinned me to the ground. Cole coming to my rescue, punching them so hard that blood was flying … His eyes burned brighter than the stars filling the night sky when he found me trembling underneath a tree.

My eyes burst open, and I sit up straight, breathing heavily. But my heart only beats faster and faster as I touch the fabric of the duvet that doesn't belong to me.

I'm not in my own bed. Or my own room.

Right then, a dark figure stretches his thick muscles beside me.

My eyes are practically glued to his skin.

Cole.

My lip quivers as I clutch the bed, watching him sit there and stare at the window ahead.

It all comes flooding back now. Him, carrying me back through the woods, into his house … into his bed.

I fucking slept here all through the night.

How? How was it so easy to fall asleep in someone

else's bed? And why did it feel like second nature to rest my head against his shoulders and drift off?

A familiar scent enters my nostrils as he gets up. His cologne. The sweet, intoxicating smell makes my heart flutter, and it puts my mind at ease.

Why? Why does it all suddenly feel so different? So … normal?

As though I was always meant to be here?

Suddenly, he turns his head and glances at me over his shoulder. "Morning."

My lips slam together as though they got caught gaping.

He averts his eyes again with his head lowered between his shoulders. It's only when I look at him in his sweatpants that I realize I'm still wearing that short, black dress that I wore to the party, and I feel so out of place.

"I …" I don't even know what I want to say. If I should even say anything.

"Are you … okay?" he asks, without looking at me. But he doesn't have to. I know exactly what he means when he asks.

The air is filled with unspoken words. My heart feels as though it got stabbed, and it's still bleeding. And he was there to witness it all.

He watched me crumple. At my weakest, he didn't come to beat me down and destroy what was left. He came to pick up the pieces and brought them back to life. With a simple gesture, a hug, he gave me back my dignity, my ability to let go.

And even though I cried there against his shoulders, he never wavered, never tried to push me back down or bully me into silence.

He was there for me when no one else was.

That means more than either he or I could ever put into words.

"I don't know," I reply.

He glances at me over his shoulder. "So you remember everything?"

I nod.

In a split second, the concern clearly shows on his face, but he quickly looks away. His fists ball, and his muscles tighten. "You said something about it happening before. Tell me."

I suck in a breath.

I've never said the words out loud. Never told this story to anyone but my therapist, and even then, it was hard. But I should let it all out. It's been bleeding like an open wound for far too long now.

"A boy drugged me at a party. Took me to his room. Used me," I say, each word feeling like I'm swallowing knives. "And he videotaped everything and showed it to his friends."

His body grows even more rigid. "Did he …?"

He doesn't finish his sentence, but we both know what he means.

I nod.

He turns to look away but not before I spotted the look

of disgust on his face. "No wonder …"

"What?"

"The cabin. When I took that picture of you … I saw the fear in your eyes." He lets out a heavy sigh. "I'm sorry." His voice is twisted, raw. Like he's trying not to fall apart. And I know the feeling all too well. "And I'm sorry about what happened to you in the woods."

I lean in and place a hand on his shoulder.

He immediately jolts up and spins on his heels to look at me, his bare, tattooed chest rising and falling with every heavy breath he takes. "Don't."

"But it's not your fault," I say, frowning.

His face contorts as though I said something heinous. "I could've stopped them. I could've gone after you, could've protected you." He shoves his fingers in his hair and marches back and forth in an agitated manner. "I was too fucking late."

I shake my head. "You were there. That's all that matters."

He makes a face. "No, it doesn't. I chased you away. You ran into those woods because of me." He points at the window, which looks out upon the forest. "You ran because of what I didn't tell you."

I know what he's talking about. The sole reason for the fight at that party. "You and Ariane were a thing."

He tilts his head, his nostrils flaring. "And now I realize she didn't tell you for a reason."

"She lied to me," I say. "She didn't even tell me this was

your home."

And boy … what a home.

There are a lot of things I didn't know about Cole.

Like that he would be the one, out of all the people there, to come to my rescue, to protect me from three boys, one of which was his own damn band member.

And as we stare at each other for a second, I can't help but say the words that have been floating in my head ever since he hugged me in the woods.

"Thank you."

His face darkens and twists into shapes I've never seen before. "Look at me, Monica. Look at me!" he yells with pain in his eyes. I've never seen him that serious. "I'm a fucking monster. A player. An asshole. A bully. Don't ever say fucking thank you."

"You saved me," I respond, clutching the blanket.

"Oh, and that's enough?" he growls.

"No, but it's a start," I retort.

He snorts and shakes his head repeatedly before picking up a lamp and smashing it into the wall with a loud roar. I jolt up and down from the noise as the glass shatters into tiny pieces.

He stands there, watching his own destruction like a beast uncaged wanting to rip through everything he can find.

Including me.

But I won't let him destroy the good inside his heart even though he so desperately wants to … just to prove to himself that it wasn't all for nothing.

That he didn't bully me for nothing.

That he didn't make me hate him for nothing.

Because that's what this has always been about.

Keeping me at bay.

But I'm not going to let him push me away anymore.

He knows my darkest secret now, the one thing I've tried to keep him from finding out.

Now it's my turn to ask.

"Do you really want me to hate you?" I drop the blanket even though it was the only thing covering my barely dressed body.

He glances at me for a second, full of unbridled fury and untethered emotions before retreating into the bathroom. The shower is turned on. I get up from the bed and follow him inside. He's already standing under the water, naked, the sweatpants casually discarded on the floor. For a few seconds, I watch the rivulets of water slide down his muscular back and along the crevice of his ample ass while he runs his fingers through his hair. He places one foot forward and one hand on the wall, his head lowered while he gazes at the water pooling beneath his feet. I wonder what he's thinking about right now. If he's still fighting the turmoil in his head.

If I can take away the pain for him like he did for me.

He couldn't answer my question, but the truth is far closer to what I said than what he'd ever dare to admit.

Hating him is the easier option. But I don't like easy. I never have.

So I pull off my dress and take off my panties, throwing them all into a corner before I step inside with him.

He glances at me over his shoulder, his eyes flickering with that same hunger every time he sees my body. I step closer and wrap my arms around him, my hands on the thick slabs of his chest, feeling every breath he takes.

They're constricted and labored as though he's struggling not to react. I push myself against him, my nipples hardening against his skin.

His body grows rigid as he fights the urge. "What are you doing?"

"What I want …" I mumble, letting the heat rush over me as I finally let myself acknowledge the truth.

I want him. I want him so fucking badly. And I always have.

Even when I said he was bad for me or that he was an asshole.

I hated him for making me lust over him.

No more.

If I don't get to choose who I fall for, at least I can choose to give in and stop fighting it.

So I lay my head against his back and listen to the sound of his heartbeat, every one of them going faster than the one before. His muscles tighten as the water rushes down both him and me.

He lets out a guttural groan, one filled with torment, as if he's forcing himself to stay put.

"All this time, you fought yourself, didn't you?" I

mutter.

He doesn't reply, but the sigh that follows my words is enough for me.

I know the truth.

TWENTY-NINE

Cole

I expected a lot of things, like that this night would blow over quickly. Instead, I laid awake to stare at her all night long, hoping she was okay. I expected her to be mad at me. Instead, she was thankful. I expected her to leave after I went into the bathroom. Instead, she actually fucking stepped into the shower with me.

She continues to defy everything I thought I knew. Not just about her but about me too.

And it fucking ruins me.

But nothing ruins me as much as her hands on my chest, squeezing so gently it destroys the cage I'd built around my heart. Her body is pressed against my back as though she refuses to let go, despite the fact that I told her everything I was.

All the bad things she should stay away from … the asshole who bullied her and made her cry.

The asshole she should hate…

Instead, she stands here, hugging me.

Doing things to me that I never thought any girl could.

Because fuck me, when those tits pressed up against my back, I wanted to turn around, grab her, and fuck her into oblivion.

I shouldn't think these things, but my mind can't help but wander to that place. I'm addicted, addicted to the sex, addicted to … *her*.

I've tried to deny it for so long, but it's impossible when she's so close to me. I can't fucking fight it anymore, can't fucking fight the hunger that wants to consume her whole.

But she's not ready. She's wounded, fragile, hurt. From everything before me and after me. Whatever she had built up as a defense, I kept destroying until nothing was left to save her from the pain of her past.

And for what? All because I was too fucking curious about what she was hiding because I *needed* to know the truth.

The truth that now stops me from doing whatever the fuck I want to her.

Because the more I learn, the more I want to protect her from bad influence.

And that includes me.

But fuck me, her tits are rubbing against my back, and

my dick is getting hard. I groan out loud, trying to shove the lust back inside, but my body won't listen to my brain.

She leans sideways, peeking underneath my arm. I glance at her only briefly, but she still surprises me when I see the same lust staring right back at me.

She grabs my arm and tugs on it until I lower it, and she slips underneath until she's right in front of me. Water pours down onto her hair, which sticks to her beautiful face. Every trickling droplet catches my attention as it rolls over her luscious lips and down the crevice between her tits. The beautiful girl standing before me undoes me with every stare and lays waste to my body with every touch. And fuck me for not being able to resist.

She leans in, her body tantalizing, forbidden, but oh, so sweet and succulent to look at. My dick hardens at the sight. If she doesn't walk away now, I don't know what I'm going to do to her. I can't protect her past this point.

"Don't," I growl when she's mere inches away from me. "You don't want to do this."

Her warm, wet parted lips coax me. "Kiss me."

Fuck.

I grab her face with one hand and smash my lips to hers.

Fuck holding back. I'm taking her.

She dared to step into my shower, then she begged me to kiss her. How am I supposed to resist? It's like she's practically begging me to. But it feels so damn wrong, and it never has. Why does it feel so bad?

My lips unlatch from hers as I attempt to decipher what

it is that I'm feeling when I kiss her. It didn't feel this way before, this … agonizing, like I'm taking something that wasn't mine to take. But the longer I look at her, the more I realize that it's not just my body reacting to her. My heart is playing along too now.

Fuck…

She pecks the side of my lips and presses a sweet, gentle kiss on top of my lips, coaxing me to kiss her back. But her presence confuses the fuck out of me, makes me feel weak and powerful at the same time, and I don't fucking understand because no fucking girl has ever been able to wreck me like this.

Another groan escapes my mouth when she grabs my cock.

I've wanted nothing more since day one than to fuck her.

Fuck her into oblivion.

But she's not ready for me, not like this.

"You don't know what you're doing," I say.

She licks her lips and bites on her bottom one, making me even harder. "If you think that, you don't know me very well."

"Fuck," I groan when she starts to rub me, my muscles clenching with need.

Clearly, I don't, because I don't think this is in her best interest.

"You should go home," I say through gritted teeth. "After last night—"

She places a finger on my lips, interrupting me. "I know what I want, and it doesn't involve talking."

Well, fuck me. How am I supposed to protect her when she won't even let me?

Her finger slides down my chest, along every ripple of my abs while she practically salivates. And when she starts fondling my cock with both hands, I do too.

I should tell her to stop. I should turn off the faucet and walk away right now.

I guess this is what they mean when they say love is like a drug … you get addicted faster than you can blink.

***

Monica

I don't need him to tell me what I want or what I should do.

I don't care if it's right or wrong, if he's an asshole or a saint, if I'm a good girl or a bad girl.

What I want right now is to show him how much I really like him … and I know he wants this more than anything. He's wanted me on my knees since day one, but I would never bow to him.

But now? Now I want to show him my appreciation.

So I slowly lower to my knees, right in front of him. His cock is huge and bounces up and down while his pupils dilate at the sight of my mouth hovering over his length.

"Monica …" he groans as I lean in and take him into my mouth.

His muscles clench as I suck him off slowly, his teeth grinding with both greed and pain. He still refuses to let go of that rage, but I'll make him release it.

I bob up and down, faster and faster, licking him off with my tongue. It's been so long since I've done this, but it feels so damn good. My pussy is already getting wet from just having him in my mouth, and my legs instinctively part to let him see.

See the entire me.

He tried before … but this? This is different. This is *my* choice.

His eyes trail down my body, every inch causing his dick to pulse inside my mouth, and it only makes me want to suck harder.

"Why are you doing this?" he whispers, a strained gasp following when I lick the tip.

"Because I want to," I say. "I already told you."

I suck him off so hard he starts to moan and bite his lip.

"I can't stop if you don't," he groans.

"Then don't stop," I reply, looking up into his devilish green eyes filled to the brim with lust. Lust only meant for me and me alone. And fuck me, if that isn't a turn-on, I don't know what else is.

One hand is still on the wall behind me while the other finds its way down to my hair. He caresses me, and when I take his cock back into my mouth, he grabs a fistful of my hair and pushes me further, groaning like an animal.

He's so big inside me it's hard not to gag, but I try. He pulls out and pushes back in again, and I let myself go to his desire. With a clenched jaw, he fucks my mouth until he's right on the edge. And I don't stop sucking until he explodes.

He roars with furor as he comes all over my tongue, the salty taste making me hungry for more. I gulp it down until the drop, and the relief shows on his face. He pants as his cock spills from my mouth, and I lick my bottom lip and lean back, eager for more.

"That's my thank-you," I murmur, looking up at him.

But the response I get is far from what I expected.

His face twists into something dark, something vicious that I can only describe as pure agony.

"Get out," he growls.

I frown and shake my head. "What?"

He lowers his head and looks away. "Get out, Monica. Go home."

I stand and try to touch him, but he leans away, disgust marring his face.

His words bring tears to my eyes. "Why? I thought that was what you wanted?"

His brows furrow, and he points at the door. "Go. Home."

A tear rolls down my cheek, but in this shower, no one will see them fall. After everything I just did, after giving my all to him, this is what he gives me? He'll make me do the walk of shame?

"I can't believe this," I mutter as I quickly pass him by, grabbing a towel and my clothes.

I don't even dry myself off fully before putting them on and running the hell out of his house.

I'll fucking walk home if I have to just to get away from here.

Fuck him and that high horse he rode in on.

And fuck him and that hard dick that made me believe he actually wanted me for me.

Fuck him for tricking me into spilling all the secrets to my past just so he could make me an easy victim.

And fuck him for making me believe I could finally let myself fall for him.

***

Later that morning

I sneak back into my home and close the door as quietly as I possibly can. Without making a sound, I go upstairs, but halfway up, my mom suddenly appears at the top.

Shit.

"Going somewhere?"

I sigh. "Mom, I can explain."

"Of course," she says, folding her arms. "And you're gonna."

I go up the stairs, and she follows me into my room.

"You weren't home last night," she says, and then she points at my bed. "You didn't sleep in this bed."

I close my eyes and breathe in and out. This is the last thing I wanted to talk about right now. "Mom ..." I sigh. "It's complicated."

"Complicated? I had to call Ariane to ask where you were." She scoffs, putting her hands against her side. "You know you're not supposed to sneak off like that. We had a deal. You come home safely."

"I know, but this wasn't planned. None of this was," I explain. "I was supposed to come home after the party, but ..."

"But what?" She frowns.

I sit down on the bed. "Something happened."

"What happened?" she asks, and she sits down beside me. "Is there something you wanna tell me?"

"No, well ... maybe ..." I look up at her. "Promise you won't be mad."

"Is this about boys?" she asks.

I nod.

"Did someone do something to you?" She grabs my hands.

Somehow, the feel of her hands on mine makes me break down, and I smash my lips together to stop the tears from flowing. "Almost ..."

Still, I fail to keep it together, and I lean in against her shoulder. She grabs me and hugs me tight. "Oh, honey. Tell me what happened."

"I was trying to get away after a fight, and then these boys chased me down into some woods," I say. "But Cole was there, and he saved me."

"Cole?" she asks.

"A boy ... It's complicated," I add.

She snorts. "Everything is complicated when you're a teen."

"Mom." I rub my eyes.

"Sorry. I just ... Do you want me to call the cops?" she asks.

"What?" I gasp, leaning away. "No. Not again. Please. Nothing actually happened. It *almost* did."

"Okay, if you're sure," she says.

"Positive. They got what they deserved."

Thanks to Cole ... who then went and shattered my heart right after.

I don't get him. I don't get his motivations, and I don't get what drives him to act the way he does.

"Well, as long as that Cole boy is there and you feel safe around him."

Safe's a big word.

A very big word.

"I'm sorry I wasn't home, Mom," I say, looking up at her.

She grabs my face. "Thank you for being honest with me." She pulls me in for another hug. "But no more parties. You're grounded for a week."

My jaw drops. "But I … we just …"

She cocks her head and gets up. "I thanked you for being honest. I didn't say you weren't going to get a punishment." She smiles. "But I love you, and I hope you know I'm only looking out for your best interests."

I roll my eyes. "Thanks, Mom."

"You're welcome!" she muses. Leaving my room, she closes the door behind her while I drop down onto the bed and groan out loud.

I really thought I'd escaped the worst there, but I guess not.

Though, if I know myself well enough, I probably won't listen to her punishment either.

Suddenly, my phone buzzes. I fish it from my pocket and read the text I got. It's from an anonymous sender, and I don't recognize the number.

ANONYMOUS: You're a slut, and you'll pay for what you did.

There's a link attached. When I click it, it leads to a folder with a picture in it … the picture Cole took of me in the cabin.

Fuck.

THIRTY

Cole

Cleaning up the mess from the party is not something I was looking forward to, but it's a cathartic experience, that's for sure. At least now I get to take out all my rage on the trash because there's plenty lying around. Stray cups, bags of chips, and food are scattered all around the house. I even found several bottles of hard liquor in the kitchen.

I don't know who brought them, but people sure came prepared.

Maybe it was Michael's idea.

Fuck that rat for ruining literally everything good in my life.

First, he tried to destroy what was left of Monica's self-worth, with him and his buddies fucking with her, and now he leaves me with this fucking mess too.

I should've never have accepted him into the band.

Now we're one guy short, and the others will hate me over it, because this ruins any and all chances we had for a successful audition.

And to top it all off, Monica thinks she has to thank me for saving her by sucking my dick.

If that doesn't prove how much of an asshole I am, I don't know what else will.

I sigh and slouch down onto the couch, rubbing my forehead.

How the fuck do I solve this mess?

I wish I knew the answers, but I have none, and it pisses me off.

I only have two days to clean up this house too because if my parents come home to this, I'm dead. But there's no way I'm gonna make this go away on my own. I need help.

I get up and search for my phone, but I can't fucking find it anywhere. I haven't actually seen it since yesterday, right before the whole party went to shit. I left it somewhere on a table, but where?

I rummage through the mess and throw everything into the bin I'm holding. Cups, liquor, snacks. Right there, underneath a bag of chips, is my phone.

"Fucking finally," I grumble, picking it up.

However, when I press the button, I notice the security is not enabled, and I'm able to open everything up without inputting a code.

"What the hell?" I mutter.

Did I do this last night? I can't fucking remember, but then again, I couldn't even fucking remember where I left it. Did I drink too much? Maybe. But not as much as the rest … or fucking Michael, that's for sure.

But then why does this make my skin crawl?

There are twenty missed calls from Tristan and Benjamin too.

Fuck.

I sit down on a chair near the table and message them.

Cole: Sorry, been busy
Tristan: Sure…
Benji: With what?
Cole: Hard to explain
Tristan: Let's meet up

I sigh to myself. Of course he'd say that. He's pissed off about last night, but I can't change what happened. I can't undo the damage that was done, and I refuse to fucking back down. So if they wanna talk, I'll talk, but it won't change a thing.

Cole: Fine, meet me at school practice
Tristan: That's Monday, I can't wait that long
Cole: Yeah, well, my parents will kill me if I don't clean this fucking house, so tough luck

I close the app and grind my teeth, looking for a cleaner online. Once I find one, I send them a message with the pay and hit sent. Pray to the fucking gods that I get help in time because if not, I'm dead.

I throw my head back, wishing I could rip myself a new one. Fuck me, I should've never let those guys convince me to let them invite more people to this goddamn not-a-party party. And I should've never, ever let Monica inside. Both in the house and my fucking heart.

Because now, both are fucking ruined beyond repair.

***

Monica

Without even thinking about the trouble I'm going to be in for ditching my mom even though I'm grounded, I go right back to Cole's home. I don't care if he doesn't want me there, he's gonna have to answer for what he did.

No one else had that picture of me, so it had to have been him.

I march up to the gate and press the buzzer. It takes him a while to answer.

"Hello?"

"It's Monica. We need to talk," I growl, looking away from the camera.

He sighs, and then the gate opens for me.

I storm up the property and ring the doorbell, but one second later, he's opening the door. I don't give him the chance to talk.

SLAP!

He stands there with a surprised look on his face as I crumple down in front of him.

"You had no right, no fucking right!" I yell, pointing at him.

"What, I don't—"

"The fucking picture!" I try to keep the tears at bay, but it's hard, so damn hard when I'm looking at him. I left my heart with him, and he threw it away and stomped on it as though it meant nothing to him. And then he went ahead and shared that damn picture anyway.

"What are you talking about?" He scoffs.

"Don't play dumb with me," I growl, and I fish my phone from my pocket and show him the text I received, including the picture. "You did that."

His eyes widen, and he tries to take my phone from me, but I quickly pull it back.

"You gonna threaten me too now?" I fold my arms.

"No, that's not—"

"Save it," I interject. "Who else did you share this with?"

"No one," he says, frowning.

"Of course." I don't fucking believe him. He was the only one who had that picture, and now it's out there thanks to him. "You're an asshole," I say. "A dirty douchebag who used me for his own pleasure. Well, I hope you're proud of yourself."

I turn around and march off, determined not to let him see me cry.

"Mo, wait!" he calls out at me, but I stick up my middle finger and keep walking, so I don't end up in more shit than I already am.

***

Cole

The next day

Not one fucking second wasted.

The moment I spot Michael, I grab him by the coat and throw him against the lockers in front of the entire fucking school.

"How fucking dare you?" I say through gritted teeth, clutching him tightly. "Snooping through my fucking phone?"

"What the fuck, Cole?!" he growls. "I didn't do shit. Let go of me."

"Not before you tell me what the fuck you did with that picture," I snarl. "Who'd you send it to?"

"What? I don't know what the hell you're talking about," he retorts, eyeing me down like he's some kind of saint. "I don't have any pictures."

When he tries to flee, I shove him farther up against the lockers. I don't care who's staring, let them watch.

"I know it was you. Admit it," I growl.

"I'm not admitting to shit. I didn't do anything," he growls. "You just fucking hate me, don't you? And now you wanna pin me for something I didn't do."

"Then who was it, huh? No one else had access to my phone," I say, not taking my eyes off him.

"*You?*" he retorts.

I get up in his face. "Like I'd ever do that to her. Stop fucking lying."

His eyes glimmer with hatred. "You care a lot about that stupid girl, don't you?"

I punch him. Hard. Right in the face. And some of the people standing around us have it on tape. But I don't fucking care anymore.

No one, and I mean no one, calls Monica a stupid girl.

"Fucking hell!" He groans out in pain. "What the fuck is wrong with you?!"

"*You*, that's what's wrong," I retort. "Now tell me what the fuck you did with that picture or I swear to God …"

"You'll what?" he spits back. "Kick me out of the band? Too fucking late."

We stare each other down for a few seconds.

"Wanna hit me again, tough boy?" he taunts, blood dripping from his nose, which he quickly wipes away with the back of his hand.

I blow off some steam and release him from my grip.

"You're not worth my fucking time."

"That's it. Walk away, pretty boy," Michael yells after me. "Go run to your stupid little girlfriend who can't even fucking have some fun."

That's it.

Without thinking, I rush back to him and bulldoze him straight back into the lockers, punching him in the gut. He buckles over and takes another blow to the face. A muffled sound leaves his mouth like a bag of chips, releasing its air, and he sinks down against the metal doors.

"Fuck you," he groans.

"Don't you ever fucking talk about her ever again," I bark at him, pointing my finger at his face. "You fuckin' hear me?"

"You two deserve each other," he says, a tepid smile appearing on his face. "You just hit an innocent guy."

"Innocent, my fucking ass." I spit on the floor beside him. "You're the worst bandmate anyone could ever wish for."

"Lucky I'm not a band member anymore then," he retorts.

"You'd better hope I find the person who did this," I say as I step away. "And that Monica is lenient on you when she decides she's going to tell the truth…"

The look in his eyes flashes, as though he's suddenly seeing red. "What *truth*?"

My nostrils flare as I stand tall above him. "You and your fucking buddies know what you did."

"Yeah, well ... where's the proof?" He scoffs, cocking his head at me.

Even though he's still on the ground, I kick him in the nuts just for looking at me.

"Waste of fucking space," I growl, and I turn around and walk off, cameras flashing all around.

I don't care anymore.

Let them watch.

I'm not the bad guy here.

Not anymore.

I walk into the practice room and march back and forth to release the adrenaline built up in my body. I look down at the floor and count the steps I take until all the rage has ebbed out, and I blow out a breath.

"Fucking Michael," I murmur to myself.

I sit down on a seat at the front and stare up at the stage where I first saw Monica as she walked past the door. And I take my guitar case off my back and place it on the table in front of me. It's a beautiful guitar ... shame it'll probably go to waste.

Suddenly, the door opens, and I turn my head.

Tristan glares at me for a few seconds.

I know what he's thinking.

He's probably heard about the fight, either from social media or through rumors. He knows what went down, but he doesn't know the full story. I don't even have all the answers.

"So ... Talk." Tristan throws his bag onto the table at

the end of the room and stares me down.

Benjamin pops in too and doesn't seem too pleased to see me even though he knew I was gonna be here.

They asked for this meeting, not me.

I already know what's gonna happen.

"I take it you saw what happened between Michael and me?" I ask.

"Oh, yeah." He rubs his lips, clearly annoyed. "It's all over social media. Wanna explain why you threw yourself at him?" Tristan asks, folding his arms. "Why you attacked him, accused him of sending pictures? Kicked him from the fucking band?"

"I can't," I say, frowning as I look away. If I tell them about Monica's picture, word *will* spread, and I don't want to do that to her. "I would if I could, but I can't. I can't do it."

"Give me one good reason," Tristan replies.

I wish I could answer his question, but it's not my place to tell them what Michael and his buddies did to Monica. That's her story.

"He did something that's unforgivable," I say.

"And it involves some pictures?" Tristan asks. "Show me then."

Like hell, I will. "No."

"Why not?" he asks.

"They're private," I reply.

The look on his face tells me that's not enough for him.

"What, that's it?" Benji asks. "Pictures? That's why he got kicked out?"

"There's more." I eye him down. "If I could say it, I would've done it already."

"Bullshit, you were just looking for an excuse to kick him out, and now you make one up," Tristan barks.

My nostrils flare. "I'm not making shit up. You know as well as I do he was a loose cannon from day one."

"That's not enough reason to kick someone out of this band, Cole. And you're not the one to decide that on your own."

"Did you forget the drugs? The bingeing? How he treated the girls?" I retort, stepping closer.

"Like you didn't do shit with girls," Tristan says, snorting. "You were just as bad."

"If not worse," Benji adds.

"Thanks, Benji." I throw him a look and shake my head. "Wow." Can't believe he's comparing me to that shithead now.

"Just saying." He shrugs. "Not judging, but you're judging Michael too now."

"I was there! Okay, I was fucking there!" I say, adrenaline still pumping through my veins. "He did something that was really fucked up. And then he shared a goddamn picture too."

"A picture? And we're supposed to believe you based on what evidence?" Tristan asks.

"I saw it myself," I say, swallowing.

"Do you even know for sure it was him that sent that picture then?"

I don't know for sure, but who else could it have been? He's the only one who had a vendetta against Monica. He probably blames her for the fact that I kicked him from the band.

"I … don't know …" I sigh. "But he's the only one with a motive."

"What motive?" Benji asks, frowning.

"I kicked him out of the band after he did some fucked-up shit at the party," I reply.

"But I was at the party. Nothing happened," Benji says. "We all were."

I look up at them both. "Yes, it did."

"Wait …" His brows furrow. "Are you talking about Monica? That drunk chick you carried inside?"

I eye him down, tilting my head. "She wasn't drunk, and she's not just a chick … but yes."

His nostrils flare as he takes in a deep breath. The air is thick with unspoken words.

"Then why won't you fucking tell us what went down?" Tristan snarls. "If it's that bad, don't you think we should know?"

I sigh out loud. "I can't … It's not up to me." I look him straight in the eyes because I can't give him what he wants.

Instead, I shake my head and look away.

He snorts and rolls his eyes. "I knew it. Course this would happen."

"Don't," I say. "Don't put this all on me."

"Why not? You were the one to make the call," he retorts. "You kicked him out. Now we're out of a guitarist, and we're supposed to be playing an audition next week!" He's enraged. I've never seen him like this before, and it hurts knowing it's because of me, and I can't do anything to stop it.

"I know," I reply. "I'll fucking find someone, okay? I can fix this."

He shakes his head and laughs. "Yeah, you do that." He starts walking backward and taps Benji on the arm. "C'mon."

"What are you gonna do?" I ask. "Leave?"

"Yeah, Cole." The disappointment in his face is unrelenting. "That's exactly what I'm gonna do."

"What about practice? The band? The audition," I say, adrenaline pulsing through my veins.

"There is no band without our guitarist," he replies, strain in his voice. "And no band without a drummer, either."

He turns around and storms out without saying another word. Benji stands there and stares at me, making me feel guilty.

"Go," I growl at him.

I know he wants to.

He makes a face at me and then shakes his head too. "I'm sorry, Cole." And he clutches his bag and turns to leave.

Rage boils up inside me, and I pick up a nearby empty

coffee cup that was left on a table and throw it at the wall while I roar out loud.

Fuck Michael, fuck this audition, and fuck this band.

Everything is ruined.

Everything I worked so hard for.

Everything I put my reputation on the line for.

Gone.

Just like that.

As if it never meant a thing.

I sit down on the stage and stare at the new guitar my parents bought me as a thank-you for watching the house and hiring a cleaner. It was earned with the drug money I hate so much, but I accepted it so I could salvage whatever we had left of our band.

And now it's all gone to shit.

THIRTY-ONE

Monica

Minutes ago

I wasn't sure I was actually going to school today. After what happened at Cole's party, I figured the entire school would know within minutes what had transpired. That I was almost used by Michael and his gang and that Cole had been in a fight to save me, only to bring me back inside and shut down the party. People were upset.

But none as much as me when I discovered he also shared that goddamn picture of me without my permission. I never asked Cole to take it in the first place. He did it to make me shut up about the drugs Michael did … and now he shared it anyway.

Who knows where else that picture ended up and who else got to see it.

That picture is out there in the world now, thanks to Cole, and what was the reason? Just to punish me for getting close? For daring to like him?

I cannot fucking get over it, no matter how much I ruminate on it while walking through the hallways. But I'm pulled from my thoughts by a ruckus going on up ahead.

Somewhere in the hallways, people are fighting, but I can't tell who as the hallways are crowded with people taking pictures and videotaping it. What's going on?

I push myself through the people huddled together, only to find Cole punching Michael in the face.

"Don't you ever fucking talk about her ever again," Cole barks at Michael, who is lying on the ground against the lockers. "You fuckin' hear me?"

"You two deserve each other," Michael replies with a half-smile that reminds me of the night in the woods. "You just hit an innocent guy."

Innocent? Far from it. But no one else besides Cole and I know the truth, and it shows. Everyone's in shock that Cole just punched him and that they're yelling at each other. But Cole doesn't even seem to care anymore.

"Innocent, my fucking ass," Cole says. "You're the worst bandmate anyone could ever wish for."

"Lucky I'm not a band member anymore then," Michael responds.

"You'd better hope I find the person who did this,"

Cole says.

The person who did what?

Send the picture?

My heart beats in my throat.

"And that Monica is lenient on you when she decides she's going to tell the truth," he adds.

Michael's face darkens. "What truth?"

Cole doesn't even seem to notice we're here, watching him. "You and your fucking buddies know what you did."

A chill runs across my spine.

"Yeah, well ... where's the proof?"

Cole suddenly kicks him in the nuts, and everyone gasps in shock, including me.

I've never seen Cole this filled with hatred ... and there's only one explanation for it.

One I threw off as impossible the moment I found out that picture had been shared.

But was I wrong about who sent it?

"Waste of fucking space," Cole growls at Michael, and he storms off through the crowd, far away from the scene of the crime, while Michael lies there on the ground like a defeated dog licking its wounds.

I'm stupefied by what just happened and stay frozen to the ground while others help Michael up and share the photos and videos they took of the incident.

I don't know everything that transpired, but I do know one thing ... Cole came to my defense when Michael ridiculed me. Even though he had no reason to. Even though he told me to leave, even though he chased me away with his anger, he still tried to protect me when it mattered the most.

When the world was watching, he didn't choose his reputation or his band.

He chose me.

I have to know what that means.

I walk into the direction he went, following the thread of fans that pursued him regardless of his actions, just to get a glimpse, a taste. But somehow, even they don't know where he went, as they're circling the hallways and checking all the doors.

Maybe he shook them off.

I walk into a different hallway, one where I will only find him on practice days.

The same room where he played his songs on the first day we met.

The door is locked, and the window shutters have been closed.

But I know he's in there.

I pause and place my ear against the door.

It's bad to eavesdrop, but when I heard Cole's voice, I couldn't stop myself. Something about Michael and the party and that he did something horrible. I hold my breath and wait for him to tell his friends. After all, they're the only ones keeping his band together. Without them, he's alone. Lost.

And I am the catalyst to it all.

His band members will believe him if he tells them the truth of exactly what Michael did to me.

But he doesn't.

He refuses, and it twists my heart into knots.

Someone grasps the door handle, and I quickly move away, clutching my bag close. Tristan and Benjamin march out and stare at me as though I'm the world's worst vixen. As if I single-handedly destroyed their band.

Maybe they're right. What if I did?

Michael got kicked out now because of what happened to me. And now they can't play anymore.

And Cole still chose to protect me instead of saving his band. He's now carrying the full brunt of the attack because of me.

I frown and walk toward the room, clutching the door handle.

Can I? Should I?

When he told me to leave, I was heartbroken.

And when I found out about the picture being out there, I was shattered.

But maybe he was mean for a reason. And maybe he didn't share that picture at all.

He kept the fact that Michael tried something on me a secret.

He didn't tell his best friends because it was my story to tell, not his.

Which means he *does* care about me, no matter how much he tries to deny it. And I won't let him push me away anymore. I need to know the truth. So I go inside and lock the door behind me.

He's sitting on the stage with a brand-new guitar lying right next to him, untouched. His hands are in his hair as he leans over, desperate to hide from the world ... from me. Because I know he saw me come in. I'm standing in the middle of the fucking room, waiting for him to talk. The pause feels eternal.

"Did you come to see me at my lowest?" he asks.

Why would he ask that question? Does he really think I hate him that much?

"You're in luck," he scoffs. "I'm down and out. Defeated. Beaten. Take a picture while you're here and post it. I don't fucking care anymore."

I put my bag down on the floor. "Why would I do that?"

He looks up at me, his eyes full of hurt. "Because it's the easier thing to do."

I fold my arms as a tiny smile tugs at my lips. "I don't like easy."

He shakes his head and snorts. "I've noticed ..."

It's quiet for some time, and I don't know what to say to make this all okay again. Even though he treated me like shit, I don't think he deserved this.

"I'm sorry," I say. "About your band."

He looks up at me with a dark frown on his face. "No. Don't fucking say that."

I shrug. "Why not? It's my fault you guys fell apart."

"Don't."

I raise a brow. "Really? So first you treat me like shit and then you won't even accept my apology?"

"You don't fucking get it, do you?" he growls. "I don't want your pity. I don't need your sorry."

"Then what do you need?" I ask, opening my arms. "Because I don't understand anymore. You keep pulling and pushing, wanting me and pushing me away at the same time."

"I need something I can't fucking have," he retorts, clenching his fist while looking up at me.

I gulp.

Does he mean me or his band?

"I don't know what you want me to say," I say. "I know I ruined things for you."

"Stop saying that!" he growls. Getting up from the stage, he marches toward me, stopping a few inches away. "You did nothing wrong. Do you hear me? *Nothing*. Michael hurt *you*. You don't fucking apologize. *He* does," he says through gritted teeth.

His chest rises and falls with every agitated breath.

I'm amazed. All this time I thought he was mad at me for ruining things, but he's mad at me for apologizing?

"I thought you were mad at me," I say. "When you told me to leave, I—"

"You fucking thanked me," he interjects, looking down at me from underneath his lashes. "In the shower."

"I thought… You wanted …" I suck in a breath.

"I don't want a thank-you fuck. I don't need you to give me what I want just because I did the right thing," he says, his voice strained with emotions.

I let go of the breath I was holding. I finally understand. After all this time, I finally realize what he was doing … Protecting me.

From *him*.

"But you used to bully me. Why did you suddenly start caring?" I ask.

He frowns and looks away, conflicted. "I always did, but I couldn't deny it anymore when you told me your story."

My heart sinks into my shoes as all the pieces fall into place. He found out the secret I'd buried for so long, and it made him care. Not just superficially, but on an emotional level. Deeply.

"And I didn't send that fucking picture," he says with an honest voice. "You have to believe me. I don't know who did, but it wasn't me, I swear."

"I believe you," I reply, and I place a hand on his chest. "Let's play a game."

"I'm done with games," he says, clenching his jaw.

"The truth. No dares," I say.

He eyes me for a moment while his thumb brushes across his lip. "Go on …"

"You care about me as more than just a friend," I say.

He raises a brow. "That's not a question, Mo."

I point at his chest. "But you don't deny it either."

He narrows his eyes at me. "Is that what you came here

to tell me? Because I think I can figure that out myself."

"It's why you pushed me away when we were in the shower, wasn't it?" I ask.

He bites his bottom lip and sighs. "Don't fucking thank me with a blowjob."

"Lesson learned," I retort.

"And it's not just a fucking blowjob … not to me. I don't … want *that* from you," he adds, swallowing.

"But I thought …" I don't even know how to respond. "I thought you were genuinely mad at me."

"I'm not, and I never was. Not at you, anyway …" he says, and his hand rises to caress my cheek briefly. "I don't want you to give me what I want when it isn't what you want. What *you* need."

I understand him now.

He wasn't mad at *me*. He was mad at himself for letting go.

Almost as if he thinks he tried to use me too.

This boy … God, this boy is so unlike everything I thought he would be.

"Everyone always told me you were a cheater. A liar."

He snorts. "What a surprise."

"Is it true?"

His eyes narrow underneath those dark lashes. "How do you think they got that information? Think hard."

I swallow. There's only one answer to that question. The person he's hated the most since the very start. The person who always got in his way. "Ariane." He nods. It's all I need to know. "But why would she do that?"

He smirks. "To ruin my reputation and my name … because she wanted to be one step ahead."

"But you two were an item, right? What was in it for her?"

"To keep her dirty little secret safe." He cocks his head. "Don't you see? *She* was the one who was cheating on *me*."

I gasp in shock. Fuck. This explains everything. No wonder they were constantly at each other's throats, why he was so angry when I called him an asshole. She spread those rumors about him and made him look like the devil.

"She hurt you …" I mutter.

"To protect herself from my fans, she threw these lies out into the world. And you know how the world works. Once the lies are out there, people believe them, no matter what I or anyone else said. So I played along," he says, and he shrugs. "Why do you think I pushed you away?"

"You wanted me to hate you," I say.

"She *forced* me to. Because she's your goddamn cousin, and she wanted to protect you from me. Because she's jealous and afraid."

"Afraid of what?" My brows furrow.

A smirk forms on his face. "That you'd make me fall in love."

My heart flutters. Does he mean that? Is this for real?

"I thought she wanted to protect me because of my past…" I mutter, completely shocked by what I'm hearing.

He shakes his head. "She's a snake. But she's also your

family."

I straighten my back. "Fuck family. Fuck Ariane and fuck Michael. They deserve each other."

That same devilish smirk spreads on his lips as his hand sneaks up to my waist. "You know, they said the same thing to me about us."

"Us … You say that like you mean it," I say as he inches closer.

"Haven't you noticed? I always did," he says, looking down at me. "Why do you think I fought so hard to stay away from you?"

I suck in a breath at that admission. "But I always thought you were only interested in quick fucks with random girls?" I lick my lips. "And I never wanted to be just another notch on your belt."

"Look at me." His face darkens, and he tips up my chin to make me look at him. "You're not just another girl. Not to me. It just took me a while to get there."

I should've known all along.

The rock star. The playboy. The asshole.

He wasn't a bully because he hated me.

He needed me to hate him so he wouldn't get close enough to hurt me.

To hurt *himself*.

Because of what Ariane did to him, he shut himself off and chose to only see girls as a form of pleasure. As a way to fight the pain.

But I could never break his heart.

And I'm done fighting the desire.

He doesn't need to protect me from himself anymore, nor does he need to protect his own broken heart.

My hand snakes up his neck. "I don't want you to stay away. I want to be yours."

"Are you sure, Mo?" he murmurs into my ear. "Because when I take you, there's no going back. And I don't want to wreck what's left of you."

I gasp when his hand slides down my ass, and I whisper back, "Destroy me."

THIRTY-TWO

Cole

Destroy me.

Two words.

Just two words … but it's all I needed to hear.

She's mine now.

I grab her face with one hand and pull her to me with the other, smashing my lips to hers. I don't fucking care anymore about the consequences or what it means when I claim her as my own. Because I need her. I fucking need her so badly it hurts.

But it hurt even more not to give in.

It hurt that I had to fight it off and push her away to keep her safe.

To keep her from being ruined.

To keep me from ruin.

But it's too late now.

Our bodies are clashing, and our hearts have locked together, and I don't know if I ever want to stop. She's always been my vice. From day one, I knew she'd be trouble. I knew whatever she hid deep within those eyes would consume both me and my band, yet I still chose to hunt her down and make her mine.

Fuck knows I tried to keep her at bay.

I tried so many times to make her hate me.

But somehow, someway, she always found her way back to me.

And I can't let her go. Not again. Not anymore.

My hands find their way around her body as I fight the urge to rip her clothes off. Every kiss is followed by an agonized groan. I've waited so long to claim her that I'm brimming with desire. My cock is already hard just from kissing her.

She does something to me no other girl has managed to do. She twists my body into knots and forces me to come face-to-face with my demons and forces me to reveal the edges of my heart.

And I no longer want to hide it from her. So I kiss her hard and fast until we're out of breath, until she opens her mouth and lets me in, and until our tongues are as entangled as our hearts.

A moan slips from her mouth, causing my dick to harden even more, and when she starts groping me through my pants, I'm done for.

"Give it to me," she mewls. "Give me everything you've got."

Fuck.

If only she hadn't said that, maybe I would've gone gentle on her.

Not any-fucking-more.

I rip open her shirt, letting all the buttons fly, and throw it aside as she lets out a squeal. Her bra comes off next, and I bury my face between her tits. She tilts her head back and moans in delight. In my greed, I pick her up from the ground and set her down on a table, kissing her as if my life depends on it.

I can't stop touching her, can't stop kissing every inch of her body. I need her like I need the air I breathe. And no amount of kisses will ever feel like enough.

I rip off my shirt and tie and lick my lips when I notice her ogling me.

"Like what you see?" I ask.

"You don't even know how much," she says, a dirty grin forming on her face.

I groan and tear down her pants and rip off her panties in one go. She squeals, but I cover her mouth with mine and nudge her legs aside. She hungrily accepts me as I step closer, her fingers desperately grasping at my pants, trying to shove them down. I help her a little, tagging off the button and zipping myself down. She quickly manages to tug down my pants and boxer shorts at the same time until my cock pops free, bouncing up and down with need.

She's still enamored by the size, and I can honestly say I'll never get used to how good it makes me feel.

I grab a condom from my back pocket, rip it open, and quickly put it on.

Our lips connect again, and her fingers coil in my hair. And even though my dick is right there between her legs, it's still not enough. Groaning, I pick her up from the table and shove her against the wall. Her legs wrap around my waist, and I push my cock against her entrance. I'm so goddamn eager, but I don't want her to regret making this decision.

"Tell me you want me," I whisper in her ear. "Tell me you're mine."

"I'm yours. Fuck me, Cole," she murmurs.

Fuck.

I thrust in, and her gasp meets my moan in a blissful explosion of lust. Like animals, we fuck against the wall, kissing and bouncing up and down. She rides me like an expert while sweat drips down my forehead, and her pussy is wetter than anything I've ever felt before.

We were made for each other, her and me, like lightning and thunder in the night sky.

And I can't fucking stop loving her.

Our mouths entangle in a furious battle while we fuck like madmen high on lust. Her body quakes with need as goose bumps scatter on her skin. My cock pulses inside her, and I'm slamming into her so hard I can barely fucking keep it together.

I move away from the wall and carry her to the table in the back of the room where I put her down and swipe everything off it. She lies down, and I fuck her against the table like a savage, my hands grasping at her waist and tits. I'm delirious with need, completely consumed by my own desire. I lean over to kiss her on the neck, drawing a line all the way down to her nipples, which peak from the attention I lavishly dish out.

And when I lean up to slam into her fully, her eyes almost roll into the back of her head.

A filthy smile spreads on my lips, knowing it was me who made her feel this way. After all this waiting, all this fighting, all this tugging and pulling, she is finally mine.

"You're fucking mine, Monica Romero," I growl, thrusting in and out as she mewls with delight. "And you'd better fucking be ready for it."

"Fuck ..." she moans. "Harder."

It turns out, she's much more of a twisted vixen than I thought.

My hand slides down her body, caressing her skin until the goose bumps create a trail all the way down to her pussy where I start to toy with her clit. She overflows with wetness. It's dripping down the side of the table. She widens her legs and raises one on top of the table, her pussy eager for more as I both slam into her and play with her until she's at the brink.

Because I don't just want her for my own pleasure, I want hers too. I want all of it.

And I don't fucking stop until she's moaning out loud, practically begging me to make her come.

I slam into her with everything I have. "Come for me, Monica. Show me how much you really want me."

Right then, her pussy contracts around my cock and delicious shockwaves make her whole body spasm while I flick her clit. The sound of her moans pushes me over the limit, and I explode inside her with a roar.

Towering over her, I plant my hands beside her on the table to collect myself for a moment, still panting like hell. My eyes lower as I contemplate what just happened. What I just did. I completely fucked her into oblivion with no remorse, no conscience. I didn't spend even a single second thinking about the consequences for her … about what it would mean for her and her body when someone would take her like that. And that it could bring up memories from the past that could seriously hurt her.

I could've hurt her.

My dick slips out of her, but she leans up on her elbows and smiles at me.

She actually fucking smiles at me. What the …?

"Don't feel guilty," she says, her hand rising to caress my cheek. "I'm okay."

I blow out a sigh of relief and grab ahold of her, hugging her tight. The first time I felt this feeling, it was unfamiliar to me. A kind of emotional connection that makes it hard not to care. But now, it makes me feel at ease, and I want her to feel good.

"I didn't want to hurt you," I say. "I don't want you to be afraid."

"I know," she says, licking her lips. "But you've never made me feel that way. I feel safe around you."

Something inside my body swells with heat, and I swear to God my heart is beating in a way it never has before.

Maybe this is what it was supposed to feel like, what I've been searching for all this time.

Suddenly, someone rummages outside the door, and we quickly gather our things and put on our clothes. Well, as much as possible, of course, because I basically ripped her clothes to shreds, and it makes her giggle when she looks at them.

"I guess I should go home and change," she murmurs.

"Hello?"

***

Monica

Someone else's voice makes us turn around.

"Shit," Cole mutters. "Someone's caught us."

"Or they just needed to be here?" I reply, quickly adjusting my shirt so that it looks at least acceptable even though it's missing a few buttons.

He cocks his head. "You think?"

I shrug. "It's a possibility."

He snorts as he puts his shirt back on and throws the used condom in the bin. I swallow hard at the thought that we actually fucked. He was inside me, and we both came like we'd been waiting for this moment for ages.

And fuck, it still makes me wet thinking about it.

"We should be happy if half the school didn't hear us," Cole says.

Both my cheeks turn strawberry red, and I gently punch his shoulder. "Stop."

He pulls me to him and presses his lips onto mine for a quick but sultry kiss. "That's what you get for being with me. Constant horniness."

What ... did he just actually say that?

"Being *with* you?"

"Yeah, haven't you heard?" he says with a smug look on his face. "According to Michael, you're my girlfriend now."

My eyes widen, and my body goes completely rigid against his. It can't be. No fucking way. "He was trying to get under your skin."

He shrugs with that same confidence that always gets my heart beating faster. "I don't care what he or anyone else thinks."

Shit. Does he ... not even mind? I mean, we're talking about Cole Travis here. Certified rock star giant among high schoolers, and here is one of his own ex-band members calling me his girlfriend in front of everyone. He should be trying to deny it vehemently, both online and offline, yet he doesn't even seem to ... care.

And judging from the smile that forms on his lips as we walk to the door, I don't think he wants to refute it.

Shit.

Fuck.

I can't fucking think straight. I'm that fucking flustered.

Cole opens the door, and Mel almost falls inside.

"Jesus," she scoffs as she falls into him. She looks up, and when she notices it's him, her eyes widen, and she quickly shuffles back. "Cole, sorry, I was just looking for the music teacher and—"

Then she sees me.

Her jaw drops slowly, like in a movie, and it makes me snicker.

"Monica," she mutters. "Cole."

"Mel," I reply.

"What are you two …?" She eyes us both, and her eyes narrow. "Oooooh …"

I rub my lips together and look away, embarrassed that she was the one who found us.

"Right," Cole says.

"Right," Mel repeats, looking severely befuddled and embarrassed, just like me.

"Please don't say a word," I ask.

"Oh, no," she replies, adding a *tsk* sound. "Who, me? My mouth is sealed."

I smile. "Thanks, I appreciate it."

"But … are you guys like … a thing now?" she asks.

Cole snorts as he sees my cheeks flare up again. "Uh, I

don't—"

"No comment," Cole interjects.

"Complicated, huh?" Mel says, winking at me. "Well, I don't mind. Y'all do whatever you want. It's not my business." Then she looks at Cole and points her finger at his chest. "But you'd better treat my girl right, got it?"

He straightens his back. "Got it."

I burst into laughter. "Don't worry. I'm all covered."

"Are you now?" She puts her hands against her side. "How covered are we talking? A little bit, or the Full Monty?"

I don't think I could get any redder, but apparently, it's possible.

"Relax, I'm just messing with you," she says, poking me in the belly. "You do what makes you feel good. I don't judge."

"Thanks," I reply.

"I just hope y'all can weather the storm," she says.

"Storm?" I mumble.

"Yeah, word goes around school pretty fast." She folds her arms. "Everyone knows about that fight between Cole and Michael, and that includes the teachers."

"Shit," I mutter, completely caught off guard.

"That's what you get with celebrities. Cameras follow you everywhere. And when you do something stupid, everybody knows." She glares at Cole for a second.

"Thanks," he tells her. "But I was defending Monica."

"I know," she says, lifting her head. "And as her friend,

I appreciate that. I just hope you don't get into any more trouble because you're in for some heavy-duty apologizing."

Suddenly, the intercom goes off. "Will Miss Romero, Mr. Travis, and Mr. Jones please report to the principal's office?"

"Jones?" I mutter.

"Michael," Cole says with a gruff voice.

My whole body freezes as Mel's face tightens. "Damn. Guess it's already too late."

Damn? Holy fucking shit is more like it.

THIRTY-THREE

Cole

"Sit down," Mr. D tells us the moment we enter his office.

Monica and I gulp as we approach the table and sit on the chairs. Moments later, Michael enters the room, and we stare at each other for a few seconds.

"Mr. Jones, sit down," the principal barks.

Michael sits down opposite me and scoots his chair a little farther to create extra space. I don't mind. I probably would've ripped his fucking head off if he came close.

"So, who wants to start?" Mr. D asks, flicking a pen back and forth while pacing around. "Wanna explain why you two were fighting in the hallway?"

Neither of us opens our mouth.

He places his hands on the desk. "Talk."

"I didn't do shit. Cole just attacked me," Michael says.

"Bullshit!" I yell at him. "You fucking harassed Monica in the woods, and then you sent that fucking picture."

"I didn't send any fucking picture!" he spits back.

"Boys!" Mr. D interrupts. "Calm down." Then he looks at Monica. "Maybe you can tell me what happened, seeing as you were apparently involved in this … drama." He adds a sigh as if it annoys him to death.

"Um …" She bites her lip. "He and his buddies attacked me in the forest."

"Okay. Tell me more. What else do you remember?" Mr. D coaxes her.

"They were trying to get on top of me," she says, sniffing a little. "And Cole came to save me."

"Who are the other guys that did this to you?" Mr. D asks. "Got any names? Descriptions? And have you gone to the police?"

"No." She rubs her legs. "And I don't know if I want to go to the police," she says.

Michael narrows his eyes at her, so I throw myself between. "Don't you fucking dare."

Mr. D nods a few times. "And this picture? What is that about?"

Monica clears her throat.

I sigh and avert my eyes. I guess this is the moment everything I did comes back to bite me in the ass. I don't blame her. It's my fault. I caused this mess, so it should be me who's punished.

"I took a picture of her body," I say before Monica has to lie.

Monica gasps. "Yeah, but I let him."

I look at her intently. She doesn't have to lie, yet she still chooses to. Why?

"Motherfuckers," Michael growls. "You took that picture to make sure she wouldn't talk, you liar."

"That's not true," Monica spits back, leaning forward to throw him a deadly stare. "You're the liar."

Michael shakes his head, clenching his jaw. "Oh, this is rich. Fuck you two. You're setting me up."

"No one is setting anyone up," Mr. D says. "And I want to know what happened to that picture."

"It got shared," Monica says.

"It wasn't fucking me," Michael retorts.

"Then who was it?" I ask.

"I don't fucking know, okay? It was on your phone, not mine. Maybe you should ask yourself."

"I would *never* fucking share that," I hiss.

"Then who would? Think hard, Cole," Michael retorts. "Got any enemies?"

"Stop," Mr. D interrupts. "You two fought enough. I don't want any back and forth on this anymore. I will find the culprit behind the sharing of this picture." He takes a deep breath. "Revenge porn? Harassment? This is not acceptable. I have no choice but to expel you both."

"What?" Both Michael and I say out loud, and we look

at each other. I want to stomp his head into the ground just for getting me into this shit.

"You've forced my hand here," Mr. D says.

"But Cole didn't do anything," Monica says, tears welling up in her eyes. "Please. He saved me. He only fought Michael because he wanted to protect me. That's it."

I appreciate that she's trying to stick up for me, but she doesn't have to. I deserve this. Besides, Mr. D looks at us like we're fodder for jail.

"Oh, fuck this." Michael gets up from his chair and throws it around. "I'm out of here."

"Sit your ass down, Mr. Jones," Mr. D growls. "Before I call the police and have you arrested on the spot for the destruction of school property."

Michael clutches the door handle and waits for a few seconds before releasing it, huffing and puffing. He slouches back to his chair and sits down in the corner of the room with folded arms and a deadly look on his face.

"You two need to solve your issues," Mr. D says, looking at both of us. "But there will be no more fighting on these school grounds, got it?"

"I understand, Mr. D," I reply, hoping he might be lenient.

Suddenly, the door bursts open, and we all turn around.

"How dare you question my daughter like this!"

"Mom?" Monica mumbles, her jaw dropping. "What are you doing here?"

Mom? Oh, wow.

"Someone sent me a video shared on social media of two boys fighting over my daughter, talking about some kind of picture. And I know what *that* means," she growls, looking at Mr. D. "You should have called *me*."

"Ma'am, I'm still investigating this matter since it only just happened," Mr. D tries to explain, but her mom is not having any of it, and I am amused.

"Do you have any idea what you just did?" her mom barks at Mr. D. "I've told you from the beginning just how vulnerable she was. You *knew*. And you let this happen in your school?"

Well, this isn't something I expected. Nor did Mr. D, judging from the look on his face.

"Ma'am, I'm trying to get to the bottom of this," Mr. D says. "And believe me when I say I am just as surprised as you are."

"My daughter did nothing wrong. She is a *victim*." There's a strain in her voice that I can only describe as overprotective.

"You don't need to sit through this," her mom says, grabbing Monica's arm. "C'mon."

"Mom! Let go of me." Monica jerks herself free. "You're embarrassing me."

"Embarrassing you?" She goes to her knees in front of Monica and grabs both her arms. "I'm trying to protect you from them." She points at us as though I'm one the bad guys.

"Mom …" Monica's face turns red. "Please, stop."

"No, I'm taking you with me. Now." Her mom drags her out of the chair and out of the room before any of us can even say a word. Before even Monica, herself, can explain what happened ... or what I am to her.

But her mom already knows who I am.

I am the boy from that video she saw, the boy who fought over some stupid picture of her daughter ... the boy who stole her fragile daughter's heart.

And I know this isn't going to go over well.

***

Monica

"Mom, stop!" I yell, coming to a full halt right in front of the car.

She made a scene in front of the entire school. There's nothing more embarrassing than that, not even two boys fighting over who shared that damn picture.

"Mom!" I yell when she opens the car door and looks at me as if I'm supposed to get inside. "No, I'm not going home."

"Monica, I'm trying to help you, please," she says.

"No, I don't need your help. I never asked you to come," I reply.

"But you got hurt," she says, trying to hold her emotions together. "Again. I knew I should've just taken you out of that school the minute things were going bad."

"What?" I frown. "Take me out? No!"

"But you were already being bullied!" she retorts.

"He was just trying to get under my skin," I reply.

"Who?" She makes a face. "I swear to God if—"

"I like him," I interject before she tries to do something stupid.

She frowns. "You *like* him? How? He's a bully!"

I sigh. "It's complicated, okay? I'm not gonna explain my entire life."

She folds her arms. "Well, you'd better explain why some boys were fighting over you and why I had to see it on social media instead of my daughter telling me herself. Those boys you're involved with, they're dangerous. Some band called TRIGGER. I can't believe you didn't tell me." She snivels, clearly upset. "I trusted you. I gave you more freedom when you told me you could handle it."

"I can," I say. "I know how to handle myself."

"But they hurt you!" she yells. "Goddammit! Now you even made me swear."

"Sorry," I mutter. "But how do you know they're dangerous?"

"Another mother called me to tell me her daughter had seen you being carried inside a house after coming out of the forest." We both suck in a breath. "What do you think is going through my mind when I hear that, Monica? After what you've been through?"

"I know, Mom, but it's not what you think. Cole actually

came to save me."

"Oh, so his name is Cole?" She scoffs. "Thanks for filling me in. And saving you? From what?"

"Other boys …" I sigh and look away. "Michael and his buddies."

"Michael?" She points at the school. "Was he that other boy inside that room?"

I nod.

"I'm going to fucking kill him."

I have to physically restrain my mom not to go back inside.

"Mom, please! Don't," I say, and I push her back to the car. "Just stop. Okay? I can handle this."

"I can't forgive this. That boy deserves everything that's coming for him. Which one was it? The dark-haired one?"

"No," I quickly reply. "That's Cole."

"Oh," she murmurs.

"And there's something I have to tell you …" I tuck my hair behind my ear. "I think we're sort of dating?"

Her eyes widen, and she makes this face I've never seen before like she's about to faint right here on the pavement. "What?!"

"Don't be mad, please."

"You're dating a rock star?" she squeals.

I try to cover her mouth with my hand. "Shh … not so loud. No one knows. Not yet, anyway."

"Monica!" She forces my hand down. "Really? That's what you're worried about?"

"I'm not worried. But this is new to me too, okay? And I'm still trying to figure it out," I explain.

She stares at me and sighs out loud. "Monica …"

I grab her hands. "Mom. I'm sorry I didn't tell you. I just needed this to be my choice. My story. You asked me if I was ready. I am."

"But these boys will never change," she says.

"But I have," I reply. "And I don't want to be stuck in the past anymore."

She looks down at my hands and gently squeezes them. "If you're sure …"

"I'm sure, Mom," I reiterate. "And Cole is in there right now, getting expelled because of me." I point at the school. "I have to go back."

"Wait," Mom says as I try to walk back. "What are you going to do?"

"I don't know. Maybe I can help keep him here." Tears well up in my eyes. "I don't want to lose this one good thing in my life, Mom."

She grabs my face and caresses me gently, wiping away the tear. "If you're sure about this boy … a thousand percent sure." She leans in and places her forehead against mine. "Then go get him."

A beaming smile forms on my face. "Thanks, Mom."

I turn and walk back, but she waits there in front of her car, watching my every step. She doesn't have to be worried about me. Not anymore.

With my head held high, I march back into that same

school that I thought would be my downfall, filled with all those students who will inevitably notice my involvement with Cole, the rumors, the picture. And it will all have been for nothing if I can't stay ...

If I can't be with the only boy who has managed to both destroy and mend my heart.

There has to be a way.

What if I can find out who sent that picture? Cole fought too hard, and he swore it wasn't him. But then who?

I grab my phone and find the anonymous message that was sent to me. The link leads to a folder on a website that has an account name attached ... AR.

AR ... who the hell is AR?

I walk inside the school without looking where I'm going as I'm too busy in my head trying to decipher who sent this to me. It has to be someone with access to Cole's phone. Did it happen at the party? It's too much of a coincidence that this happened just a day after. But who would do that? It could've been anyone.

Except if it were just anyone, I'd assume they'd send this picture around to anyone they could to make fun of me and have a laugh. But I don't think that happened because no one in this school even glanced at me when I walked in. No one seems to have noticed this picture going live.

So that begs the question ... did they only send it to *me*?

As a threat?

Suddenly, I bump into someone. "Oops, sorry," I mutter.

"Monica?"

I look up into Ariane's eyes.

"I didn't think you'd come to school today," she says, frowning. "I mean, after what happened at the party…"

My lips part as I'm struggling to find the words. My brain is trying to mesh things together into a cohesive story while also trying to react to what she's saying. I should go to the principal's office and find Cole.

"Are you okay? You look like you've seen a ghost," Ariane asks.

"I …" I'm still dumbfounded, staring at my phone.

Ariane follows my gaze down.

I stare at the symbols again. AR.

Ariane. Romero.

THIRTY-FOUR

Monica

My eyes rise to meet hers, and in a split second, it all comes flooding in.

Ariane hated Cole. Hated him because she always told everyone he cheated on her. But Cole said she was the cheater, and she tried to blame it all on him to save her reputation.

And now she's trying to sabotage my relationship with him too.

"It was you …" I mutter, lowering my phone.

Our eyes connect, fury spilling from us both.

One second passes before she grabs my arm, whisks me into a bathroom, and shuts the door.

My heart beats in my throat as I press a few buttons on

my phone, trying to find what I'm looking for.

"Look, I don't know what you got into your head, but this isn't happening," she says.

I struggle to keep my anger contained. "AR. That's you, isn't it?"

She doesn't reply. She stares at me with her brows raised. "Monica ... really?"

"You sent this," I growl. "Admit it."

For a moment, there's only silence. Then a devious smile forms on her face.

"You shouldn't have gotten close to him," she says.

My nostrils flare. "So it *was* you. You tried to make me think he did this. You *wanted* me to hate him and blame him!"

"Oh, please." She folds her arms and takes a provocative stance. "I didn't take that damn picture of you."

"No, but you were the one who sent it around."

"How?" She scoffs. "How would I have done that, hmm?"

"You were at that party. You could've opened his phone."

"And why would I do that?" she asks. "Why the hell would I need a picture of *you*?"

"Because you wanted to threaten me so I would stay away from him."

She rolls her eyes and sighs. "Oh, Monica." She turns to the mirror and starts redoing her lipstick. "You really are naïve. And here, I thought you'd finally learned your lesson."

"Shut up," I retort.

She's a goddamn snake.

"No," she says, throwing me a look. "I don't think I will. You see, you did something that no girl should ever do." She walks toward me and points at me. "I told you to stay away from him, and what did you do?"

"All this time, I thought you wanted to protect me," I say, shaking my head. "But you were just protecting yourself."

"I don't need protecting," she hisses. "But you do."

"Oh, what? I stole your boyfriend?" I spit back. "He hates you. And you knew. You knew what you did to him, and you flipped the story to make him look like the bad guy, so you'd get away with your scheme."

"You think I care?" She cocks her head, her jaw tightening. "He deserved it after how he treated me. He never gave me one ounce of the attention he gave his fans. So I thought I'd give him a taste of his own medicine. He wanted attention from fans? He got it."

"You're sick," I growl. "I can't believe I trusted you."

"Honey, I told you, you were too naïve."

"My mom chose this school because you said it was safe," I reply. "But you were the one person making it unsafe here."

"Boohoo," she taunts. "Cry me a river."

"So you're gonna admit that you sent that goddamn picture?" I ask. "You wanna be ballsy, but you can't even admit you were trying to push me away from him. Why? Why couldn't you let me have this one good thing in my life?"

"*Yours*?" She scoffs. "He was *mine* before he was ever yours."

Suddenly, she pulls a knife out from her pocket, and I step back in fear.

"What, scared now?" she muses. "Weird, because I recall him doing exactly the same thing to you."

I gasp. "How …?" But then it hits me. Michael.

He was there, and she had started dating him right after that whole ordeal. He must've told her what had happened after Cole told him what he had to do. An eye for an eye. Payment for my silence.

And now it's come full circle.

"Yeah, I'm not an idiot. Cole tried to shut me out, but I have my ways," she says.

"You were using Michael to get to him," I hiss. "And now you're using me."

"I'm not doing anything." She shrugs. "You brought this all on yourself."

I glare at the knife she twirls in her hand. "What are you going to do then? Cut me up? I'm your cousin!"

"Do I look like I care?" she retorts.

No, she looks like a goddamn psycho bitch. "What the hell do you want, Ariane?"

She snorts. "I think you know exactly what I want." Her eyes travel down to my phone, but I clutch it tightly in my hands.

Fuck no.

I immediately turn around and head for the door, but she immediately rushes past me and blocks it with her body, pointing the knife at me.

"Oh, no, you're not getting out of here."

"You're not getting away with this," I growl.

"Oh, yes, I am, and you're giving me that phone."

"Why? So you can erase the evidence?" I look her dead in the eyes. "Over my dead fucking body."

"Don't tempt me, Monica," she says.

"Tempt you? Have you lost your fucking mind?" I yell. "I'm your fucking family!"

"Not anymore." She shakes her head. "You lost that privilege the moment you tried to hook up with him."

"But you're the one getting him expelled. Right now. Don't you want to keep him here?" I ask, trying to reason with her.

"He had his shot. He wasted it," she replies. "I tried. Believe me. But if I can't have him, you can't either." Her face darkens, and she beckons me. "Now give me that phone."

"Or what?" I snarl, standing my ground.

"Don't make me do this, Mo," she says through gritted teeth.

"I'm not making you do anything. You can stop at any time. You can walk out there and tell Mr. D exactly what you did."

She laughs. "And ruin my reputation? Never mind my entire fucking education?" She throws me a look and laughs some more. "Bitch, please. Hand me the goddamn phone, and you can go on your merry way to another fucking school. I'll tell your mom just how badly you fit in."

"She'll never believe you," I say, clenching my fists in rage.

"Oh, but she'll believe you? The fucked-up, damaged goods over me, the pretty perfect princess?" she mocks. "Yeah, I don't think so."

She inches toward me with the knife still firmly clutched in her hand. What the hell is she thinking?

"C'mon, Mo. Last chance," she says, pointing the knife right at me.

"Or what, you gonna stab me?" I growl. "What the fuck is wrong with you?"

She suddenly lashes out at me, and I jump back toward the door.

"What the hell!" I yell.

"Give me the fucking phone, Monica," she barks.

If only I'd known she was a goddamn psychopath sooner.

Maybe I wouldn't have gotten so deep into this shit.

"Fuck off," I retort, trying to find anything I can use to defend myself—a plumbing tool, a toilet roll holder, or even a fucking soap dispenser—anything will do. So I pick up the nearest object in my vicinity, which happens to be a broken-off piece of the faucet.

She laughs. "What are you going to do with that? Hit me?"

"Stay away," I hiss.

"I tried that, and it didn't work. And you know? I don't even care anymore," she retorts.

She's closing in on me, so I chuck the piece of faucet at her head, but she dodges just in time.

Fuck.

My eyes widen at the sight of the knife coming straight for me.

Suddenly, the door bursts open.

***

Cole

I storm inside after hearing the ruckus from down the hallway. I was just about to leave the school property after Mr. D kicked me out, but Monica's distraught voice stopped me in my tracks and made me barge straight into the bathroom.

And when I find Ariane threatening her with a knife, I lose my shit.

"Get the fuck away from her!" I yell at Ariane.

Ariane turns toward me. "You ruined *everything*!" she squeals, turning the knife on me instead.

But I grab her arm and twist it until she drops the knife.

"Ow! Stop! You're hurting me!"

"Cole," Monica mutters in complete shock.

"Get back," I warn her.

Ariane's off the rails and completely unhinged. If she gets close, maybe Ariane will try to hurt her again, and I don't want to risk it. I'd rather have her focus on me.

"Get off me," Ariane snarls at me, trying to free herself from my grip.

"Don't you fucking dare," I growl at her, fiercely protective of Monica. "You tried to fucking knife Mo?! She's your own goddamn cousin!"

"Let go of me!" she yells, and she rips away from me in one go, falling back to the corner of the bathroom like a snake retreating to its shelter. "She deserved all of this. She brought it onto herself," Ariane hisses. "She tried to take you from me. She doesn't deserve you. Don't you see?"

Take me from her?

I was never hers, not even when we were together. She didn't want to be mine, yet now she decided she doesn't want anyone else to be mine either.

My face contorts. "What the hell is wrong with you? You did all this just because you're jealous?"

"You," she replies, tears welling up in her eyes. "You did this to me."

"You did this to yourself," I spit back, and I beckon Mo to step aside so Ariane can't suddenly twist around and try to hurt her.

Monica quickly passes by Ariane and stands behind me,

grabbing my waist.

"Yeah, you run back to daddy," Ariane hisses. "You're pathetic. Both of you. I should've shared that picture with the whole goddamn school when I had the chance, but I wanted to be merciful and give you a chance to stop this from getting out of hand. Guess you chose the hard way."

My jaw drops, and rage overcomes me. "So it was you? You stole that picture off my phone?"

She cocks her head. "You should really change your stupid code. It hasn't changed since we dated."

She's really lost her marbles. All this time, I thought it was Michael who stole the picture and sent it when it was Ariane pulling the strings from behind the scenes all along.

"She tried to push me to end things with you," Mo explains, "because she wants to keep you to herself."

"You cheated on me!" I growl. "Fuck you for making everyone think it was me. You'll pay for this," I say. "You're not gonna get away with any of this."

She makes a disgustingly snooty face. "Who do you think they'll believe? The attention junky and the poor little frightened victim or the most popular and respected girl in school who was thrown away like some used-up doll by the school's own boy band?"

"They'll believe this," Monica sneers, and she holds up her phone.

A recording of the entire conversation plays.

Ariane's pupils dilate as she stares in disbelief.

"When ... how ..." she mutters.

"The moment I saw your initials, I knew it was you." Mo scoffs, her head held high, even in the face of danger. "I don't trust snakes, never have."

Ariane's face completely melts off like a goddamn fiery volcano just went off in front of her. "You pushed me to confess."

"Yeah, and you were dumb enough to fall for it." Monica presses the button and lowers her phone. "Your reign over this school is finished."

THIRTY-FIVE

Cole

It took only minutes for Mr. D himself to come see what the ruckus was all about. Of course, Ariane denied every allegation we threw her way, but Monica had the proof. After we told Mr. D exactly what had happened and made him listen to the recording, he immediately had her restrained and called the cops.

It didn't take long for them to arrive and haul her back to their police car in the full frontal view of the entire fucking school.

I guess in her words, you get what you deserve.

As for me, since Mr. D was provided with proof of Ariane's misconduct, he agreed to put me on suspension for the fight in the hallway instead of completely kicking me out, which I accepted. Michael is still expelled for what he did to Monica in the forest, along with his two friends, so I'm glad I won't ever have to come face-to-face with them again, or I might've ripped them all a new one.

The only thing that never managed to come back together, though, is TRIGGER.

And now I'm sitting here on the floor in front of my bed with that letter in my hand, wondering if I should throw it in the trash. I suppose it wasn't all for nothing. I got a lot of fans, and maybe I can start up again someday. But I don't think Tristan and Benji will be so easy to forgive me.

"Is that ... an invitation?" Monica asks.

I look up. She's lying right behind me on my bed. "You know snooping is against the rules."

"What rules?" she taunts, winking. Then she snatches the paper from my hand. "Lemme see."

"My rules," I growl, and I turn around and try to steal it back, but she keeps jumping across the bed to get away from me. "Monica, give that back," I say with a stern voice.

"An audition for TRIGGER?" she muses with raised brows. "And next week!"

"Doesn't matter, just give it back," I say, sighing.

"Why not? This is important! Why didn't you tell me?" she asks.

"Because it doesn't matter anymore," I reply, lowering my head when she looks at me with the same pride I wish I could feel. "We're not going."

"What?" she gasps. "Why not?"

"We kinda broke up," I say.

She snorts. "Broke up? You make it sound like a relationship."

I shrug. "As a band, we're married to the music." I sit down on the bed. "Or we were. I haven't actually talked with either of them since that whole thing with Michael went down."

She stops running and lowers the paper. "Well, then go talk with them." She sits down behind me and wraps her arms around me, the paper still in her hands. "This is worth it." She sighs. "Besides, I don't want to be the reason for your breakup. Can you imagine? Monica Romero, destroyer of TRIGGER. Your fans would kill me."

I laugh. "It's not your fault. It was my choice to kick Michael out."

"Yeah, but if I hadn't gone and walked out of the party, they wouldn't have—"

I turn around and quickly place a finger on her lips. "I don't wanna hear any of that shit. You hear me? None."

She lowers her eyes at me, and I slide my hand to her cheek and give her a gentle but enticing kiss. And she smiles against my lips in appreciation.

"But what about TRIGGER? You're just gonna give up?" she asks.

"I appreciate that you wanna fix things, but what's done is done. I made a decision. And there is no way in hell I ever want Michael back in the band. And I simply don't have a replacement that's as good as him with a bass guitar," I reply, leaning my forehead against hers. "But I have you. And that's enough for me."

I kiss her again, this time even slower than before because I wanna savor what I have.

Suddenly, she leans back, her eyes springing open like a light bulb just went off in her head.

"Wait," she says. "I think I know someone."

I frown. "What are you talking about?"

She jumps up from the bed and fishes her phone from her pocket. "Someone to replace Michael."

"You know a bass player?" I raise my brows.

"Well … technically …" When I eye her hard, she starts backtracking. "Maybe."

"Monica," I murmur, giving her a stern look.

"Just let me do this, okay? It's worth a shot, so let me try, please?" she begs with such a cutesy voice that I can't say no.

God, if only I hadn't fallen so hard for her, maybe I would've been able to resist.

I rub my eyes and groan. "Okay, fine."

"So you'll meet him?" she squeals. "Yes! I'll set up a meeting for today."

Shaking my head, I laugh. "Oh, brother."

***

Monica

My nerves are killing me as I walk into Spark's Curve Diner, which looks like it was designed by an older couple in the 1950s. Apparently, they have the best ice cream in the neighborhood, but more importantly, this is where Sam, Nate, and I agreed to meet.

Cole clears his throat and adjusts his hair while I look around until I find them sitting in a red booth in the back. When she looks up and spots me, she waves, and a beaming smile appears on my face.

"C'mon," I tell Cole, and I walk toward them with pride.

Sam gets up from her seat and immediately runs to hug me, almost choking me with her strong grip. "I missed you!"

"I missed you too," I reply. "But have you worked on your muscles or something? 'Cause damn girl, you're squeezing me to death."

She snorts and pulls back only to poke me in the belly. "Thought I'd give you some of your own medicine for a change." She licks her lips and glances at Cole over my shoulder. "Who is …?" Then her eyes widen. "Wait a minute."

Cole's eyes flicker, and he taps his foot. "Here we go."

"You're that dude from TRIGGER, aren't you?" Sam's jaw slowly drops. "Oh my God, it really is you."

She looks like she's on the verge of squealing, but the sound never manages to slip from her tightly sealed lips.

"Yep, it's me," Cole replies, raising his brows.

"Oh my God, I can't believe it," Sam says, completely ignoring me. "But what are you doing here?"

Cole snorts. "I'm with her, actually."

Sam looks mortified. "With ... *you*?" She looks at me now, and my whole face turns red as a beet. "*He's* the boy you've been talking about?"

Okay, I didn't think I could get any redder, but here we are. Especially with Cole looking like he wants to laugh over my embarrassment.

I rub my lips together. "Yep."

"Oh, my God," she mutters, still in shock. She leans in closer. "Can I ...?"

"Sure," I say, and I look at him over my shoulder. "She wants an autograph."

He snorts and grabs a pen from his pocket. "Hold out your arm."

She does what he asks, and he scribbles his signature onto her skin.

A squeal escapes from her mouth. "Eek." She can barely contain her excitement. "Thank you!"

"You're welcome," Cole replies, a bit embarrassed because everyone in this diner is looking at him. I'm pretty sure not everyone knows who he is ... yet. But most people of our age do, and that apparently includes my best friend.

Behind Sam, Nate stares at all of us. "Hey, Nate," I say.

He throws up a hand without saying a word, so I guess we'll get to that later. He was always the quiet type.

"I didn't know you were a TRIGGER fan," I say to Sam.

"Only since like a few months," she says, rolling her eyes at me. "But we don't talk about music that often."

"Sorry about that." I scratch the back of my head. "Been a little busy with my new school."

She smirks. "Yeah, I can see that." She leans in, and whispers in my ear, "Good catch."

I almost choke on my own words. "Thanks."

"I mean it, he's hot. And famous," she whispers. "How did you do it?"

Cole snorts.

So he could hear it. Damn.

"Long story," I reply.

She grabs my hand and pulls me to the bench. "C'mon, tell me all about it."

I sigh, and we all sit down so I can tell her everything that happened since I left school for Black Mountain Academy, but I leave out some of the details that put Cole in a bad light. I'll tell her someday when we're alone, but I just don't want to make him feel bad.

When I've mentioned all there is to know, she's still leaning in, barely having touched her ice cream. "That's it?"

"That's it." I lean back against the seat, and Cole throws his arm around my shoulder.

"I still can't believe you managed to get a fucking rock star for a boyfriend."

"Hey," Nate interrupts while throwing Sam a look.

"This here is just as fine."

She snorts and lowers her eyes at him. "Yeah, yeah, no need to get jealous." She pecks him on the cheek. "I'm already yours."

"Good," Nate retorts, and he smiles when he sees Cole pulling me closer to him.

"I'm not the catch. She is," Cole says, making my heart flutter. "I'm the lucky one here."

I place a hand on his chest and give him a little kiss against the jaw. "That's sweet."

"Sweet?" He leans back, raising a brow at me. "Don't start swearing at me now."

When the laughter dies out, Sam finally picks up her giant cup of ice cream and spoons some into her mouth.

"So, I heard you were looking for a bass player," she mumbles while looking at Cole. "That true?"

He shifts in his seat and clears his throat. "Yeah, well …"

"He has an audition, and they desperately need an additional guitarist to make it. Temporarily, until they find a new permanent one," I fill in. Cole's always trying to protect his image, but he doesn't have to be ashamed of losing one of his band members, not in front of my friends.

"But you'll keep it tight-lipped, won't you?" I ask.

"My lips are sealed," she replies. "Don't worry."

"Good," Cole replies a little too snarky. "So who is the guitarist then?"

Sam leans back and eyes her boyfriend.

Cole frowns and narrows his eyes. "What ... him?" He points at Nate as if he can't believe it.

"I rap, mostly," Nate replies. "But I've been playing the bass on my off days for years. My dad forced me to focus on football while I was in high school, but music ... that's my real passion."

"Music?" Cole cocks his head as if he didn't peg him to be that type.

"Don't believe me?" Nate raises a brow at him. He leans under the table and fishes out an actual guitar case that was stuck between their legs.

"Interesting," Cole says. "You've got some surprises up your sleeve."

"I can play some if you want," Nate replies with pride in his eyes. "Just a few notes, I don't wanna bother the other people here."

"Sure, why not?" Cole says, leaning back in his seat. "Let's hear it."

Nate pulls out his guitar and puts the case away. The moment he begins to play, everyone's watching him with perked ears and wide eyes, each note more beautiful than the one before. Cole's noticed it too, judging from the glimmer in his eyes.

I smirk as Sam and I stare at each other, knowing these two are gonna be a great match.

And maybe, just maybe, it's not too late to save TRIGGER.

***

Cole

With my guitar strapped to my back, I meet up with the guys at TRIGGER's last hangout ... the club we first played at and the same one where Monica broke my old guitar. It's a place filled with memories that I'm not ready to lose.

Tristan's already there, drinking a Coke at the bar with Benji, who's casually playing with his phone. I blow out a breath and head toward them. The looks on their faces darken when they spot me. Tristan shifts in his seat, ready to listen, but not for long.

"Took you long enough," he says.

"I know, and I apologize." I raise my hand.

"I don't even know what I'm doing here, to be honest," he replies.

"Yeah, I'm only here because I don't want to stop playing," Benji adds. "But I don't like what happened here."

"I know, guys, and I'm sorry," I say. "Can I sit?" I point at one of the chairs next to Tristan.

Both he and Benji nod, but Tristan looks away once I sit down beside him.

"So are you inviting Michael back?" Benji asks.

"No," I swiftly reply. "Not a chance."

Tristan sighs out loud. "Why? What could he possibly have done?"

I throw him a look and rub my lips together. "I can't tell you ... but I can invite Monica in, and *she* can tell you."

He frowns and looks at the door the moment it opens. Monica steps inside, clutching her bag.

"Hi," she says, waving.

"What is she doing here?" Tristan hisses. "All she did was distract you from what was important."

"She gave me something to fight for," I retort, looking him directly in the eyes. "If it weren't for her, I would've gone off the deep end, and you know it."

He's quiet for some time, and I know he knows exactly what I mean.

Monica comes toward us and looks at them both. "I'm sorry for ruining your band," she says. "If I'd known this was going to happen, I would never have left that party the way I did."

"The party?" Benji frowns. "You mean when Cole carried you back inside while you were passed out? *That* party?"

She nods and looks down at her feet. "I was ... exhausted from crying. Crying over Michael and what he and his buddies did to me."

Tristan shifts in his seat. "What did he do?"

"He attacked me," she explains, her head held high. "Chased me into the woods behind the house, and watched while his buddies sat on top of me, egging them on to do ... to do ..." She chokes on her words again, so I jump off my chair and grab her hand.

"You don't have to say anything else if you don't want to," I say.

"Thank you," she replies with a genuine smile on her face.

"Michael tried to assault you at the fucking party?" Tristan asks.

Monica nods, and he immediately slams his hand onto the bar so loudly even the bartender is spooked. "I can't fucking believe it. I trusted that motherfucker."

"I didn't," Benji says. "You should've seen him alone with fans. He always went too far."

"I know, but he only did it to willing fans. Not like this," Tristan says.

"I knew he was like this," I say, inserting myself back into the conversation. "And that's not the only thing he did. You both know about the drugs. She did too. He even forced me to make sure she wouldn't talk, or it would ruin our band."

I look at Monica feeling the guilt sweep through me once again.

I wish I had never put her in that position.

That I had never treated her the way I did.

I was foolish, overcome with the protectiveness of the only thing I knew I had … my band.

But I didn't know back then what I'd be willing to lose to keep her safe.

Everything.

"It's my fault that it got this bad, and no, I can't make

up for the lost time, nor can I change what happened. Michael is out, and Mr. D kicked him out too."

"I heard. He wouldn't shut up about it." Tristan takes a sip of his drink. "I had to mute him to stop the constant barrage of texts."

"He was the problem all along," I say. "He's what ruined our band."

"Yeah, but we can't do anything without a guitarist," Benji replies.

"I know, and that's why I actually wanted to meet up." I look at Monica and nod at her, and she turns around and quickly runs to the door.

"I want to try to fix things. I know this isn't perfect, but it's something," I say as Monica brings in Nate. They both stare at him like he's an uninvited guest.

"This is Nate," I say while Nate waves. "He's gonna be our new bass player."

Tristan makes a face. "A *new* guitarist?"

Benji cocks his head. "Really?"

I nod a few times. "Best chance we have at making the audition."

Tristan hops off his seat. "We don't just need to make the audition. We need to earn it. Win it. And the only way to do that is through hard work and perseverance." He eyes Nate up and down. "You think you got what it takes to join TRIGGER?"

Nate pulls his guitar out of the case, puts on the strap, and winks at me while Monica and I step aside. When he begins to play, both boys are completely stupefied, and their jaws practically dropped to the floor.

"But how did you find him?" Tristan mumbles in awe.

Monica folds her arms, and I wrap my arm around her shoulder. "Thanks to this ... distraction over here." I pull her close as we watch Nate play a song for us with pride.

When he's done, they both clap. Then Benji asks, "But can we really do this in time for the audition?"

"Of course," Nate replies. "I can practice the songs at night and rehearse them during the school's lunch break."

Tristan frowns, then licks his lips, eyeing us all, but mostly me. "And you're sure this is going to work?"

A smug grin spreads on my face. "Thousand percent. It has to ... because there's no fucking way I'd ever give up on TRIGGER."

Slowly but surely, a genuine smile forms on Tristan's lips. "If you say so, I believe you."

"Aw ... c'mere," I say, and I hold out my arms. "Group hug."

"Really?" Tristan frowns, but I still give him the biggest of bro-hugs possible, Benji included.

"I'm sorry, man," Benji says. "We should have trusted you."

When I release them, Tristan starts to stumble over his words too. "Yeah ... I'm ... sorry on my part too. I didn't mean to be so cruel, but it's hard when there's so much at stake, you know?"

"I get it," I reply. "No hard feelings."

Tristan throws me a playful punch. "Michael sure did a number on you. You're covered in bruises."

"Small price to pay to finally be rid of him," I say, winking.

"Thanks," Benji says. "For bringing Nate in, I mean."

"Oh, you don't have me to thank for that." I look at Monica and beckon her to join us. "She did all this."

"You?" Tristan raises a brow and lifts his head. "You brought TRIGGER back together?"

She bites her lip and anxiously steps forward. "I didn't want this to mean the end. Especially not when I know you guys will make it big."

A tepid but certain smile lights up his face. "I guess you're not as bad as I thought." He playfully pats her shoulder a few times, which turns everything into an awkward mess.

"Thanks, I guess," she replies.

"That's the way you're gonna treat the girl who saved our asses?" I mock.

His cheeks start to glow. "Well, maybe, I mean, she did kinda distract you … a lot." When we both throw him a dirty look, he adds, "But she's also a good influence on you. And she brought an amazing bass player into the building."

"Thanks, bro," Nate replies, as he takes off his guitar strap and puts his guitar back into the case. "But just know, I don't play for free."

Everyone starts to laugh. For the first time in a long time, I'm confident we're gonna make it. I'm convinced I made the right decision.

Because without Monica Romero, I would've probably given up on myself by now. I would've given up on trust, on my future, my school, and even this goddamn band.

But I pulled through, thanks to her and those sweet kisses that make me forget everything bad about my life.

And I grab her and press my lips onto hers, claiming her in front of everyone.

I don't fucking care anymore what anyone thinks. I'm doing this for me. For *us*.

She's the reason I do this.

Why I fight.

And I won't stop fighting for her.

Not until she tells me to.

EPILOGUE

Monica

The club is booming with people, as we all gather to watch TRIGGER performing on stage. It's a much bigger venue than the last time I saw them play, so their efforts to stick together and keep going really paid off.

The audition was a success, and the record label has asked them to write more songs, which they will now produce professionally and market to the world. Of course, the boys were ecstatic. Even Nate couldn't stop celebrating this hard-earned win.

Nate has blended in so well that it's hard to believe he only joined them a few weeks ago. He plays their songs as though he's played them his entire life, and he seems to love being on stage.

Cole and the others even let him have his own few songs where he's allowed to rap, and the crowd always goes mental when he goes up to the mic. Cole doesn't even seem to mind sharing the fame. He looks much happier and more content than he did before ... before Michael was kicked out ... before he met me.

I smile at him as he plays his guitar like a pro while the crowd goes wild with excitement, hollering their names, chanting along to each of their songs. It's a thrill to be able to witness his rise, and it's humbling to know that I was a part of that. That I helped keep them together, despite all the odds being stacked both against them and me.

But you know what they say ... never give up on hope.

And I'm far from ever surrendering.

Being with Cole has taught me that no matter what trouble gets on your path, you can get through it, as long as you keep breathing and have people around you who care about you, who will help you get back on your feet again when you need them.

Cole was there for me when I was at my darkest, and now I'm here for him at his lightest.

And I can't help but smile when I watch him perform on stage with the entire crowd's eyes set on him while his are focused solely on me. And I can't help but stare right back at him with wonder in my eyes, completely mesmerized by his performance just like the very first time I saw him play.

"My God ... I still can't believe *he's* your boyfriend,"

Melanie suddenly says, and I almost lose my shit.

"Boyfriend?" I stutter.

"Yeah, aren't you two kind of *officially* a thing now?" she asks, winking. "I saw you come out of the practice room, remember?"

My entire face glows. "Uh ... I guess."

She throws her arm around my shoulders. "C'mon, Mo, there's nothing to be ashamed about."

"You two having fun without me?" Sam just crept up behind us, almost giving me a heart attack. "Here." She hands both of us a Coke. "On the house."

"Thanks," I say, and I take a huge sip.

"I think I said something I shouldn't have," Melanie jests while ogling me.

"What?" Sam muses, and she looks at me now, because I'm only getting redder the more they talk.

"She and Cole are secretly a thing," Melanie whispers.

"Yeah, I knew," Sam says.

"Okay ..." Melanie frowns and throws me a look. "So I was the only one who didn't know?"

"Sorry," I say, making a face. "We never officially labeled it. It just sort of happened." I shrug. "It's complicated."

She takes a sip. "Doesn't have to be if you two just talked."

"That's what I always say," Sam says. "But she never listens."

"Hey! I didn't bring you two together so you could gang

up on me," I interject.

They both laugh, and Melanie throws an arm around Sam too. "I'm glad you did, though, because I can totally see this being a thing. The three of us against the world."

"Don't forget Cole and Nate," Sam says, dreamily staring at Nate on stage.

"Everyone can be a part of our little club," Melanie says, "but we need a name."

"Noooo, please God, no," I retort, and they both burst into laughter.

"I'm just messing with you, Mo." Melanie throws me a playful punch, and I poke her in the belly to get back at her.

The last song finishes, and the boys take a bow on stage, and the fans give them a final round of applause. Cole jumps off the stage and immediately comes toward us while the guards in the front hold back the fans from flocking after him.

Without a second of hesitation, he grabs my face and kisses me on the lips in front of all my friends, and it's the most sultry, sexy kiss I've had in a long while. These performances really get him riled up.

"Fuck, that was beautiful," he groans against my mouth.

I smile, but when he leans back, and I see the looks on my friends' faces, I'm mortified.

"Well, if that isn't an intro, I don't know what is," Melanie muses, sipping her Coke like it's nobody's business.

As our lips unlock, the others stare at us while hiding laughter, and I blush again, knowing they saw him practically eat me up.

"There's a room in the back if you need it," Sam jests.

"Oh, stop," I growl, punching her shoulder. "Like you and Nate weren't fucking smooching nonstop every day after you just met."

Now it's her time to blush. "We were sensible about it."

I snort. "Sensible my ass. You two were groping each other at lunch and skipping out on classes just to make out in the bathrooms."

Sam's eyes widen.

"Yeah, I said it," I add. "Out. Loud."

"That was once. Maybe two times," she retorts.

"Every. Damn. Day," I say, and Nate grabs her by the waist and nuzzles her.

"I remember …" The way he groans makes me think he gets just as horny from performing as Cole does. Is that a guy thing or what?

"Hey, I don't mean to be a party pooper, but don't we have somewhere to be?" Cole suddenly says.

I gasp and check my watch. "Shit!"

I grab his hand and drag him toward the door while simultaneously waving at my friends, hollering, "Sorry! Got to go! Promised Mom I'd meet her after!"

"Talk later. Have fun!" Sam yells while groping Nate.

"You too!" I yell back.

"Thanks!" Melanie calls out, still casually sipping on her drink while waiting for the next band to come up to the stage.

"C'mon," I say to Cole as we walk back to his car. "Mom's waiting."

"Oh boy …" he groans as we sit down and close the doors. "I forgot about it."

"I know."

"I don't like remembering," he adds.

I snort. "It'll be fine." I lean in to press a sweet kiss to his cheeks. "It'll be over before you know it."

He raises his brows at me and starts the engine. "Yeah … or I'll be dead."

***

"So … you're finally here," Mom says as she opens the door.

I clutch Cole's arm while all his muscles are tightening. "Hey, Mom, sorry we're late."

She arranged a special meetup with the three of us while my dad's still at work, just so she could personally grill Cole.

"As usual," she mumbles, but she steps aside anyway. "C'mon in."

We quickly pass her by, and she scoots in front to escort us to the table. "I made a late-night snack. Hope you don't mind."

Of course she did. She wants to persuade him to lower his defenses, and then she'll go full-on attack mode. It's what she does, how she won over my dad when they were still teens.

She's not a woman you mess with.

"Nice, I'm famished," Cole spits out before he realizes it, and he immediately backtracks. "I mean, thank you, ma'am."

It's hard to hold the snorts inside.

He's probably trying to be the best version of himself so he doesn't disappoint my mom, but this is hilarious because it's so not like him.

We sit down at the table, and we all stare at each other without saying a word while Cole keeps staring at the chips, cookies, and cake as if he hasn't eaten in days.

"You sure look … fantastical," Mom says, clearing her throat while ogling Cole.

He's still in his leather outfit, complete with sparkly makeup. "Sorry, I just came off stage. Didn't have time to get dressed."

"Ahh …" She nods a little. "Yeah, I read about that. You're a musician, right?"

"I'm the lead singer and guitarist in our band TRIGGER, yeah. Heard about them?" he asks, sweat dripping down his forehead, which he quickly wipes away.

I don't think I've ever seen him this tense, this nervous. Not even for an upcoming performance. But my mom is just … my mom.

"I've read a few things," she replies, and she picks up her wineglass and chugs it down before planting it down on the table. "Like you were in a fight over my daughter."

My eyes widen. "Mom!"

Cole grabs my hand and smiles. "It's okay." He turns his gaze back to my mom. "One of my band members betrayed us and hurt Monica in the process. He did some pretty horrible stuff, which ultimately resulted in the fight you probably saw online." He swallows. "I had to do something to stop him."

"So do you do this often?" she asks.

"Mom, it was not his fault. Michael was an asshole who was only in it to get high and use girls."

My mom's jaw drops. "And you let this boy play with you in *your* band?"

"I didn't realize how bad he got until it was too late," Cole replies, trying to keep his cool. "But he got kicked out. I don't want that toxic stuff anywhere near us."

"Good." She pours herself a new glass. "But you're dating my daughter now."

He gulps, and my face turns completely red.

"Well?" Mom pushes.

"I … I …" I mutter, not knowing how to answer.

"Yes," Cole answers without hesitation. "And I'm not going to stop."

I look at him and breathe a sigh of relief, but my heart swells to immeasurable proportions knowing that he just told my mom out loud something I could not even admit to myself.

"I know you don't like me, and you may not approve," he says, and he squeezes my hand. "But I'm in love with your daughter. And I won't let anything come between us."

I bite my bottom lip and lean in to give him a short peck, before returning my attention toward my mom.

"Mom ... please ... I know our start was rocky, and I know what you've seen online might muddy the waters. But trust me when I say this, us, Cole, is the best thing that has happened to me since I went to my new school."

She takes in a deep breath, clutching her glass. "But he hurt you ... so many times ..."

"To protect me ... from him." I swallow. "But I don't need any more protecting. I'm done with that. I'm done with crying, done with hurting. I'm done with my past."

"And you're sure you can handle whatever comes with him and his band? All the jealous fans, the screaming girls?" she asks, in complete denial at this point. "Because I don't think you can, Monica."

"I don't know. But I will try. And dammit, I won't give up," I say and look up at Cole. "Not with this."

Mom places her glass down and cocks her head. "Well, it seems you managed to do something no one else has done up till this very day, Cole."

"And what's that?" he asks.

My mom throws him a look. "Steal her heart."

We both tighten our lock on each other's hand.

A slow but tepid smile finally forms on her lips. "If you're sure about this, Monica—"

"Yes, a hundred percent," I interject. "And I want you to be okay with it. That's all I ask. Just let me be me, and let me love the people I want to love."

Her shoulders relax, and she leans back in her chair. "If you put it like that, how am I ever going to say no?"

The smile grows bigger and bigger, and so does mine, and I jump up from my seat to get to her side of the table for a big hug. We squeeze each other tightly, and she rubs my back.

"Oh honey, I'm just trying to look out for you. I'm scared. I don't want you to get hurt. I don't want to lose my baby."

"I know, Mom. But I've dealt with my demons, and I need to move on. On my own terms." I lean away and look her in the eyes.

She grabs a strand of my hair and tucks it behind my ear. "You've grown up so much. I barely recognize you." She leans her forehead against mine. "But if you're happy, then so am I."

"Thanks, Mom," I say as she gives me a quick kiss on the forehead.

"All right … you've got my blessing."

I do an inner happy dance as I quickly sit back down beside Cole.

"But don't bring that whole charade into my home, got it?" She points at Cole. "I don't want any of that TRIGGER stuff happening here. No fans. No paparazzi. You do that shit somewhere else."

Cole smashes his lips together. "Yes, ma'am."

I snort at his obedience.

My mom knows how to whoop some ass, and she's not

afraid of him.

"Good," she retorts, and she picks up the bread basket and holds it out to him. "Now have some fucking bread. You look like you haven't eaten in days."

I have to hide my laughter behind my hand.

"Thanks," he mumbles as he grabs a bunch and places them on his plate.

"Well? Dig in!" Mom says, grabbing a cookie for herself too.

I grab some chips while Cole shoves a whole bread into his mouth.

"God, I'm hungry," he groans. "And this is delicious. Did you make these yourself, ma'am?"

"I wish," she muses.

"Well, either way, I love it," he says.

Mom takes a bite of her cookie and says, "But no fucking under my roof, got it?"

Cole starts to choke on his bread and coughs it up while I burst into laughter.

"I'll try to remember that," he says, trying not to die inside.

"Good, because I'm not gonna clean up after your mess."

"Mom!" I scream, mortified, and I grab his hand. "Okay, let's go upstairs. I don't need or want to hear any of this."

"But no fuckery or else!" she yells after us as I rush upstairs with him.

I don't say another word.

I'm not gonna make promises I can't keep.

And when the door closes behind us, Cole immediately grabs my face and kisses me hard, smashing me into the door like nobody's business. His lips are on my neck and chest, while his hands travel down my ass, squeezing hard until I moan with delight.

"God, I fucking love you," he whispers, our lips barely able to unlatch.

"I love it when you say that," I say, smiling against his lips. "Say it again."

"I love you, Monica Romero," he says with a guttural moan as he whisks me up in his arms.

He was right when he said he'd catch me one day. I didn't realize it then, but I know now. I've fallen hard for Cole fucking Travis. I've fallen all the way in love with him.

I pull away and whisper into his ear, "I love you too, Cole Travis."

The groan that emanates from his body makes my pussy thump with need as he carries me toward the bed.

"Do you really think we can stop?" I mumble as he showers me with kisses.

I don't think I care or want to know the answer to my own damn question because even if I wanted to, I can't fucking stop, and I won't fucking stop.

"You know me," he murmurs, licking his lips in a way that still manages to make my heart skip a beat. "I don't play by the rules."

THANK YOU FOR READING!

Thank you so much for reading Rowdy Boy!

I have plenty more books available right now on Amazon.com.

You can also stay up to date of new books via my website: www.clarissawild.com. Make sure you sign up for the newsletter while you're there!

You can also find me on Facebook: www.facebook.com/ClarissaWildAuthor, make sure to click LIKE.

You can also join the Fan Club for more sneak peeks of upcoming books: www.facebook.com/groups/FanClubClarissaWild and talk with other readers!

Enjoyed this book? You could really help out by leaving a review on Amazon and Goodreads. Thank you!

ALSO BY

CLARISSA WILD

Dark Romance
His Duet
The Debt Duet
Savage Men Series
Delirious Series
Indecent Games Series
The Company Series
FATHER

New Adult Romance
Fierce Series
Blissful Series
Ruin
Cruel Boy

Erotic Romance
Hotel O
The Billionaire's Bet Series
Enflamed Series
Unprofessional Bad Boys Series

ABOUT THE AUTHOR

Clarissa Wild is a New York Times & USA Today Bestselling author with ASD (Asperger's Syndrome), who was born and raised in the Netherlands. She loves to write Dark Romance and Contemporary Romance novels featuring dangerous men and feisty women. Her other loves include her hilarious husband, her cutie pie son, her two crazy but cute dogs, and her ninja cat that sometimes thinks he's a dog too. In her free time, she enjoys watching all sorts of movies, playing video games, and cooking up some delicious meals.

Want to be informed of new releases and special offers? Sign up for Clarissa Wild's newsletter on her website www.clarissawild.com.

Visit Clarissa Wild on Amazon for current titles.